MVFO

D0338584

THOUGHTS
&
PRAYERS

NATIONAL BOOK AWARD–LONGLISTED AUTHOR
BRYAN BLISS

THOUGHTS & PRAYERS

GREENWILLOW BOOKS
An Imprint of HarperCollinsPublishers

Thoughts & Prayers
Copyright © 2020 by Bryan Bliss

The text of this book is set in 11-point Goudy.
Book design by Paul Zakris

Library of Congress Cataloging-in-Publication Data

Names: Bliss, Bryan, author.
Title: Thoughts & prayers : a novel in three parts / Bryan Bliss.
Other titles: Thoughts and prayers
Description: New York : Greenwillow Books, an Imprint of HarperCollins
Publishers, [2020] | Audience: Ages 13 up | Audience: Grades 10–12 |
Summary: "Three high school students attempt to repair their lives after
a school shooting"— Provided by publisher.
Identifiers: LCCN 2020024432 | ISBN 9780062962249 (hardcover)
Subjects: CYAC: Grief—Fiction. | School shootings—Fiction. |
High schools—Fiction. | Schools—Fiction.
Classification: LCC PZ7.1.B63 Th 2020 | DDC [Fic]—dc23
LC record available at https://lccn.loc.gov/2020024432

20 21 22 23 24 PC/LSCH 10 9 8 7 6 5 4 3 2 1

First Edition

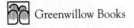
Greenwillow Books

For everybody who continues to fight.
You give me hope.

We are still here. Everywhere. All around you.
Some of us are children and some
are older, but we all pretend to be okay.
We survive.
No matter what,
we stand beside every one of you.
The next ones, too. There will always be next ones.
We cry.
We scream.
And when it feels as if our skin is on fire and
the only thing we can do is burn—
well then, we'll burn.
Bright, hot, forever.
Until something changes.
Because every single one of us should've been a reason.
Should have been enough.

PART ONE
The Monster

CHAPTER ONE

BEFORE SHE MOVED TO MINNESOTA, CLAIRE DIDN'T KNOW the inside of your nose could freeze, that cold like this even existed. It started at your feet and climbed up your legs, seizing your chest, until every part of your body was completely frozen.

Before, she didn't take the bus, which appeared at the corner, its headlights cutting through the haze of the morning snow falling in silent clumps.

She used to love the snow.

Waking up, finding the world covered. Refreshing the browser on her laptop and jumping when the phone finally rang, the automated voice saying those sweet words of freedom—*Catawba County schools have been cancelled.* . . .

Nothing short of a miracle, nothing better. Not even Christmas.

But that was before, and now the snow was just another thing that disappeared.

The bus stopped on the corner and Claire turned up her music, loud enough that the other students at her stop— laughing like they'd never had as much as a paper cut— wouldn't talk to her.

The doors shushed open, just like always. And just like always, the slow march toward the yellow bus started. Claire tried to join them. Tried to make her body move, but it was as if the snow had gone solid, seizing her feet.

She looked into her bag, letting person after person pass (breathing, breathing), trying to ignore the panic as it began to swirl, rushing into her ears like storm water.

She looked up, realizing she was alone.

The whole bus was a choir of stares and whispers, and the driver was giving her a look like, *I'll leave you, I swear,* so instead of making him choose, she shook her head (breathing, breathing) and started to back away. She expected that first step to require a Herculean effort, something to crack concrete. But it didn't and the force—the snow, the ice, all that cold—brought her down hard on the sidewalk.

The stares and whispers turned to laughter.

Before those kids would've been her friends. *Before* it wouldn't have been impossible to get on the bus. *Before* she

Bryan Bliss

had friends and she would've laughed as she sat in the cold, the snow, rubbing the pain out of her ass and barking for everybody to shut the hell up, or else.

Her brother found the carriage house online and rented it sight unseen before they'd even arrived in Minnesota. They were still in North Carolina then, only days after, the panic swallowing them both. It was as if everything familiar had suddenly sprouted a fuse, already burning.

So, they left.

They left nearly everything, save a few boxes of clothing and pictures—their entire life crammed into Derrick's small hatchback. They didn't stop until the ground was flat and white, and when they pulled up to the carriage house, behind a legitimate mansion in the heart of St. Paul's old-money neighborhood, Claire was sure it was a dream.

Mark-O, one of Derrick's best friends from his skating days—and the owner of the Lair, a local skate park—had promised a job and enough money to cover the carriage house, which was bigger and nicer than any place they'd rented in North Carolina.

She had her own bedroom, her own bathroom; the entire place was heated by an antique woodstove that wrapped her in a warm embrace every time she came in from the cold. At first glance, the house was perfect, just like the job at the Lair was perfect—a chance for Derrick to focus on skating again finally. And, maybe, if you weren't looking closely, you'd even think their life had snapped back to the way it had always been before. Perfect? Well, no. But safe. And when was the last time she'd actually felt safe?

She knew the exact minute of the exact day.

Claire kicked the snow from her shoes and opened the door. Her brother was staring at a table full of opened bills. As if he was summoning the courage to begin paying them. At first, he didn't look up, and when he did, it took a second for the usual concern to flip onto his face.

Derrick was older by eight years, enough that he was already out of the house and living in Los Angeles when their parents were killed in a freak car accident. He ditched LA, a skating career that was about to take off, to make sure Claire didn't end up in foster care or, worse, with one of their backwoods extended relatives who dotted the hills and hollers of West Virginia. Sometimes Claire wondered if it would've been easier if their parents were still around. If she and Derrick hadn't run away as hard and fast as they could.

"What happened?"

To Derrick's credit, he didn't sound angry or even tired. At

Bryan Bliss

this point, either would've been justified. But his tone was patient and kind—as always.

"I couldn't get on the bus and then—" She motioned to her pants, the damp circles at her knees.

Derrick stood up and ran his hands through his long, brown hair, not looking at her, which was a good thing because Claire couldn't look at him, either. It had been a year and she was still sabotaged by the simplest things. Walking through the hallways at school. Ordering food at the mall. Getting on the bus. She wasn't okay, she wasn't better, and the weight of it had pulled Derrick underwater with her.

Claire stared down at her jeans. She'd had them for years, rescued from the rack of a thrift store in Chapel Hill. A one-day adventure Derrick let her tag along on. There was a fray on one of the pockets, small enough that you'd never notice it. Been there from the start. Claire would mindlessly pick at it during class, at lunch, while watching television. But now, as she stared at it, she realized it was just the start of something bigger.

"Hey," Derrick said. "It's good. We're good. Okay?"

Claire forced herself to look up. To say, "Okay."

CHAPTER TWO

CLAIRE HELD HER BOARD ON HER LAP AS DERRICK DROVE. The Lair was on the other side of the Cities, tucked between steel-sided buildings that housed manufacturing companies and office-supply distributors. When they pulled up to the entrance, there wasn't another car on the street. Derrick shot her a smile.

"The benefits of skating at eight a.m."

Claire didn't mention how many other random times they'd shown up here. Before sunrise, after midnight—the benefits of having a key to the building. And she didn't mention how skating had become their way to escape, to momentarily forget, to never actually talk about why they were at the Lair at two a.m. on a school night.

Because skating worked.

It didn't matter if she couldn't get on the bus or off the light rail, if somebody's puffy jacket froze her to the carpeted hallways at Central High School, or she simply woke up and found herself unable to function. If she needed it, they skated. For as long as it took to empty everything out of her.

Before they got out of the car, Derrick hesitated as if he wanted to say something. Claire braced herself, staring at her board, which had been left behind by some long ago LA girlfriend. Before, Claire would've asked Derrick why he still had it—needled him until he smiled and told her to give him a break.

But he didn't say anything, just cracked the car door and sat there for another second as Claire felt the cold wind kick through the car, a rogue snowflake floating in and disappearing almost immediately.

The Lair didn't have hours, not really. Instead, Mark-O would open the doors as early as he got there and close them whenever he finally tapped out, which usually was hours past midnight. Mark-O liked to say that a skate park with its doors closed was useless, especially in a place like Minnesota.

"Look at this degenerate," Mark-O said, looking up from the tattered paperback he was reading only to reach across the counter and punch Derrick in the dead center of his chest.

"At least I haven't made a career of it," Derrick said, which made Mark-O smirk.

Claire left them to their macho ritual and disappeared into the skate park—a cathedral of wood, concrete, and iron, every inch of it tagged by spray paint and stickers. It was her chance to have a space to herself for a few moments. To know that she was completely alone, completely safe.

Soon enough, of course, Derrick would come in and kick his board to the ground. And while he rarely talked to Claire when they skated, getting lost in his own past—in the joy she knew he felt every time the board was under him—a small part of her heart dropped every time he came into the room and that rare seclusion ended.

Depending on the day, other skaters would trickle in, some of them skipping school just like Claire. Eventually the entire room echoed with the metallic grind of trucks against rails, the wooden slap of boards, and the laughter, the laughter, the laughter—always rising up above the music, no matter how loud.

Claire put her board down and stared into the empty skate park, trying to visualize her path, her "line" as Derrick called it. When she first started skating, she'd get stuck in one spot

Bryan Bliss

for five, ten minutes, trying to figure out which direction to go—which path wouldn't lead to a collision. Derrick always said skating meant claiming your place in the room, claiming your line, whether you were good or not.

She put a foot on the board, took a deep breath, and pushed off.

When she heard other people talk about the important things in their lives, the big things like family and friendship and love, they always described it as a feeling. Something electric and pulsing with life. You felt it in your ears, your heart. And maybe she had felt that before, when she played basketball. The thrill of a made shot. A last-second victory.

But skating was different. It emptied her and made the world quiet. Manageable, if only for a few moments at a time. When she inevitably fell, everything came back so powerfully, Claire was unsure if it was the rush of sound or the impact of the fall that took her breath away.

This time, she was up for only a half a minute before she fell, harder than usual, her helmet smacking against the concrete floor with a hollow *pop* that echoed across the cavernous space. She laid there for a second, watching her board continue dutifully on its original line when a voice said, "Oh, *shit*. Are you okay?"

No moment in her life passed without Claire being

hyperaware of anyone and everyone who entered into an enclosed space. She sat with her back to the wall at restaurants, got on the bus or train last. If someone moved or reached into their jacket to pull out gloves, a book, anything, she would jump like the planet had lurched off its axis.

So, she knew Derrick was still talking to Mark-O. This room should be empty.

The voice called out again (breathing, breathing), but she could barely hear it now. The storm shot toward her like a missile. When a tall, rangy boy with long hair appeared at the top of one of the vert ramps, everything just stopped.

He slid down the ramp on his knees, picking up her board in one fluid movement as he stood up and walked toward her. She tried to yell for Derrick, but her voice stuck in her throat like a ball of ice.

The boy—he must've been close to her age—smiled nervously, holding the board out toward her. But Claire was essentially cowering below him (breathing, breathing), unable to move except her eyes, which darted around the room, up and down his body, looking for an escape, a threat, anything.

"Whoa—are you . . . guys! *Guys.*"

The boy looked back to his two friends, who were now standing at the top of the ramp, watching. One by one they

Bryan Bliss

slid down the smooth plywood, laughing as they walked toward Claire. The first boy seemed trapped now, too, as if her fear was a live wire that conducted through her body, paralyzing anyone who dared to get close.

The three boys looked no different than the countless skater boys Derrick had always called friends—no different than the ones who gave her casual glances when she managed to make it across the park without falling. The same boys who laughed at stupid jokes, using their sarcastic shorthand against each other like a straight razor.

The first one said, "I think she's—I think there's something wrong with her."

This made the other two laugh.

"Don't listen to what anybody says, Dark. This is *exactly* how you get a girl to go out with you."

The kid—Dark?—knelt down in front of Claire slowly, hands out like you'd approach a cornered animal. "Are you here alone?"

This only made his friends howl with more laughter, but he ignored them. His eyes—deep blue and a striking contrast to his dyed-black hair and equally black clothes—were fixed on her. Claire tried to swallow, to push against the storm, but it was rising higher and higher and higher until it was just her nose and mouth above the water, barely pulling in air.

(Breathing, breathing.)

"Whoa. Hey . . ."

One of them went running to the lobby.

The other knelt down next to Dark. It might've been thirty seconds, maybe thirty minutes before Derrick and Mark-O came sprinting toward her. The five of them stood around her, asking questions, saying her name.

Looking like they'd seen a monster. Something worse.

Bryan Bliss

CHAPTER THREE

CLAIRE SIPPED WATER AS DERRICK TALKED TO THE BOYS. She could hear him telling them the basics. The broad strokes. He whispered, but it didn't matter. She knew the story better than anyone.

It was right at the beginning of the day and it sounded like popcorn. She was pressed against two other students—Eleanor, her teammate for nearly ten years, and a freshman she didn't know—under one of the giant metal staircases that had only been installed at Ford High School in the last five years.

She huddled beneath the metal as the popcorn (*pop-pop-pop*) went off around her, the sound slowly being overthrown by something new—a storm rushing into her ears. A silence that was neither quiet nor peaceful.

The next thing she remembered was screaming, throwing fists and kicking feet—they'd always told them to fight back— as the police tried to pull her out. Adrenaline rushed back into her body in one sudden jolt. Almost a year later, she could still feel the pain of that exact moment. The moment she became something different, something outside the rest of the world.

Of course, Derrick wasn't saying that.

He'd use words like *processing* and *healing* and *the event*. She didn't know if he dodged the real words—*four dead, broken, school shooting*—as a way to protect her or to protect himself. Either way, the three boys looked like they'd seen a ghost. And maybe they had. Maybe she wasn't real anymore, and all of the past year was nothing more than a kind of residual energy, electric impulses. Leftover brain activity.

Derrick gave one of the kids a fist bump, which probably seemed cool to him in the moment, but made all the boys laugh under their breath when he turned toward Claire. He came over and picked up her board, fiddling with the trucks and checking the grip tape. When he was satisfied with it, he put the board back down and looked at his hands for a moment, as if he didn't know how to fix them.

"We can go whenever you're ready."

Claire nodded. Sipped more water.

Bryan Bliss

Derrick started packing up her board, the tattered elbow and kneepads, when Dark came rushing over. No, *rushing* wasn't the right word. He walked like somebody was chasing him, but also like he was acutely aware that everybody was paying attention to how he moved. The result was almost bashful, incongruous with his lanky frame.

"Are you leaving?"

"Yeah, bud. Claire's probably had enough for today."

As he was talking, one of the other boys came up. "But you only got in one run."

Behind them, the final boy yelled out, "Half a run, technically!"

When they laughed, it was different from the kids on the bus. The kids in her classes. This was familiar, bringing her in instead of pushing her out. For the briefest moment, it was a ray of warm, thawing light.

"A run's a run," the second kid said, reaching a hand toward Claire. "They call me Leg. That's God. And you know Dark. But one run? That's not a day. Especially if you're skipping to hit up the Lair."

As soon as he said it, Leg looked at Derrick like he might call the principal. As if he wasn't complicit.

"I mean, school's cool and everything," Leg stammered. "But sometimes you need a mental health day. You know?"

"Your whole life is a mental health day, Leg," God said.

They all laughed again, and it made Claire smile.

"Leg's, like, the opposite of perfect attendance. What do you call that?"

"Community college," Mark-O said.

The boys offered up a collective "*Oh shit!*" and immediately began riffing on potential merchandise. T-shirts. Stickers. The Lair would make a killing, they all agreed.

As they were talking to Mark-O, Derrick leaned close to her and said, "Up to you."

Every single muscle in her body, every single cell, played a constant message: run, hide, go. At first, this response had been necessary for survival—for healing, they assumed. But she could no longer tell the difference between the constant panic that steered her away from everyone and everything and three seemingly nice guys who just wanted to skate.

So instead of talking she picked up her board (breathing, breathing), strapped on her helmet, and walked back into the ramp.

Leg and God didn't stop talking to her, even as they traded tricks, trying to one-up each other—to impress Derrick, all of which made Claire smile. Dark sat on a couch just off the lip of one of the smaller ramps, writing or drawing in a

Bryan Bliss

black-and-white composition notebook. Every so often, he'd look up, catch Claire's eye, and then go immediately back to the notebook.

It was as if the skate gods noticed her distraction and reached down to nudge her, just enough to lose balance. She hit the ground hard.

God got to her first, followed by Leg. After the initial check-in, the perfunctory *"Damn, you really ate shit"* acknowledgment, God yelled out, "She's fine!" before Derrick could even get to them.

After that, they took turns rolling up next to Claire, encouraging her, giving her pointers, and once, God grabbed her hands and took her flying across the skate park. When God saw she was stable, he let go and she rode all the way to the ramp where Dark was sitting.

She tried to get off her board without falling, fell anyway, and then sat there watching Derrick and the other boys before Dark said, "You can come up here if you want."

Claire tried to climb to the top of the ramp, but her entire body was torched. Dark reached down to help her up and, once she was on the couch, they sat there silent and awkward, watching the others.

Eventually, he gave her a long look before he exhaled and said, "So . . . why do you skate? You're really, you know, bad."

It made her laugh, the sound ringing across the nearly-empty park. Derrick shot her a glance, a smile, at the surprise of her voice. And it had surprised her, too. When was the last time she'd laughed? Actually *laughed*.

"Shit." The pained look he seemed to always wear deepened. "That's not what I meant. I mean, I don't skate but I still come. I guess I wanted to let you know you don't *have* to skate."

Before she knew what was happening, Claire started talking.

"I just keep thinking some of Derrick's genes might show themselves. Maybe? Hopefully?"

They both watched as Derrick rode his board high above the top of a ramp, turning an effortless 360, before dropping back down onto the ramp with barely a sound. The boys slapped their boards against the ground in appreciation.

"He's pretty amazing," Dark said. "I think God and Leg are in love."

"He was pro. Before."

Claire almost laughed again at the way Dark's jaw dropped. Leg must've seen it, must've thought something important was happening, because he flew toward them, taking the ramp too fast and nearly falling when he tried to stick the landing right next to Claire.

He jumped up, snapping his fingers and then fixing his hair in one fluid motion.

"Meant to do that, anyway. Dark, you trying to get me a prom date over here?"

"Jesus, please don't start."

Claire gave Dark a look, but he was already staring at the cover of his journal and shaking his head. She couldn't tell if he was nervous, embarrassed, or something else.

"Her brother is a pro," Dark said, obviously changing the subject.

"What? With who?"

Leg dropped next to Claire and stared at her like the question was a test—one Claire wasn't sure how to pass.

Her anxiety spiked but she pushed through it and, trying to sound casual, said, "Dirty Version."

Leg jerked back, like she'd just asked him if he wanted to know Jesus as his personal savior.

"*Dirty Version*? Holy shit."

Claire nodded, but Leg was already standing, yelling for God. Even Dark looked impressed. Derrick rolled up, kicking his board into his hand as he tried to figure out what was going on. She smiled quickly and shook her head—it's nothing—but before Claire could say anything, Leg yelled out, "Shit, bro. Dirty! Version! They make the *best* videos. Respect."

Derrick smiled at Claire, as if she'd been trading secrets to score points with Dark and Leg. It embarrassed her, because it was true and because now Dark and Leg were staring at her, too, probably thinking the same thing.

"For a bit. Then I got old."

"You still look pretty solid to me," God said.

"You sound like Mark-O," Derrick said, pulling off his helmet and pushing the hair back from his eyes. "But shit. Who knows what will happen?"

"Do they, like, have an old man division?" Leg asked, completely serious.

"Bro," God said, shaking his head. "He's, like, twenty-eight."

Claire laughed with the rest of them, but she couldn't help but notice how tired Derrick sounded. How uncertain he looked, as if he didn't believe things would ever change. Both of them stumbling and feeling their way through a dense cloud with no end in sight.

Bryan Bliss

CHAPTER FOUR

CLAIRE WOKE UP SORE THE NEXT MORNING, A FACT THAT announced itself suddenly when she first stood up. She had a flash, a memory, of basketball practice—long summer runs through the hills of North Carolina that made her legs rubbery. A time she could barely remember.

And for a split second, her brain turned itself off and functioned normally. She was sore, end of story. There were no other messages, no low-grade terror.

For a single moment, she felt fine.

Derrick was dressed and sitting at the kitchen table when she came into the room. As she was pouring cereal into a bowl, he casually suggested that he could drive her to school, no big deal.

Claire stopped pouring and swallowed once. The bus

yesterday. The train a few weeks ago. He was trying to protect her. He didn't think she was fine.

"That sounds good," she managed, keeping her back to him as she ate her cereal—so he couldn't see how hard she was working to fight off the tears of frustration.

They drove slowly through the snow-covered streets.

Derrick turned up a song on the radio, nodding his head thoughtfully with the beat as they waited for the cars in front of them to pull forward in the drop-off lane, every other kid getting out of their car and rushing through the cold without a second thought.

"Well, shit. Look at this."

At first she thought Derrick was pointing to the school resource officer huddled in the concrete crook of the main building, slowly bringing a steaming cup of coffee to his lips. But just above him were three boys mimicking and mocking every movement the man made.

"Maybe the community college comment got to them," Derrick said, just as the resource officer looked up and Dark, God, and Leg pushed away from the railing, laughing.

Claire didn't understand the urge to get out of the car. And maybe it was because she hadn't moved that fast in months, but when she reached for the door, she couldn't get it open.

Bryan Bliss

Derrick took in the whole sad struggle with the handle.

Then he laughed and unlocked the door with a push of a button. Claire shot him a dirty look.

"What?" Derrick said, still smiling. "Go to school already."

Once she was out of the car, she tried to walk normally. Not fast, not slow. Just *normal*. She was so focused, she nearly jumped when she reached the top of the stairs and Leg called out her name.

He held his arms out like he wanted to give her a hug. At first Claire mistook God and Dark's obvious shock for coldness, the distant way people seemed to treat everybody who hadn't lived in Minnesota for generations. But then God smiled and, finally, so did Dark.

"So. You go here." Dark looked even more uncomfortable than he had at the skate park.

"Nah," Leg said, "she's stalking you."

"No . . . I go here," Claire confirmed, just as the first warning bell rang above them. None of them moved, even though Claire instinctively took a half step toward the door.

"Did you bring your board?" God asked. Claire shook her head. "We're taking the bus to the Lair after school. You should come."

Claire was about to say something when the school resource officer came huffing up the stairs.

"The—bell—rang," he managed.

Leg looked at his wrist, where there was no watch. "Is it that time already?"

Dark smiled and mumbled something to God, who laughed.

"You guys think this is a joke?"

"Not *this*," Dark said, nodding at the security guard. "More like, you."

The cop must've thought Claire was an easier target, because even though the three of them were nearly doubled over with laughter, he took Claire by the arm (breathing, breathing) and started pulling her toward the door.

"Bro, let go of her," God said.

"You need to get to class," the cop said, ignoring God, Leg, all of them.

Claire was dive-bombing to the bottom of the ocean, unable to speak or do anything other than be dragged to the front door.

"Don't you see what you're doing?" Dark asked, wrenching her arm away from the cop.

As soon as he did, Claire shot up to the top of the water, gasping. She ran to class and didn't look back, didn't acknowledge the teacher (breathing, breathing) who told her to slow down.

Bryan Bliss

She could barely see when she sat in the too-small desk, trying to pretend that everything was fine.

She was fine.

Dr. Palmer, her language arts teacher, was up at the front of the room trying to keep a large stack of books from falling from her hands, which they did almost immediately.

"Okay, *okay* . . ." She gave the class a shrug and then swept her hands across the books that now littered her desk, the floor. "Behold the tools for your summative project!"

There were a couple of stereotypical groans, which Dr. Palmer ignored with such completeness they died immediately. She picked up one of the novels and showed the cover to the group.

"*Lord of the Flies.* Who wants it?"

Nobody raised their hand. And for good reason, Claire thought. She'd read the book as a freshman, writing a paper about Piggie and how he was essentially the only female character, as he was always quoting his aunt.

Dr. Palmer tossed the book toward a kid in the front row. "Okay, Argus. You probably need to read that one." Claire didn't know Argus or whether he knew the plot of the novel, but the look of shock on his face was enough for Dr. Palmer to crack a smile. Before he had a chance to respond, complain—anything—Palmer picked up another book.

"*The Bluest Eye.* Toni Morrison. Never heard of it? Well, now your life is about to be changed." She threw the book to a girl in the corner, who gave a legitimate shriek when it landed on her desk. "I know. Wait until you read it."

Dr. Palmer continued throwing books across the room, one by one, until it was just Claire and a kid who was somewhat sleeping in the back of the classroom, despite all the flying literature.

Dr. Palmer held up two more books—*Frankenstein* and *Leaves of Grass.* Claire didn't hesitate when Palmer tossed both books between her and the sleepy boy. She grabbed *Frankenstein* and quickly went back to her seat.

The boy looked up at Dr. Palmer dreamily.

"Andrew, your life just got a lot more complicated."

The assignment sounded simple enough. Read the book. Find a personal connection. Write, draw, construct a demonic temple in its honor—it didn't matter what—but respond in *some* way. It was the oldest of teacher tricks and, normally, Claire would be thankful, if not downright jubilant, for this sort of slam-dunk project.

Instead, she stared at the back of the book and read the synopsis for the thousandth time.

Bryan Bliss

She'd first read *Frankenstein* her sophomore year for a similar, equally forgettable assignment. But unlike so many things in high school, the book had stuck to her in a way she hadn't expected—in a way that had brought some ribbing from her friends when she kept reading it again and again, carrying the tattered paperback everywhere.

And now it lit up parts of her life that she'd forgotten, like a pinball shooting through her. Had she almost gotten into a fight with Chris Thompson because he'd made fun of the cover's dramatic illustration? Did Coach Harris tell her to "close that book and get your mind right" on the bus before the Maiden game? For months, the book—the sheer audacity of it—lived inside of her.

But eventually she just stopped carrying it around. Eventually she moved on, chasing whatever new thing had traipsed into her brain. Back when she didn't feel like the one being chased.

She was still staring at the description when the bell rang. And when Dr. Palmer asked if she was okay, she jumped up—feeling the weight of the book in her hand as she walked through the hallways. The weight in her backpack when she got to her next class and the teacher told them to clear their desks for a test. It was something like nostalgia, but not quite, hovering over her and begging her to . . . what?

Open the book? Remember that time in her life? Whatever it was, she spent the next three periods trying to shake the hold it had on her brain.

At lunch she saw God waving at her across the cafeteria—no, waving her toward a table that was already packed. Claire shook her head out of habit, even smiled, but God didn't hesitate. He stood up and jogged over to her.

"Hey, I didn't realize you had C lunch. Come sit with us."

Claire opened her mouth to say something, come up with some excuse that would make it clear how much she didn't want to join a table of people she didn't know, thank you very much. But God was too quick again.

"What else are you going to do? Sit alone?"

"Well, yeah," she finally said. "Exactly."

God started laughing hard and loud.

"C'mon."

And then he started walking back to the table.

Claire knew she could easily just walk to her normal spot in the corner, a sparse table of garden-variety introverts. People who barely made eye contact, let alone risked starting up an actual conversation. She'd have to force herself toward God's table, and it would take every ounce of strength and determination she had. But the first step didn't. And neither did the second. And soon she was following God. Just a girl walking across a cafeteria.

"This is Claire," God said to the table, which greeted her collectively. Leg gave her a nod but went back to the animated discussion he was having with a girl sporting hair dyed such a deep blue it was almost black.

"You're in my language arts class," another girl said, pushing up her chunky glasses as she spoke. "Dr. Palmer. First period?"

Claire nodded, realizing that she was still standing, and suddenly her body wouldn't work in that same effortless way it had only moments ago. She was so concerned with trying to make her body sit down, she completely forgot the girl talking, who was looking at her friends like, *Does it speak?*

"Yes," Claire forced out. "Dr. Palmer."

"Have you seen her YouTube channel?" Leg said, suddenly interested in the conversation. It drew the girl away enough that Claire could breathe for a second and when she did, something loosened inside her.

One more breath. A second. By the third, she could sit.

"Yeah, it's all about, like, how she and her husband make ancient weaponry."

"She's so fucking cool," the girl with the glasses said.

"Like, they're building an actual trebuchet in their backyard," Leg said, absolutely giddy to share this information.

"I keep asking for an invite to her house, but you know . . . teacher-student boundaries and all that."

They were still talking about Dr. Palmer when God reached over and got Claire's attention.

"So, after school. You in?"

Before, in North Carolina, Derrick liked to give her hell about her social schedule—he annoyingly called it her *calendar*—but she'd had the same friends since kindergarten.

She went out all the time. Driving through the warm North Carolina summer nights with the windows down. Shouting lyrics to their favorite songs. It wasn't every single night, the way Derrick would claim, but it was pretty close.

Sometimes it rose up and presented itself to her in the middle of the night. Everything she was missing. How she wouldn't walk across the graduation stage between the two people she'd been stuck between for nearly seventeen years— Lona Cooper and Chad Dell. It used to annoy her whenever seating charts came out at the beginning of the year, but now it made her ache for home.

"And besides, you kind of owe Dark," God said.

"What?"

Her voice shot up unexpectedly. God laughed again. She looked up and down the table, expecting to see Dark smiling

Bryan Bliss

sheepishly, in on whatever gag they were trying to pull. But he wasn't at the table—had he been?

"The rent-a-cop got him. I don't know if he's suspended, but it wouldn't surprise me."

"That dude's not even a rent-a-cop," Leg said, momentarily looking up from his phone. "More like a layaway cop."

Some people laughed, but not God.

"I guess you don't touch cops," he said. "No matter if they're rented or not."

"What's going to happen to him?" Claire asked.

Before God could answer, the bell rang above them, and the entire cafeteria exploded with movement, every kid pushing away from their table to beat the rush into the hallways, which would soon be choked with bodies. God and Claire didn't move.

"Here's the thing about Dark," he said carefully. "They're always on him for something. *Always*."

God didn't give Claire a chance to respond. He stood up and gave her a weak smile. "Anyway, come skating with us. It will be fun, you know?"

And just before she agreed—just before he walked away—Claire noticed the briefest flicker of worry flash across God's face.

CHAPTER FIVE

CLAIRE GOT ON THE BUS WITHOUT A SECOND THOUGHT, ignoring the look of concern from the driver. Her mind drifted toward a moment that now seemed more like dream than reality.

She'd accepted a social invitation.

If Claire was being totally honest, she hadn't planned on actually going through with it. But God and Leg had been waiting for her after school with their phones out, ready for her number and address. The whole transaction had happened so quickly that, before she could stop herself, muscle memory had taken over, and she'd fired off a text. She'd given God her address.

And now she was kind of freaking out.

But this wasn't like the storm that raged unpredictably

and inconveniently. This was more of a dull dread that refused to leave her stomach. Normally, she could hide in the carriage house and simply wait for the sun to fall and to come up again—one more day. But as she was getting on the bus, God wagged his phone in front of her face—Leg laughing beside him—and reminded her, "We know where you live."

She got off the bus and hurried back to the house.

Inside, Derrick was watching a skating video on his phone. He mumbled a distracted "hello," as if he too had forgotten the need for daily—if not hourly, by the minute—check-ins. So, Claire went into the kitchen, dropped a piece of bread into the toaster, and leaned against the counter, trying to figure out how she would tell him that she was not only going out, but going out with a bunch of guys she'd just met the day before.

What could go wrong?

Her toast hadn't even popped up when there was a hard knock on the door. For a brief moment, she lied to herself and said it must be Mark-O or maybe a Mormon missionary— somebody else. But then she heard the laughter. The jostling of bodies. And that strange, empty panic returned to her stomach.

When Derrick opened the door, God and Leg fell into the

room, already mid-conversation, as if both she and Derrick were up to speed.

"Yeah, but that's not the *spirit* of the award, man." Leg turned to Claire and Derrick. "Right?"

Claire flushed and searched for something to say.

Thankfully, Derrick sat down and said, "What award? You up for the Nobel Prize, Leg?"

Leg lit up like a lightning strike. "Oh, hell no. Something way better. I'm trying to letter in prom."

This time it was Claire and Derrick's turn to laugh.

"Are you high?" Derrick asked, cocking his head to look into Leg's eyes.

"Lettering in prom, man!" If possible, Leg was even more excited now. "Like, if you go to prom all four years, they give you this sweet-ass engraved martini glass and it's a really big deal."

Derrick turned to God who, almost regretfully, confirmed.

"*Big deal* might be an overstatement."

Leg slapped at his arm playfully and said, "Don't you dare denigrate prom."

"So, this is a real thing?" Claire asked. "Isn't prom, like, months away?"

"Hell yeah, it's real, and we're at threat level red, yellow, midnight—whatever's the worst."

Bryan Bliss

"He can't find a date," God said, answering Claire. "And I told him he should just go by himself. You're still going to prom, even if you're alone. And bro, *nobody* starts looking for a date in February."

This time God punched Leg, who ignored it and reached down to pick up Claire's toast. He took a bite and said, "Against the spirit of the award, bro. We're seniors! And besides, if I don't act soon, all the good dates will be gone."

"By *good* he means, any girl that would go with him," God once again clarified.

"Whatever," Leg said, finishing off the toast, "I'm not getting this close only to go down like a chump."

Derrick, clearly amused, realized that God and Leg had essentially just appeared in their living room, because he kind of shook his head and gave each of them a look.

"So, I'm confused. Are you here to ask one of us to prom?"

Leg didn't hesitate. "Would you go?"

"Sorry, bud."

"Just take your cousin like last year," God said. "Anyway, are you ready?"

Claire was too befuddled by the conversation to realize that God was talking to her. And that's when Derrick got interested, too.

"Ready? For what? What's happening here?"

"We're going to the Lair," Claire explained, unsure how Derrick would react.

And it took him a few seconds. He gave God and Leg a deeper look, as if he were trying to discover any ulterior motives. Whether they might actually be high. Whether "lettering in prom" was some kind of euphemism. But eventually, he relaxed and he smiled.

He gave Claire one more quick glance before he said, "Just be home before midnight."

The Lair was busier than she'd ever seen it, which made sense. She and Derrick intentionally went during off times, when the lines would be open and the chances of her accidentally colliding with another skater were at their absolute lowest.

Now she could barely make it through the door to the main room, let alone find a comfortable place to drop in and ride.

"Is Dark here?" she asked as God was tying his shoes. When he was finished, he checked his phone and then said, "Up on the couches."

Claire looked and saw Dark sitting next to another kid but obviously wishing he was alone. He was head down, furiously scribbling in his notebook.

"I might go up and talk to him," Claire said, taking another wary look around the packed room.

Bryan Bliss

"Don't get entranced by his innate charms!" Leg said, cackling as he and God rode off into the crowd.

It took Claire nearly five minutes to make it down the narrow hallway that was barely big enough for a couple of wiry skaters, let alone the thirty who were trying to push in different directions.

She finally made it up to the couches just as the boy who'd been sitting there was carrying his board to the lip of the ramp. With a loud whoop, he dropped in and began zipping around the park. Dark barely looked up when the boy yelled out, so he didn't notice Claire at first. When he did, he closed his notebook quickly and nodded at her.

"Hey," he said. "They said you were coming."

"I'm supposed to apologize," Claire said, sitting down next to him.

Dark smiled awkwardly and all he said was, "No."

And then he sat there, quietly watching the rest of the room. Claire wasn't sure he would speak again until he said, "So what did I miss?"

"What?"

"At school. Did anything happen. Besides, you know, the entire place being overrun by fascist police officers looking to wield what little power they have against children."

"Oh, wow."

"Sorry," Dark said, suddenly embarrassed by the outburst. "But I mean . . . "

Dark looked as if he wanted her to agree—to give him permission to continue. But Claire wasn't sure how to respond so she said, "Do you have Dr. Palmer? She gave everybody a different book to read. Plus, a project."

"I had her last year. Have you seen her YouTube channel?" Dark fumbled with his phone, trying to pull it up. But the Lair was like a concrete box—no service. "Anyway. It's about, like, weapons. Old weapons, so not the good kind. Anyway, what did she assign you?"

A momentary panic washed over Claire. *Not the good kind* was the sort of comment that she might not have paid any mind before. The boys at Ford High School—hell, half the girls—were gun obsessed. And maybe it wasn't obsession, but something different. Hunting, clay shooting, target practice—guns were sewn into the fabric of the school, the town, the entire culture.

But *not the good kind* would never just pass by her now.

"You okay?" Dark said, looking like he was worried she might stroke out again in front of him. She shook her head, clearing her mind, and then nodded.

"Sorry. *Frankenstein.* That's my book," Claire said. Before she could say anything else, Dark cut her off.

"You know Frankenstein is the *scientist* and not the *monster*."

Claire rolled her eyes. "Uh, yeah. I'm not an idiot. Jesus."

Dark dropped his notebook and then his phone when he tried to pick it up. When he had them both in his hands, his mouth was obviously trying to form an apology, but he was so flustered he just sat there looking like a grounded fish sucking for air.

Claire swallowed her irritation.

"I'm sorry. It's just . . . I know that book. Better than most people," she said. "And I haven't really, you know, talked to people in . . . well, in a long time."

"So, what's my excuse?" Dark asked.

He smiled and then became embarrassed again, turning down to his notebook, which he opened and began flipping through the pages. When he found the page he wanted, he paused, looked up at Claire, and then cautiously passed her the notebook.

The page was filled with thick, black lines that swirled together, crossing over one another in an almost manic collection. Upon first glance, Claire wasn't sure it was anything more than a poor attempt at abstract art. But when her eyes began to focus, when she could really make out the specific choices—a scar above what looked like an eye, a gruesome mouth—she could see that it was a drawing, a furious drawing, of a face staring off the page.

"It's the Monster," Dark said.

Claire was in bed, staring at the wall above her head, the overly ornate woodwork that lined the edges of her ceiling, when she finally found the words she'd tried to say to Dark.

After he showed her the picture of the Monster, a cold and creeping dread reached across her body. She'd never been a fan of horror movies, but they also never bothered her. Never affected her on a visceral level. She'd see a monster and say "That isn't real," putting it into some sort of mental box and never letting it escape. But the immediacy and power of Dark's drawing plucked something deep inside her.

It wasn't fear, necessarily. But it also wasn't *not* fear.

Dark must've known he'd rattled her, because he spent the rest of the time in the skate park—not to mention the entire bus ride back to St. Paul—showcasing his lighter drawings. A cartoon man and woman, holding an umbrella as tiny hearts fell across the page like raindrops. A spot-on caricature of a biology teacher nobody at the school liked. Dark had lingered over that page for a second before, finally, flipping to a fairly graphic depiction of two anime characters Claire didn't know. Whatever made him

Bryan Bliss

pause on the picture of the biology teacher quickly gave way to embarrassment, which got Dark so tangled that he closed the notebook and mumbled, "Well, anyway."

Now, as she stared at the ceiling and listened to the intermittent sounds of cars passing on the road in front of the carriage house, the words she wanted to say to him came quickly.

Are you dangerous?

It seemed dramatic even to her, alone in her bed. *Dangerous.* It was a drawing. A pretty damn good one, too. She'd tried art freshman year, and even among the advanced students, she hadn't seen a drawing with the complexity of Dark's.

She hadn't seen that sort of ferocity, either.

Claire tried to shake herself off this path because, frankly, it was one she'd been down a thousand times in the last year.

Seeing a problem where there wasn't one. A weapon, aggression in the smallest degree, even malicious intent, in every and any possible movement. Nothing was sacred or safe, not anymore. She lived her life on the head of a pin, an exhausting balancing act.

But she hadn't been right. Not even once. Every single time she was wrong, and the *threat* turned out—once again—to be something broken deep inside of her. Something that she had no idea how to fix, or whether fixing it was ever going to be possible.

She fell asleep at some point. And when she dreamed, it mimicked her reality once again. The entire night she felt like she was being chased by something she could not see.

Bryan Bliss

CHAPTER SIX

THE NEXT MORNING CLAIRE WAS UP EARLY, CLANKING around in the kitchen loud enough that Derrick appeared and sat down at the table with a cup of coffee. It took a long time—two cups' worth—before he finally said, "It's five thirty in the morning."

She didn't want to tell him that she couldn't spend another minute in bed, that she wanted to get to school as quickly as she could to give Dark a once-over. To really look at him. At that notebook. To decide.

Basically, she knew it was nuts and she wanted to get out of the house before Derrick got a whiff of it.

"Skating was good," she offered up. Derrick nodded, head in his hands. "I don't know if they'll ask me back, though."

"Why?"

She didn't have a reason, now that he'd asked. But eventually she'd freak out in front of them. Eventually she would create a reason not to go out. Maybe she already had. So, she shrugged and plucked a box of cereal from the cupboard instead of answering.

"Those boys don't know what to do with themselves around you," Derrick said. Before Claire could object, he added, "They seem like good dudes. It could be worse. You could be hanging out with the wrestling team again."

Derrick chuckled when Claire spun around to glare at him.

She'd never "hung out" with the wrestling team. Yes, she had threatened one particularly obnoxious guy named Chris when he'd made a comment about the "evolutionary position" of women and their need for protection. He was lucky that she hadn't knocked him out right there, honestly. Coach O came to apologize and when he saw the fire in her eyes, he asked her if she wanted to be the first female state champ in the history of North Carolina. She could do it, he said, just needed a little training.

After that, the wrestlers—Chris especially—gave her both a wide berth and a respect that made Claire think good old Coach O had run them into the ground. Either way, Derrick never let her hear the end of it.

"I never once hung out with a wrestler, let alone a group of

Bryan Bliss

them," Claire said, picking the marshmallows out of the box of cereal and eating them one by one. "Besides, they were all terrified of me."

"With good reason," Derrick said.

It took a few seconds and then he casually said, "I know basketball wasn't realistic this year, but have you thought about going out for track? I'm sure some workouts or something are coming up in the next month or two. You've always been fast as hell."

Claire didn't wait for Derrick to finish. She was already thinking about the crowds, not being able to see each person, to make sure that she was safe. Nothing but screaming and chaos and the constant sense that everything could end before anybody could stop it.

She shook her head quickly, trying to muster up some of Derrick's same casualness as she put the box of cereal into the cabinet.

"I don't know, we'll see. Can I get a ride to school?"

Claire charged up the front steps two at a time, expecting to see God and Leg standing at the top, just as they had been the day before. When they weren't and instead a bunch of girls were watching her side-eyed, she felt the first flush of foolishness.

The second came only a few seconds later when she saw God standing in the doorway, clearly amused, at her rushing a group of sophomores like she was on a SEAL team.

"I think you seriously scarred them forever," God said. The girls were still staring at Claire with what she now saw was complete and utter bewilderment. "Like, they may need to go see the school counselor."

"I was . . ."

What? Her initial plan had been to come and ask God and Leg about the notebook, about the drawings—to see if they shared a look. Or reacted in any way, subtle or significant, just *something*. Now, standing there, she saw the flaws in her reasoning. Dark was their friend. She was overreacting. Again.

Take a few breaths and regroup, she told herself.

"Is Dark back?"

God sighed. "No. They got him for two days this time. So, it'll be Monday."

"Is he . . ." Claire didn't mean for it to be a dramatic pause, but it happened all the same as she figured out what to exactly say. "What's with that notebook?"

God shrugged. "I mean, first things first. It's not normal for him to show it to anybody. So, you obviously made an impression on him."

Claire must've looked upset, or at least confused, because God reached over and touched her on her shoulder. "Hey, that's a good thing. Trust me."

Claire stepped closer to God as the bell rang and the girls at the top of the stairs pushed by them. God did not seem in a hurry, though. He scanned the street, as if he expected to see someone—Dark, perhaps. Claire couldn't read the expression on his face. It could be concern. But it could very well be nothing. A teenage boy trying to muster the energy for another early morning of high school.

"I don't like the drawings, if I'm being completely honest." God continued watching the street, the emotions on his face now clear as the cold winter day—he was worried. "Dark needs people like you in his life. People he can trust. People who are willing to see him for who he is *now* and not just some kid who did something in middle school once."

"What did he do in middle school?" Claire asked.

God hesitated. "Something stupid. Something he's paid for a thousand times since then."

Claire wanted to push him for more answers, she wanted to grab God by the shoulders and force him to answer the same question that had kept her up for hours last night—was he dangerous?

God shook his head and said, "Please just trust me? Just

give him a chance and don't do what everybody does."

"And what's that?"

Just then, a teacher's aide Claire didn't know—but who obviously had dealt with God before—came outside and told them to follow her to the office. And before she knew it, God's face had transformed. He was smiling and talking to the aide, all while he directed Claire to the doors behind him, saving her from whatever would happen next.

Claire was still thinking about God and Dark and so she didn't see Dr. Palmer until she was standing right above her desk.

"Are you deep in thought or completely ignoring my gracious offer of a free period full of nothing but enjoying classic works of literature."

Dr. Palmer gestured dramatically as she spoke, unfazed by the way the entire class was now staring. Claire sunk down in her desk.

"I've already read it," Claire managed. "Multiple times."

"Multiple times. Really . . ."

Claire could tell Dr. Palmer was sizing her up, so she went against standard operating procedure and rattled off some trivia.

"Shelley wrote it when she was eighteen, almost on a dare.

Bryan Bliss

And a lot of people didn't think she'd written it because, you know, she was a woman and *obviously* a woman couldn't have written something so popular and insightful and revolutionary."

"Revolutionary?" Dr. Palmer pulled an empty chair next to Claire's desk and sat down. "That's an interesting word choice."

Claire was sitting up in her desk now, her voice beginning to rise with a passion for the book she hadn't felt in years. If people were still watching, she didn't care.

"I mean, look at the Monster. It switches to his point of view. Suddenly we're in the Monster's head. So, I don't know, it feels pretty . . ."

"Revolutionary. I hear you. I hear you."

Dr. Palmer leaned back in the chair, staring off into the distance. This was more than Claire had spoken in the entirety of the past school year. And now, in the wake of her sudden outburst, she wanted to disappear inside the neck of her T-shirt. She could feel every single set of eyes on her, their stares heavy and burdensome. But none more than Dr. Palmer, who was smiling like she discovered a secret.

"So, what do you think the Monster is feeling?"

The question surprised Claire, not because she didn't know the answer. It was something she'd spent many nights thinking about and, during one eventful language arts class, it had caused her to verbally annihilate a kid who implied that the Monster was nothing more than a thoughtless beast.

But those were old words from an old world. And maybe she'd spent her allowance for the day, because she suddenly couldn't talk. So she shrugged instead and sat there, hoping that Dr. Palmer would save her and just walk away. When she didn't, Claire simply said, "I don't know."

"Well, I guess you've found your project, then."

And then she stood up and returned to the front of the room.

God and Leg were waiting for Claire at the front door after school. As soon as they saw her, Leg said, "Right" and started walking down the staircase. She nearly fell trying to catch up with them, dodging students and teachers as they wove through the crowd, down the sidewalk, and away from the long line of yellow busses.

"I'm going to miss my bus," Claire said.

"Good! School busses are instruments of institutional control!" Leg was looking back as he yelled, seemingly about one second from raising his fist in the air and exhorting his fellow students to rise up, rise up! And then he started laughing and dropped his skateboard to the ground, slowly rolling a few feet in front of Claire and God.

"He's an idiot," God said.

They were almost to the corner before Claire asked, "Um, where are we going?"

God didn't say anything, just pointed across the street. A large truck was passing, momentarily blocking her view of the intersection. When it was clear, she saw Dark, head down and drawing in his notebook.

"What is he doing?"

"He can't be on school property. That's officially *not* school property."

Dark looked up as Leg shot across the street on his board, nearly getting hit by an oncoming car. The driver hammered his horn, to which Leg gave a classy, almost royal, wave. When he got close to Dark, he faked a few punches. Dark didn't respond at all, just stood there enduring it.

Once Claire and God made it across the street, they all started walking down Lexington Avenue, a road that would eventually land them at Claire's house. And for a moment, she thought maybe they were walking her home. That they expected to come over and sit around in her living room— an idea that made her breath catch.

But then they turned left on to Selby and made a right

onto a street Claire didn't know, and then another left, until suddenly Claire had no idea where they were. She tried to note every side street (breathing, breathing), hoping that she'd be able to string them together in case . . . what? She needed to escape? The word was an invocation, transforming her body into a jelly-filled panic. Every single muscle told her to run, even though she felt like she could barely walk.

"Hey . . ." God was staring at her. Leg and Dark were halfway inside the door of an apartment building. "This is Dark's spot. We were going to go in and chill. Are you . . . good?"

Claire managed a thumbs-up, but when God turned to follow his friends into the apartment building, she didn't move. Couldn't, actually. Maybe God remembered the skating park. Or maybe Derrick had told them more than she knew, and God had been prepped for a classic Claire freak-out moment. Either way, he let the door close and stood there, waiting.

And that was the problem, wasn't it? She didn't know when a new nightmare would pounce out of the dark corners of her mind, gripping her entire body in a terror that might last thirty seconds or the rest of the week. She didn't know why she couldn't walk to Dark's apartment, or why she simultaneously felt foolish and under attack.

Bryan Bliss

God wasn't fazed. "Do you want to call your brother?"

"Yes," she said, pulling out her phone. "Where are we?"

God gave her the address and watched as she nodded and hit the button for Derrick, smiling as the phone rang (breathing, breathing) and she tried to quiet everything down.

"Hey, what's up?"

"Hi. I went with God and those guys. To Dark's apartment. We're at"—she looked at God again for the address—"the corner of Milton and Portland. Next to a church that looks like it should be in a BBC miniseries about friars and nuns."

The last part had just come out, making Derrick laugh. When Claire looked at God, he was trying to keep a straight face as he mouthed, "What are you talking about?"

And just as quickly as the panic had come, it began to drain out of her. Maybe it was talking to Derrick. Or God, trying so hard to honor her freak-out, but failing utterly. His entire body was shaking with laughter. Or maybe it was the realization that she wasn't trapped—she was safe.

"Are you okay?" Derrick asked. "Do you want me to come get you?"

"I'm good," Claire said. As she did, God smiled and turned around to push the button for Dark's apartment. When the buzzer sounded, he held the door for her.

"Hey, Claire—" Derrick paused, taking a full beat before he finally said, "Have fun. Okay?"

Dark's apartment was dimly lit and smelled like take-and-bake cookies, which were waiting for them on a paper plate in the center of a cheap coffee table. A lamp with a missing bulb stood in the corner, barely putting off enough light to see the room—which was smaller than Claire's bedroom. Leg was fiddling with the back of the television, trying to connect an old video game console and swearing every few seconds.

"I wish she wouldn't unhook this, man. It's a real pain in the ass to strip the wires and get the connection to your old-ass TV."

"Grandma thinks it's going to start a fire," Dark said, looking to the kitchen where an older woman leaned against the counter, smoking.

"I'm going to go on record and say that this Nintendo 64 is less of a fire hazard than, say, falling asleep on the couch with a lit cigarette," Leg said, cussing again.

"She's old," Dark said, his voice flat and lacking emotion. He did look at Claire, as if he was embarrassed by—what? Leg? His apartment? The fact that his chimney-smoking grandmother wasn't going to be a member of an IT team anytime soon?

"My brother is scared of lightning," Claire offered, giving Dark a quick smile. A quick moment of solidarity. "Like, he won't sit near windows during a storm because he thinks the lightning is going to come in through the window."

Leg stopped messing with the television. "What."

"That's, like, physically impossible," God said.

"Meteorologically impossible, even," Dark mumbled, which made everyone laugh. God slapped him on the shoulder and Leg went back to the work of connecting the N64, which after a few more seconds, lit up the dark room in one brilliant flash of light.

Leg and God played a game called *Tony Hawk's Pro Skater 2*, which Leg proclaimed "the best damn game of all time" before he cut himself off and immediately started swearing.

"My controller is broken. These things are old, and my *controller is broken*."

"The controllers work fine," God said. "And stop complaining. We have *company*."

Dark sat on the floor, his back against the couch. Every few seconds Claire would peek at what he was drawing—the same heavy black lines. The same chaos.

"Can I use your bathroom?" Claire said. Dark nodded and jumped up, rushing in front of her to close doors on the way down the hallway. It was the fastest she'd ever seen him move.

"It's right here," he said. "Sorry. The whole place is kind of gross."

"Stop apologizing," his grandmother said, stepping out of what must've been her bedroom at the end of the hallway. Claire hadn't even seen her leave the kitchen. Before she could stammer out an apology, the woman snapped, "Nobody walks into a place like this and expects Buckingham Palace."

Dark cringed as his grandmother trudged past them, lighting another cigarette on her way back to the living room.

"You should've seen our trailer in North Carolina," Claire said. "The bathroom was a total pit."

"Yeah?" Dark said, looking at her through his dark hair. "Well, tell me how it compares. Wait. Is that weird?"

"I mean, it *wasn't*."

Claire smiled and Dark smiled, shifting his weight to his other foot before saying, "Okay, well. Good. I mean, let me know if you need anything."

He cringed again.

"I should be fine," Claire said, pointing at the bathroom. "Over a decade of experience."

Bryan Bliss

Dark laughed uneasily before walking back down the hallway, checking the doors a final time before he disappeared into the living room.

The bathroom was small and, in striking contrast to the dim living room, was lit by a bright and obviously new bulb. Claire had to squint as she washed her hands, looking at herself in the mirror when she was finished.

She was thinner, maybe by ten pounds. Her eyes seemed darker, too. As if something inside of her had changed and was only now pushing itself out. She fixed her hair and smiled at her reflection, wondering if that, too, had changed.

She could hear the boys playing their game as she stepped out into the hallway. As her eyes adjusted, she almost tripped and fell over a large, fat cat that had decided to sit right in front of the bathroom door. He looked up at her lazily, as if to say, "Step over me. Or wait there, I don't care."

Choosing to step over the yawning cat, Claire noticed a door was now open in the hallway. The cat must've been in there and pushed his way out. She wasn't planning on looking, let alone opening the door. But a faint red light caught her attention first. And then it was the eyes, bone white and piercing. Spotlights in the otherwise shadowy room.

The Monster.

Its head seemed to push through the back wall of Dark's room, expertly drawn around the twin windows that looked down into the street. And from the corner of the room, two arms reached forward, trying to catch her before she could run away. Its face, unlike the ones in the notebook, was plaintive—almost pained. Like it could be crying or screaming, depending on what happened next.

She knew that look.

They'd only been in Minnesota a few days, back when she still believed they could run away. Derrick had the television on—they always had the television on back then—and in a moment of either confusion or misplaced excitement, he'd said her name.

It was Eleanor, her friend. Her teammate since second grade. But she looked different, as if she'd been changed in some fundamental way. She was screaming, crying, right outside the front doors of their high school. Of course, everybody would end up focusing on the *FUCK GUNS* that she'd scrawled across her T-shirt. The pure fury that seemed to shake the otherwise still picture.

But for Claire, it was Eleanor's face. Something universal, traveling across the thousands of miles between Minnesota and North Carolina to perfectly capture the pain and the

Bryan Bliss

fear and the grief that all of them felt. That Claire still felt every single moment.

"Hey . . ."

Claire would've run God over fullback style if he hadn't caught her by the shoulders. She couldn't stop herself from shaking in his hands.

"I'm fine," she said automatically.

God followed Claire's eyes into Dark's room and, after a second, closed the door. He looked like he wanted to say something, but instead he let go of Claire's shoulders and looked back to the other room.

"We're going to run over to Grand Ave.," he said. "Get something to eat."

And then he left her in the hallway to calm herself. To push back the storm. To breathe.

CHAPTER SEVEN

CLAIRE IGNORED HER BURRITO BOWL, WAITING FOR Derrick to come pick her up, trying to dismiss every red flag rising inside her. Calling every fear a liar.

It didn't help that God had watched her the entire walk to Chipotle—a look she knew all too well. She'd used that same microscope to dissect every movement and intention of every person she met, these boys included. She expected him to turn one of the lamps on her and begin the interrogation any minute.

Instead, the three of them ordered food, found seats, and generally acted the same as usual—loud and unabashedly idiotic. Still, every so often she caught God staring at her. He never let his gaze linger, always smiling at something Leg or Dark said and turning away as soon as she caught him. At first she thought it was actually in her head—a fiction her anxiety was knitting together.

"I mean, they do make you pay for guac, which is total bullshit. But otherwise?" Leg lifted his burrito, as if to consecrate it before the food gods, and let loose a too-loud *ommmmm*. "Best restaurant in the entire world, fight me."

A couple shot him a rude look, but he didn't notice. He stared reverently at his burrito for a moment before taking a huge bite.

"I prefer Taco Bell," Dark said, looking up from the table only to catch Leg's incredulous face.

They were still arguing when Derrick walked in and started bumping fists and swiping rogue pieces of steak from their bowls.

"What up, degenerates?" he said, dropping into the seat next to Claire.

"No context," Leg said. "Chipotle or Taco Bell?"

Derrick said, "Wow, I mean—how does one gauge his response? Affordability? Freshness? The ability not to spend the rest of one's life on the toilet after consuming?"

"See?" Leg said, slamming his hands down on the metal table. "You don't *ever* get the shits after eating at Chipotle. It's, like, in their business plan. This matter is settled."

Derrick was laughing with the boys when he turned and

saw Claire, halfway out of her seat and obviously waiting for him to be done. She didn't need to say anything. He stood up and said good-bye for both of them, but just as he was about to walk away, he snapped his fingers and pointed at the three boys.

"I almost forgot—Mark-O had somebody cancel at the product demo tomorrow. So, me and Claire are going to hit up the Lair tomorrow night. If you guys are down, I'm skating. Plus, if you don't make a big deal about it, after I'm finished I'll let you walk off with some of the promo gear."

Leg was nodding before Derrick had even finished his first sentence, and now he looked like he was on the verge of choking himself with enthusiasm and a mouthful of burrito.

"Hell yes," he managed. "We'll be there."

God was staring at Claire again, and she forced a smile. Forced cheer into her voice, hoping it would be enough to end this conversation and get them out the door.

"You guys should totally come," she said, her voice all wrong.

Derrick looked from Claire to the boys, before finally saying. "Okay, well. It starts at seven o'clock. Maybe we'll see you guys."

As they were walking outside into the cold night air, it started snowing once again. Big, fat flakes that fell from the sky and disappeared as soon as they hit the ground—a singular thing returning to the masses.

When they got to the car, Derrick put his hands on the roof and looked over at her.

"So, what was that about?"

The lights inside the restaurant made it seem warm for a second. Leg was gone from the table, getting another soda. And God was talking to Dark intently, neither of them looking toward the window or Claire.

She had no idea what they were talking about or how she should feel.

"Nothing. I'm just ready to go home."

At school the next day, Claire was too distracted to focus on her project. And when Dr. Palmer once again stopped by her desk, she didn't need another conversation. So, she wrote "The Monster" at the top of her page, which was enough to appease Palmer, who moved on to bother the kid in the back who was obviously flummoxed by *Leaves of Grass* and had taken to just staring at the unopened book, as if waiting for inspiration.

She opened *Frankenstein* and started flipping pages, toward the section she knew was written in the point of view of the Monster. The first time she'd read the book, she'd been shocked to discover that the Monster wasn't, well, a monster. She could still remember the moment—in her bed, Derrick asleep in his room—realizing the profound loneliness of the Monster and not understanding what it would be like to be that much of an outsider.

A little over a year ago. Only months before she became an outsider, too.

In the months after, people used Monster language a lot. *The monster who did this*, that sort of thing. She hadn't known the kid and now could barely remember his face, even though sometimes he would appear to her in dreams, nothing but a shadow. Something she never thought she could escape.

She could feel tears beginning to well up and she wiped at them quickly, hoping nobody saw her. Trying to stem the tide, to give herself a distraction, she quickly wrote, *The Monster was created.*

She stared at the words, which felt truer than she'd expected. The Monster was unable to experience the world in even the simplest of ways. The joy of discovery was always mixed with the pain of rejection, the sudden and brutal reminder that the Monster would never be the same—a continual life of *after*.

The bell rang and kids stood up, hurrying into the hallways

Bryan Bliss

for their five minutes of cramped freedom between classes. When Claire didn't join them, Dr. Palmer came over and rapped her knuckles on the desk.

She opened her mouth to speak but noticed the words on the paper. Her face changed ever so slightly, from playful to thoughtful to, maybe, impressed.

"It must be difficult to be a creation," she said. "To lose all sense of . . . I don't know. Agency, maybe? Control?"

Claire didn't want to look up. Didn't want Dr. Palmer to see her face, the shadow of her tears, which were surely evident. The undeniable truth that she'd lost control of even the simplest parts of her life.

"Claire . . . are you okay?"

Claire wanted to say it exactly right, so she didn't answer right away, even though kids were coming into the classroom now. She forced all the emotion out of her voice, trying to sound more robot than human.

"Do you think the Monster would've ever been, you know, able to live in the normal world?"

Dr. Palmer sat down in the desk in front of her and waited for Claire to look up. When she did, Dr. Palmer smiled gently and said, "Well, what happens in the cottage at the edge of the village?"

Claire thought for a second. "He listens to the family."

"Right. And more importantly, he *learns*. He becomes educated. And education leads to . . ."

"College?"

Dr. Palmer laughed.

"Well, sometimes. But I was thinking *empathy*. The more we know, the more difficult it becomes to ignore our surroundings—to ignore things like suffering and joy and pleasure."

"So, he's becoming less of a monster," Claire said.

"In a sense," Dr. Palmer said. "I think he's growing, maybe. Evolving. The point is, it's impossible to stay static, no matter what happens to us. We're always changing. We're always growing. And we're always healing."

She held Claire's gaze for a long moment, before smiling one last time.

"You're going to be late," she said. "I'll write you a pass, okay?"

Claire nodded, standing up and following Dr. Palmer to her desk. The kids in the class were buzzing behind her and it made Claire nervous (breathing, breathing) to stand with her back to them. Dr. Palmer handed the pass to her. Claire took it and stood there, thinking.

"What do you think the Monster would be like today?" she asked quietly. "If he got the chance to live happily ever after?"

Bryan Bliss

Dr. Palmer didn't hesitate.

"He would do the best he could, every day."

Claire spent most of her trigonometry class thinking about Dr. Palmer's statement, a decision that submarined her on multiple fronts. First, her teacher—a squat man with an impressive braided ponytail—said her name three times before she shook herself out of her own brain and, as the class tried to muffle its laughter, had to admit that she wasn't listening.

But perhaps more importantly, the Monster had once again taken up residence in her imagination. Before, she empathized with its struggle—constantly reacting to a world that never felt safe. It had been an intellectual exercise, something that would keep her up at night. But now it pushed too close to her own life.

If that wasn't bad enough, she couldn't separate that Monster from the menacing monsters of Dark's notebooks. He'd given shape to something that, until now, had been formless. And while Dr. Palmer's statement—*he would try his best*—made her feel hopeful, she couldn't keep herself from focusing on the sharp hands and reaching eyes that seemed to crawl out of her subconscious until every part of her body was humming with anxiety.

The rational explanation was that Dark simply connected with the book—probably the movie, but maybe the book—in not quite the same way she had, but in *some* way. And if she wanted to be stereotypical, she could point to the evidence—black clothes, pale skin, dyed black hair. He looked the type.

But the fury of his drawings. The lines that seemed to come from a different, almost needful place. It didn't look like passion. It looked like anger.

And that's what worried her. That's what tied her in knots and had teachers calling her name, period after period, until she was coming down the stairs for lunch, stuck in that same fog.

God was standing against the wall, waiting for her. When he saw her, he jumped forward and matched her pace.

"Hey, can we talk for a minute? Like, in private?"

Claire looked around the hallway. There wasn't a private place in this entire school, a fact that routinely laid her low. The hallways were eternally clogged, forcing Claire to press herself against the walls just to keep moving against the constant traffic jam. She couldn't help but wonder what would happen if they all had to move fast.

"We can go to the choir room. The teacher hates me, but I'm sure she's forgotten about *the incident*."

"The incident?" Claire asked, forgetting the hallway for a moment. She laughed nervously.

"Freshman year. I sang a solo and . . . it didn't go well. Just leave it at that."

Claire tried to imagine God in choir, dressed in a matching outfit with his hair just so. Singing and pantomiming for parents and grandparents. The smile that appeared on her face disappeared when she saw the look on God's face.

"Yeah, sure," she said.

The choir room was only a few steps down the hallway, on the other side of the main entrance to the school. And like God promised, it was mostly quiet other than a couple of boys who were working their way through a piece of music on the piano. They ignored God and Claire, save a cursory glance when the door opened.

"Okay, I don't know how to say this."

Claire could feel her heart rate climbing as he spoke. She'd never been good with conflict, not even before. She always wanted to control the situation, no matter how small. And now, after, she couldn't tell how much was control and how much was simple fear.

"About Dark—"

"I didn't open his door. The cat did it. But I'm not sure

what to think about that drawing or the notebooks and . . . help. Please."

She had to take a breath after she finished talking, and God closed his eyes for a second before he spoke.

"I understand. I do."

God paused again and Claire recognized the look on his face. It was hesitation mixed with the need to say something really important. Her brother. Those early therapists. Teachers. She'd seen it plenty of times before.

"They're fucking scary, okay? And I don't know why he draws them. And I don't particularly care because . . . those drawings? They keep him balanced somehow. Before he started drawing them, I literally worried about him all the time."

God shook his head, like he was trying to get rid of a bad dream.

"Leg and I have spent a lot of time protecting him from, well, everybody. From their assumptions. Their accusations. All of it. And, if I'm being honest, I don't want to have to protect him from you, too."

"What are you protecting him from exactly?" Claire asked.

God looked over at the two boys, who were really starting to amp up their volume—their enthusiasm.

"If there's a problem in this school, they always look at

Bryan Bliss

Dark. Doesn't matter what it is. All people see are the clothes and how aloof he is"—God smiled here, as if he was remembering something—"and it makes me tired. It pisses me off. And I just want people to see him the way I see him."

"And how's that?" Claire asked.

She studied every muscle twitch, every blink of his eyes—looking for even the slightest tell. The slightest evidence that God was trying to hide something.

He looked her straight in the eye and said, "He's the best person I know."

Whatever sincerity had powered his response quickly turned to embarrassment. God rubbed the back of his neck, as if he could massage the redness away.

"Look. I just wanted to clear this up, you know? We think you're cool. Hell, Dark thinks you're cool—and that dude hates *everybody*."

God patted Claire on her knee, which seemed a little too familiar while also being oddly formal at the same time. And then he stood up, stretching his back and giving the two boys a brief look that, for a moment, bordered on panic. A distant memory, rearing its head. He reached a hand down to Claire.

"So, what do you think? Lunch? Maybe we start all over?"

CHAPTER EIGHT

WHEN CLAIRE GOT HOME FROM SCHOOL, DERRICK HAD all of his boards out in the living room and he was meticulously checking the grip tape, adjusting the trucks, inspecting every part of every board. She fell down onto the couch behind him and closed her eyes.

"How was school?" he asked, using a knife to work some grime from the inside of a wheel. When Claire didn't answer, he turned around so he could see her. "Hey—you good?"

"I'm just tired," she said.

And it wasn't a lie. Every single part of her body felt ragged. She'd spent half the night and most of the day worrying about Dark and reminding herself of every single moment where she'd been frozen by fear and how, always, it turned out to be nothing more than a trick of her splintered head.

Like when she went yelling for a security guard at the Mall of America because a father was pulling a baby bottle out of his diaper bag. Or at school, when she refused to go into the auditorium because the exits were too far from the seats. Or the one time she took the light rail alone and every single person that stepped onto the car represented a new threat that couldn't be properly observed or neutralized or anything.

And now, Dark.

So, she was exhausted. She wanted to go to sleep and stay in bed until winter finally ended in this frozen state and she could hear the songs of new birds outside her window in a world that, for a moment, seemed unspoiled.

"Listen, we don't have to go tonight," Derrick said.

But even Claire could tell he was hoping she would rally. He'd already given up so much, competing when he had time and never complaining as sponsor after sponsor decided a pro skater in Hickory, North Carolina, wasn't exactly capturing skate culture's imagination. And that was before the move to Minnesota, before he became, essentially, a glorified front-end clerk at the Lair.

He wanted this and she knew it. Plus, skating had saved her before. So maybe it would one more time, if not for her sake, then for Derrick's.

"Somebody has to bring home a paycheck around here,"

she said, forcing her voice to seem light. And it worked, because Derrick laughed, which infected the room—pushing itself inside of her until she, too, was laughing deliriously and wondering if this, too, might fix whatever was broken inside of her.

The Lair was packed—more than usual, which was a good sign for Derrick. He always skated better when there was a crowd. However, as soon as he saw the room, he gave Claire an uneasy look, which she shook off like the snow from her jacket, and told him to "go rip it up," which made him laugh again.

She put her board on the ground and, without thinking, pushed off and tried to disappear into the throngs of skaters. She had a clean line for about five seconds before a kid on a scooter came flying past her, not only knocking her over but nearly putting a crack in her helmet, too. She sat there for a moment, trying to push down the anti-scooter mentality she'd developed—and Derrick stoked—in the last year. She was still swallowing all the unsavory words she wanted to yell out, when Leg and God came rolling up.

"Fucking scooter kids," Leg said, reaching down to help her up. "They're a menace to society. Not just the skate park. *Society.*"

God gave her a quick nod as he scanned the skate park. "We want to get in a few runs before your brother starts tearing shit up."

"Okay," Claire said. "I don't want to slow you guys down."

God gave her a look. "What? No. Come skate with us."

This time, Claire scanned the park. Still full. Still intimidating. Still impossible.

"I don't think you're prepared for how bad I really am."

God rolled his eyes. "Trust us. We're nearly professionals."

Then he took her by the hands and they were going fast—faster than she thought was possible after only a few feet of buildup. For the first few seconds, Claire couldn't breathe enough to tell him to stop. But seconds passed, and she realized it wasn't panic, but, something different. Something closer to exhilaration.

Every few feet, God would yell out, "Left!" And she'd shift her weight to the left, hoping the board would respond, which it always did. Despite her inability to stay upright, she still had innate athletic talent and that, combined with God's natural instincts on how to maneuver the board, seemed to be enough.

Leg came screaming up next to them, laughing hysterically and giving her fist pumps, hand claps—truly excited. And then God let go of her hands, and for a brief second it felt like she was flying, like she couldn't be stopped.

A second later Leg had her by the hand and they were once again shooting toward the other side of the skate park. Claire was laughing now; it came in bursts between breaths, an uncontrollable action.

Leg passed her off to God again. As they were coming up to the ramp, she expected him to once again give her a direction, but instead he said, "You got this!"

And then he let go.

She told herself to breathe.

To focus.

Shift your weight, watch your feet, don't be afraid to eat shit because none of that matters, just having the courage to *go for it*.

All of the lessons Derrick had taught her.

When she hit the ramp, she pivoted—a move she'd seen countless six-year-olds perform on their first day on the board—and came back down the ramp toward God.

The entire place exploded into applause. People slapping their boards onto the ground in appreciation, respect, the unspoken language of the skate park that acknowledged and applauded any growth—any moment of checking fear and all that other shit in the hopes of landing a trick you've never landed before.

Claire didn't notice Dark sitting on the couches, head in his notebook, until she and Leg and God climbed up the ramp, still feeding off her success.

"Derrick better watch out!" Leg said loudly, clearly hoping his voice would carry to where Derrick was warming up. When it didn't, he turned to Claire and said, "Next time we're skating the bowl."

"Yeah, no," Claire said, but she couldn't deny her excitement. "But maybe I'll make it across the park without falling?"

"Perfect," Leg said.

They dropped onto the couch next to Dark, who gave a momentary grimace and then scooted to the farthest cushion.

"Dark, did you see Claire?" Leg asked. "If she can do it, I'm a hundred percent certain your never-wants-to-go-out-in-the-sun ass could ride a board with your best friends every once in a while."

"Moral support," Dark said, turning his notebook to the side to shade a drawing. When he noticed Claire looking, he closed the notebook and avoided her eyes.

"What."

"Nothing. I'm just—I don't know. Sorry."

God tapped his board on the ground. "But you're going to come watch Derrick, right? Dude is brilliant."

Dark mumbled something incomprehensible before opening his notebook once again. But he didn't draw this time. Instead he began flipping through the pages, pausing only a second or two on certain pages the way her grandfather used to read the newspaper.

"Well, we're going to go get a seat on the lip of the bowl so we can watch." God looked at Dark and then at Claire. When neither of the moved, he slapped Leg on the shoulder and said, "Race you."

And then he took off, cackling as Leg started swearing loudly and proclaiming that any result would have an asterisk. The last thing Claire heard him say before he was swallowed up by the sound of the room was, *"Asterisk!"*

Before she could even turn—and say what? She didn't know, but she felt like she needed to say something—Dark said, "They're both certified idiots."

"I know—"

"Why were you looking in my room?"

Claire sighed. "I didn't mean to. The cat opened the door and I couldn't help but see . . . it."

Dark grimaced again. "It's not like it's porn or something. Jesus."

"Why do you draw them?"

Claire was surprised by her own question and Dark seemed to be just as shocked. He stared at her like she'd asked him to speak against the dead.

"Why do you freak out when you see people at the skate park?"

It hurt Claire, because he already knew the answer. And Dark saw it immediately, his face softening. Everything about the way he was confronting Claire changed.

"Aren't there things that just make you feel better?"

Claire nodded, but the truth was, there weren't many things that made her feel better.

At first, it was running—moving to Minnesota. Getting as far away as possible and never looking back, no matter how much it hurt. And once they were in Minnesota, it was hiding under the covers, on their couch—blaming the cold—as they watched old movies, until that no longer worked and they turned to the demon-freak speed of skating.

But none of it was permanent. None of it ever truly stamped out the dread that snuck back into her veins, snaking through her entire body until she was once again unable to forget why they were doing any of it.

"So, it works?" she finally asked. "You feel better?"

He shrugged, and in the immediate silence, Claire thought

she'd unwittingly stepped out of bounds. Instead, Dark stared at the closed notebook on his lap, trying to find the words.

"I don't know. And, like, do you think I *want* to be like this? Do you think I don't know what people say—what they think? I've been called every name you can think because of it. Freak. Psycho."

"*Dark.*"

Dark laughed.

"Well, yes, actually. Did they tell you what it stands for?"

"No. I just assumed it was in reference to, you know."

She motioned to his hair and then down his body.

"Wow. I feel so attacked right now."

Before Claire could apologize, Dark waved it away and said, "They used to call me the Lord of Darkness. Fucking *Satan*! And these are my friends!"

He was laughing, but Claire could tell there was more to the story—more to the way he attempted to keep her next question at bay with the laughter. He gave her a guarded look and shrugged.

"So, I guess I'm just *Dark*," he said. "Forever."

Bryan Bliss

CHAPTER NINE

ON THE WAY HOME, DERRICK COULDN'T CONTAIN HIS excitement. Even before he was skating full-time, he'd come home from a session, or one of the early promotional tours, and it would be as if he was bouncing on the clouds. So, she hadn't seen him this way in years. And she sat there, trying to hide her smile—why?—as he told her about the event, even though she'd been sitting on the lip watching with Dark, God, and Leg.

"When I hit that impossible, and everybody lost their mind?"

He smiled even bigger, cherishing the moment, which had admittedly been pretty amazing. Leg nearly had fallen into the bowl, drawing both Mark-O's and the announcer's ire.

Afterward they all stood around talking, laughing—normal.

When Dark had finally closed his notebook and agreed to watch Derrick, he seemed fine, as if they'd cleared the air and now had an understanding. But when they got to the lip, she noticed the way God and Leg seemed to relax. How they constantly seemed to flank Dark, almost by instinct, always keeping tabs on him. And they snuck looks at the notebook, too. They tensed up when his usually monotone words suddenly turned aggressive.

Whatever had happened with Dark had made an impact on God and Leg. It was the sort of thing you saw in movies, a life-changing experience that binds a group of friends together in a way that is stronger than steel. Leg, God, and Dark had that. And they obviously cared about one another, even if it meant hiding something big.

"Claire . . ."

They were at a stoplight and Derrick was watching her. "Yeah, sorry."

"I asked if you were hungry. We could stop at the taco place. Or maybe that Greek spot over on Snelling. What do you think?"

She wasn't hungry. Her stomach was already full of birds, fluttering around—occasionally jumping into her throat suddenly and making her want to cry out from the surprise

Bryan Bliss

of it. But instead she said, "Up to you," and Derrick made a quick left turn toward takeout.

Claire was running and the hallways were filled with smoke. She heard the popcorn (*pop-pop-pop*) and it rattled her teeth, like biting down on tinfoil or touching a low-grade live wire.

She ran.

She ducked.

She listened as people she barely knew screamed and tripped over one another, some of them struggling to get up—some of them already on the ground.

Her foot slipped on the newly polished floors. Or maybe it was the blood. She slipped again, trying to turn a corner that would've been a straight shot to the doors that—even though she couldn't see them now—she would later learn had already been chained shut.

She climbed under the stairs first, barely making it underneath before Eleanor was next to her, shaking and crying. Both of them listening as the popcorn went off even louder.

Pop-pop-pop.

And when she started screaming, she wasn't sure if it was happening then, now, or in some in-between place she'd never be able to escape.

* * *

Claire woke up to the sound of laughter—a whole room of it. And when she stumbled into the living room, she was greeted by the smell of pancakes.

"Claire!" Leg had two whole pancakes on a fork, and he lifted them toward her in greeting. "Your brother is the shit. You know this, right?"

Dark and God were also at the bar that looked into the kitchen, both of them too busy eating to acknowledge her beyond a quick wave.

"Hungry?" Derrick asked, holding up a tall stack of pancakes. When she nodded, he dumped three onto a plate and handed it to her. She sat down next to the boys at the bar, her head still foggy.

She hadn't slept more than a few hours and, while the pancakes would help, all she wanted to do was go back to bed. But Leg wasn't having it. He pushed in between her and God and looked her directly in the eye.

"Are you ready for today to be the greatest day of your life?"

Before she could respond, he held up his phone—too close to her face, honestly—and then cussed when the video didn't auto-play. He hit the small triangle button on his screen and then held the phone for Claire once again.

Bryan Bliss

A jaunty acoustic guitar kicked off the video, quickly followed by some sort of Celtic-sounding instrument, and finally a fiddle. In the background a castle rose from the darkness and suddenly there was a picture of Dr. Palmer's head—quickly joined by a man who was presumably her husband—and together they began trying to knock the castle down. When it fell, the debris spelled out, "Storming the Castle."

Claire turned to God for an explanation and he motioned back to the video, which now showed Dr. Palmer smiling and wearing what looked like a homemade tunic with StC emblazoned across the chest. She looked absolutely giddy.

"Storm Mob, time to get hyped!"

The camera swung nauseatingly to the left and at first, it looked like she was aiming it at the legs of a picnic table before the video began to expand to show . . .

"The trebuchet. Is. FINISHED."

Dr. Palmer and her husband cheered, putting the camera down and jumping into the foreground of the video to break down possibly the Most Awkward Dance Ever. At least, according to Leg, who was already howling with laughter.

"Shut up and let her watch it," God said, smiling.

She went back to the video and saw Dr. Palmer holding an apple. "We could fire this . . ."

A buzzer sounded, followed by a studio audience–recorded "NO!"

Her husband lifted up an orange, "Or maybe this . . ."

The buzzer. The studio audience.

And then Dr. Palmer lifted up an oversized teddy bear with a gigantic red ribbon tied around his neck. "Or maybe we could launch Mr. Poofy Pants!" The camera cut to a close up of Mr. Poofy Pants, who admittedly looked unmoved by the possibility.

"Just kidding. We'd never hurt Mr. Poofy Pants."

"But Storm Mob!" Her husband again. "You know we didn't build an actual trebuchet without the intention of launching something *proper*. Martin Luther King Jr. Park in Minneapolis. Today. Two p.m.

"Kids and families welcome. But we reserve the right to launch any small farm animals that are brought to the scene."

The video cut to both of their faces in a freeze-frame, ending with the sound of a goat bleating.

"Get ready," Leg said, shoving the phone into his pocket. "Because we're not missing this."

They took the bus to Minneapolis, hopping off at the entrance to Martin Luther King Jr. Park, a fairly standard-looking park, save the giant trebuchet that had been wheeled into the center of the baseball field.

"Jesus, *look at it.*" Leg was absolutely giddy.

It was twenty feet tall, easy, and built with an expert craftsmanship that Claire didn't anticipate. The video didn't do the actual device justice. Even from a distance, it was both impressive and a bit intimidating.

"There's no way that thing is legal," God said. "Like, it can't possibly be legal to own a fucking catapult."

"*Trebuchet,*" Leg said. "Show some damn respect."

"Okay, whatever. But that thing could literally kill somebody."

"You'd have to really aim," Dark said.

Leg and God gave him a look and then fell apart laughing.

"What? It's a siege weapon. Not like she's going to launch an offensive against Central, as much as *that* sounds appealing."

Claire looked at God and Leg, who didn't visibly react to what sounded like a threat. Dark caught Claire's eye momentarily and then started talking to God.

"Are we going down there? Or are you too scared to get close to the 'scary' weapon?"

Leg didn't wait for a response. He yelled out, "STORM MOB!" and charged down the hill, holding his skateboard above his head—ready for battle.

When they finally caught up to Leg, he was running

around the trebuchet, asking questions, and generally acting like a toddler on a trip to the fire department. Dr. Palmer didn't seem thrilled to see them, even if Leg kept saying they were all devoted members of the Storm Mob, but when she saw Claire, she smiled broadly.

"I think it's cool that you showed up," her husband said, holding out his hand. "I'm Greg, Wendy's husband."

"Well, we're big fans of you and Wendy, Greg." Dr. Palmer stared at Leg and he held up his hands in defeat. "I meant *Dr. Palmer.* Big fans."

Dr. Palmer considered all of them for a second before she said, "I'm going to answer the question that I know is coming: No, Francis, we will not use the trebuchet to shoot you across the park."

"Your name is *Francis?*" Claire asked, finding the information amusing for some reason. It wasn't a particularly strange name, but it was just the context—Leg's unfaltering swagger—that made her think his real name was something like Hawk or Jersey.

"We don't speak of Francis," Leg said. "And actually, all I want is to be in the video. Come on Dr. Palmer. You'll increase my social standing by, like, a hundred percent."

"Doubtful" is all Dr. Palmer said.

* * *

Bryan Bliss

Over the next thirty minutes, a crowd began to form around the trebuchet. Some were passersby, but most seemed to be dedicated fans of the YouTube channel. Leg, God, and Dark got a huge kick out of the fact that Dr. Palmer had this not-so-secret celebrity life.

Claire thought it was interesting, if not cute, that Dr. Palmer was willing to be so public with her interests. There was no shame, no embarrassment, just pure passion for the things that she found interesting. And while Claire intellectually understood it, she knew enough about her fellow high school students to want to pull Dr. Palmer to the side and be like, *Are you sure you should be doing this?*

But even in person, she was enthusiastic—an entertainer, working the gathered crowd until suddenly the camera was out and they were going live.

"Hey there, Storm Mob," Dr. Palmer said. "We're live at MLK Jr. Park in Minneapolis getting ready to test out the trebuchet. Can I get a What-*What!*"

God looked at Dark and then Claire and they all had to cough and choke back the laughter. Not that anybody noticed. They were all too busy giving Dr. Palmer a hearty *What-WHAT!*

"And I want to introduce a special guest to the livestream— one of my students."

Dr. Palmer paused here, as if steeling herself.

"Francis Custerman."

Another *What-WHAT!* from the crowd.

This time Claire couldn't hold back her laughter. Whether it was the live audience, the hundreds watching along from home, or finally somebody calling him on his bullshit, Leg looked absolutely stricken. He stood there, holding the watermelon they planned to launch—unable to close his mouth as Dr. Palmer introduced him.

She paused, quickly determining that he was not up for the cameo, and went to continue when Leg started talking.

"Hey there, Storm Mob, this is Leg—don't call me Francis—and I want to take this opportunity—"

Dr. Palmer tried to stop him, but he was already in front of her, addressing the Storm Mob in its entirety.

"—to ask for some help. I'm looking for a date to prom. One more date and I letter in prom. You might be thinking, Why does a good-looking guy like Leg need help from the Storm Mo—"

Greg came from the side and politely moved him off camera, but not before the crowd gave him another enthusiastic *What-WHAT!* for the effort. Dr. Palmer continued, unaffected by the improvisation.

Bryan Bliss

"Thanks for the help, Francis. Now, who's ready to launch this watermelon?"

The crowd was still losing its shit when Leg came up next to Claire and said, "Nailed it."

"You're going to end up with a forty-year-old medieval weapons enthusiast as your date," God said.

"I'm not picky. Equal opportunity. As long as she shows up and I get my damn martini glass."

"She'll probably show up in a suit of armor," Claire said.

At first God just stared at her and then he and Dark started laughing.

"Claire!" God said. "Coming alive!"

She laughed, too, thinking about the way she used to crack on her friends—how she would have to be careful, to figure out who could take the cuts, because when she felt comfortable with someone, it was open season. Nothing was sacred. And she expected nothing less from them in return.

Sometimes she wondered if her friends in North Carolina—Eleanor, the rest of them—were still fractured, too. She had mostly given up on social media, the pain of seeing all of them was too much. What would she post? How would she react when one of them said they missed her or asked when they were coming back from the Great North?

If the rest of her body and mind were broken, it was all a

reminder that her heart, to some extent, had been spared. And she couldn't stand the idea of having to engage with all of them in that way. To make them real, living people once again and not figments of some imaginary past life.

And so, as God and Dark—and eventually Leg—laughed, she wondered if maybe this was the first real step toward who she was before.

"Okay, Storm Mob—enough with the talking. Let's chuck this thing!"

Greg went over to the trebuchet and began working the giant winch, slowly bringing the arm closer to the ground with every turn. As it descended, the crowd began to cheer louder and louder. And when Dr. Palmer ceremoniously raised the watermelon above her head, they nearly lost their mind. Claire couldn't even hear what she was saying, could only see her fingers giving a countdown—three, two, one—before she pulled the lever and in a slow, loping motion, the trebuchet began to fire.

At first Claire wondered if it wasn't working. The physics of the way it was rising seemed off, as if somebody had forgotten to attach a key piece. Still, the crowd was focused and all in, the only sound being the cars on the interstate in the distance.

And then in one sudden movement, the arm shot forward,

Bryan Bliss

whipping the watermelon into the air so high that, at first, Claire could barely see it.

The watermelon kept rising, kept barreling forward. Past the park. Over the neighboring houses. And finally, above and across the interstate.

"Oh, fuck," Dr. Palmer said. And then remembering that she was still live, that students were present, she turned to the camera and said, "Sorry, Storm Mob. But that was just . . ."

"Shocking," Leg said to Claire.

In the distance, the sound of honking horns. And a few minutes after that, the first siren could be heard in the distance, slowly getting louder and louder.

"I'm out," Leg said, grabbing his skateboard and taking off without a second notice. Pretty soon God was dragging Claire across the park, both of them laughing hysterically as Dark attempted to keep up with them.

The last thing they heard was the Storm Mob giving Dr. Palmer one final *What-WHAT!* before they disappeared around the corner.

CHAPTER TEN

CLAIRE FELT ELECTRIC ON THE BUS BACK TO ST. PAUL, watching Leg turn around in the seat next to her so he could face God and Dark, all of them laughing and speculating on whether they'd ever see Dr. Palmer again.

"How can you explain something like that to the police?" God asked. "I mean, who builds a trebuchet and attacks Saturday afternoon traffic? Plus, how did she even get it there?"

"Probably towed it behind her Subaru," Leg said. "You know she drives a Subaru."

The bus dropped them only a few blocks from Dark's apartment, so they walked over there because Dark's grandmother had promised cookies or something that was baked, warm, and filled with sugar. When they opened the door, however, they were met with the sickeningly sweet smell of alcohol.

Dark stopped immediately and turned around, trying to push them out the door before his grandmother called out, "Peter? Is that you?"

Dark sighed and closed his eyes. "Yeah, Grandma. I just came to—"

Before Claire knew what was happening, a metal pan was crashing at their feet. Dark's grandmother—dressed only in a robe, cigarette hanging from her mouth—was livid.

"You didn't come home last night," she yelled. "Is that what I signed up for when your parents left? Answer me."

Dark stammered a few words, but they were unintelligible. God and Leg had frozen, their eyes planted on the ground in front of them. Claire didn't know what else to do but watch.

"So, you're out with your friends all night? That it?"

"I was—"

"He was at my house, Ms. Klatchky," God said. Claire didn't know if it was true or not, but it sounded convincing.

"Does your house have a phone?"

"Yes, ma'am."

"Because even a shithole like this has a phone—isn't that right, Peter?"

"It's not a shithole, Grandma," Dark said. His face was blank, free of a single emotion.

His grandma laughed and walked away for a moment. Claire heard the refrigerator open and then the unmistakable sound of a can being opened. Dark didn't hesitate. As soon as she was out of sight, he turned around and pushed Claire and the others out of the apartment.

They were barely through the door when his grandmother started screaming again. Dark didn't stop. He was leading the group now, his chin up—as if he was willing himself not to be affected by any of this. They could still hear her yelling in the stairwell, rumbling down the steps until they were finally outside.

Claire expected Dark to start walking, but he didn't. He stood outside, as if he needed to catch his breath. God and Leg didn't speak, but God put his hand on Dark's shoulder and kept it there until a window above them flew open and about twenty of Dark's notebooks landed on the ground.

Dark didn't even look up as he quickly began gathering them. But the more he picked up, the more came falling from the window—his grandmother screaming the whole time.

"You don't want to live here? Fine! Take all of this shit with you!"

Dark's arms were full and even with God and Leg helping,

Bryan Bliss

there were still at least fifty notebooks on the ground. She looked at the boys, who were busy finding places to stash the notebooks—pockets, on top of Leg's skateboard. Anywhere they would fit. So Claire did the same, tucking them anywhere she could think, until her arms were full.

Either Dark's grandmother ran out of journals or got tired of throwing them, because suddenly they weren't falling any longer. Dark was busy trying to scoop up the last few when God told him they should go.

"To my house, man. You can spend the night."

Dark nodded quickly. He didn't look embarrassed or even angry—just resigned.

Claire kept dropping journals on the way to God's house, bending down to pick them up and then—realizing she needed to catch up—walking faster, only to drop some more and fall even farther behind.

Every time the journals fell, she'd catch a glimpse of different pages—mostly the Monster, staring up at her from a different perspective. Those same arms, the eyes, trying to see through her. But every so often, there would be a different drawing. Sometimes just a random word—never anything with discernible context—written with the same furious pen strokes.

When they got to God's house, Claire did a double take. The entire block was tree-lined and put together. And while the houses didn't rival the literal mansions on Summit Ave., they weren't small. The sort of houses occupied by the happy families in lighthearted television shows. She stood there on the big porch, probably looking as wide-eyed as she felt.

"What?" God said. Usually there was an innate amusement in his voice, but the words came out thin.

"Nothing. You have a nice house."

God nodded and carefully put the notebooks down so he could unlock the door. As soon as he did, Dark came over and collected them—checking the spines and arranging them in some kind of order, oblivious to everything else.

"Dark, it's cold out here," God said. "Why don't you bring them inside?"

Dark didn't acknowledge him, so God shrugged and then opened the door for Claire and Leg. Before she could move, Dark mumbled something to her.

"What?"

"The journals," he said, and Claire handed them over.

Once inside, Leg fell onto a large leather couch and closed his eyes with what was either a groan or a sigh. Claire sat across from him, in a nice armchair that looked more comfortable than it actually was. When she sat down, the

Bryan Bliss

journals she'd stuck in the waistband of her jeans poked her in the back. She almost pulled them out and rushed them to Dark, but God came back into the room with four cups, a pitcher of steaming water, and some hot chocolate packets.

Leg didn't open his eyes. "Thanks, Betty Crocker."

"Go fuck yourself," God returned. "And you're welcome."

God made a cup of cocoa and handed it to Claire. Then he kicked Leg and told him to take off his shoes or his mother would skin both of them. Leg, eyes still closed, obeyed— giving God an enthusiastic, if not condescending, thumbs-up.

Claire drank her hot chocolate, watching the shadow of Dark through the curtains.

"This hasn't happened before," God finally said. "Like, his grandma is always kind of either over-the-top sweet or . . . like that. But the whole throwing his shit out the window is new."

Leg sighed or groaned again. "And I know he didn't sleep here last night."

God shook his head. "So, that's a problem."

"Where was he?" Claire asked, unsure if they wanted her to join the conversation. Leg finally opened his eyes and looked at God, who took a drink of his own hot chocolate without answering.

"Maybe he snuck into the Lair. Or maybe he spent the

night just walking around. The thing about Dark is—"

He stopped talking as the door opened and Dark, his face and hands blue from the cold, came into the room and stood there, still blank. But when he spoke, his words were full of something different, something Claire heard for the first time—actual anger.

"What's the thing?"

At first God was confused. And then Dark said, "You were just about to tell Claire 'the thing' about me. So what is it?"

"Man, c'mon—you're upset. I get that. But there's no reason to take that out on me."

"No, *you* c'mon. What were you going to explain? How I've always been fucked up? Oh, wait—how about how my grandmother is a drunk and probably bipolar, but that's the best option I've got as far as family goes. Or maybe you were going to tell her about middle school?"

"You know I wouldn't—"

"Wouldn't? *Wouldn't?* You're the one who fucking sold me out!"

God stood up and got in Dark's face. For a moment Claire was sure they were going to fight right there in the living room. Leg must've sensed the same thing, because he jumped off the couch and pushed God away two times before God knocked his empty mug off the table and disappeared up the stairs.

Bryan Bliss

"Fuck this. Fuck him." Dark started walking outside and Leg followed him, down the porch and halfway up the block before stopping and yelling his name one last time.

Leg came back into the room and gave Claire a quick smile, before going upstairs to find God. As soon as he was out of sight, she pulled the notebooks out from behind her with the intention of putting them on the pile with the others.

The two notebooks were meticulously labeled on the spine in neat silver ink. One said XXVI-11.12, the other, XXVI-2.12, only a week ago. She looked at the stairs and without a second thought, opened the first notebook.

It was filled with, as she expected, different drawings of the Monster. And once again, the same chaotic word clouds. Every few pages there would be something blacked out in thick ink, whatever had been there, now obliterated. She fanned through the last few pages, turning them into an unplanned animation—the Monster jumping and lurching from the page.

She opened the more recent notebook, thinking she'd find more of the same. Instead, the first page was a picture of the Monster holding the decapitated head of a man with glasses. The next page the Monster towering over a cowering woman, a look of menace on his face that hadn't been in any other drawing. And then, more pictures of the Monster, once again reaching out in his almost helpless way.

She flipped through the book, wondering if she would find more pictures like the first, but she didn't. When she heard movement upstairs, she paused momentarily and then stuck both notebooks back into the waistband of her jeans as God and Leg came down the stairs, both pink in the face. Claire didn't know if it was anger, concern, or just the cold.

"We need to tell you about Dark," God said.

God and Leg and Dark knew one another before they'd earned their nicknames. And as they grew up, Dark was always getting in trouble. The one whose reputation got sent up the chain to every new teacher in every new grade—not even getting spared in the transition from elementary school to middle school.

Dark was a troublemaker. A trouble starter. A trouble finisher.

"But fuck all of those teachers and their fathers," Leg said. "Because they didn't know him. All they saw was the dirty kid wearing the same clothes with the grandma who—"

He looked at God and they both seemed to have a mental conversation right in front of Claire.

"You don't have to tell me," Claire said.

"I mean, you already saw it," God said in one breath, exhaling at the end. "Except, sometimes it's in the parking lot after our fifth-grade graduation."

"And other times it's the cafeteria in front of everybody," Leg said.

Hearing all this felt voyeuristic and sensational—a feeling she knew all too well from the aftermath of the shooting. Every person wanted something from every kid in her school. A quote. A picture. A video of them crying about their lost friends. And while Claire had missed the brunt of it—they were gone within weeks—she still saw it in the faces of people who knew why she'd moved to Minnesota. She saw it on the right-wing websites that were still obsessed with Eleanor and her FUCK GUNS T-shirt. She saw it every time another shooting happened at another school, the whole circus starting up in the exact same way.

Still, she wanted to know about Dark. She wanted to know why he drew the Monster, why he seemed so disconnected despite having two friends who would do anything to protect him. And maybe she wanted to make sure that he wasn't disconnected in the same way as the kid who'd come into her school with what might as well been an automatic rifle.

The panic hit her right in the chest.

"So, seventh grade," God said. "I was so worried about him. He started getting into fights—"

"Or, more specifically, getting his ass kicked because Dark isn't a fighter," Leg said.

"Yeah, well. He was intentionally doing shit to get himself in trouble—and it worried both of us."

"So you . . . told on him?" Claire asked.

She expected Leg to jump in, give God shit for ratting out his friend. But Leg was staring at the ground, intentionally not looking at either her or God.

"Tell her about the bathroom," Leg said, still looking at the floor.

Claire's heart jumped into her throat and maybe God noticed, because he gave her a smile before he started the story.

"Like I said, it was rough. He was disappearing for days at a time. And when he'd come back, he just didn't look good. Too skinny. Too pale. Probably living outside."

"And then one day we come to school and he's got a knife," Leg interrupted. "Just a pocketknife, but he had it in his hand in the bathroom of the school and, like, he was just *sitting* there. Like he was waiting for something."

Claire froze. In the aftermath of every shooting, the same bullshit talking points were trotted out—no matter how

Bryan Bliss

many kids had died. How many more would. It's a mental health tragedy, they said. You can't stop criminals from buying guns, they cried. Hey, look—a psycho with a knife could do just as much damage.

She'd always thought they were bullshit, a way to let overgrown boys keep their killer toys. And yet, her reaction to the mental image of Dark sitting in his school bathroom with a knife in his hand made her entire body go rigid.

"So I took the knife and brought him to the office," God said. "We were kids. Telling the adults is what you were supposed to do, right?"

"We thought they'd help him," Leg said. "But instead, they just— "

It was the first time Claire had ever seen Leg anything other than lighthearted. He was so angry he punched the leather couch.

"Well, they didn't do shit," Leg said.

"That's when we decided it was our job to protect him," God said. "Pretty soon after that, he started drawing the monster pictures and they helped him. So, here we are."

Claire nodded.

(Breathing, breathing.)

Yes, the Monster might be therapeutic. A way to express something that couldn't otherwise be expressed. Hadn't she felt the same way? And what would it mean for her to have some release valve, a way to export all of the shit that clogged her mind and pushed the storm water higher and higher in her body until she could barely function?

But the Monster could also be something else entirely. Something that's been inside Dark since that moment, clawing its way out with every drawing.

God and Leg didn't seem to think he was dangerous. They'd rationalized him into a friend who needed help and maybe protection. But how many other times had people not said something—had they waited until it was too late (breathing, breathing) and another kid walked into a school wearing body armor and carrying a cannon.

She stood up and ran outside—but stopped, unsure where to go. So she laid down in the snow and let the cold and the wet take over her body, numb everything until she couldn't feel the pain, the fear. The voice that was telling her nothing can stop the inevitable, nothing can stop the inevitable, nothing can stop the inevitable.

Bryan Bliss

CHAPTER ELEVEN

CLAIRE STAYED IN BED ALL OF THE FOLLOWING DAY, responding to Derrick in single words, refusing everything he offered except solitude. The next morning, minutes before the bus would lurch to a stop on the corner, Claire was still in bed and staring at her ceiling, hoping for a sudden cough or maybe a slight fever—some new symptom that might help her explain why she still felt so sideways.

Of course, this was no different than any other time she'd spent the weekend hidden under her covers. The image of Dark in the school bathroom, even though it was years before, made her stomach clench with the fact that, this one time, she'd been right. This one time, she'd sussed out danger—been so close it had become her friend—and now she could still barely move. Could barely stand to think about any of it.

When Derrick saw her at God's house, the shock was visible on his face. This was different—and not good. She was wet and shivering, still lying in the snow. But even though he wrapped her in a blanket, it wasn't the cold that paralyzed her. No, it was that she couldn't stop the panic from racing through her mind like a razor blade. Making ribbons of the minimal progress she'd made in the past year.

Normally Derrick would take her home, feed her whatever she wanted, and let her melt into her bed—becoming a fully formed person on her own time. It might take a day, or even two, but there was always the expectation that she was getting better, no matter how incremental. That she would stand up and try again.

But this time, she didn't feel even a stitch better. This time, she wanted to ignore the litany of texts God and Leg had sent, and stay in bed, forgetting about Dark and all his pain. The Monster, the notebooks, which were stuffed deep in her backpack, all of it. She wanted to stay in bed, to spend the rest of her life right here, listening to the quiet snow fall outside her window.

When Derrick knocked on her door—five minutes before she would need to leave and still make it to school, a timeline they'd pretty much mastered at this point—she didn't answer at first. He cracked the door open and said her name softly.

Bryan Bliss

"You up?" he asked.

"Yeah," Claire answered.

Derrick took a step inside the room and leaned against the doorframe.

"We probably need to get going if you want to be on time. Or if you want a chai or something, we can be late. I just . . . "

He trailed off, running his hands through his hair.

"I just want you to be okay," he finally said. "Whatever that takes."

"Getting up now."

Derrick smiled and then pushed himself off the doorframe and walked out of her room. She heard him open and close the front door, followed by the sound of the car starting in the driveway. In a burst of energy, she stood up, threw on a sweatshirt and some track pants, grabbing her bag as she rushed out the door to meet Derrick in the car.

Claire sat in Dr. Palmer's class with her hood up, hoping she could avoid attention, or at least look as if she was focused on her project. However, every time she looked at *Frankenstein* on her desk, or the mostly bare piece of paper that was supposed to be her project, it brought back visions of Dark and the Monster. It made her want to pull the notebooks out and flip through the pages, hoping to find some clue—a *gotcha!* moment that would put her mind at ease.

When Dr. Palmer walked up to her desk, Claire nearly fell out of her chair. Dr. Palmer looked equally surprised and gave her a quick once-over, like she was checking for wounds, before she spoke.

"I just wanted to check in with you and the boys after, well, you know. Everything this weekend."

The inside of Claire's body jumped this time, every single part of her skipping a beat until she remembered the trebuchet. The police. Another *before*.

"We got on the bus and went home, that's it."

Dr. Palmer seemed relieved. "Well, the trebuchet is now officially in the custody of the Minneapolis Police Department, which I guess is for the best." She smiled and leaned closer to Claire. "But did you see how far it launched that watermelon?"

When Claire gave her a weak smile, Dr. Palmer stopped smiling and sat down in the empty desk next to her. She hadn't even noticed that the normally sleeping kid was absent.

"Are you sure everything is okay?"

Claire almost started crying. She wanted to tell Dr. Palmer everything—but where did the story start? Saturday? When

Bryan Bliss

she first saw the notebook? Or months—a year—before now, when everything in her life got jigsawed apart, leaving her with no way to find the corner pieces. No way to figure out the rules of the game.

"Do you want to go out into the hallway? Talk about it?"

Claire could already feel the stares of the other kids, could practically hear their laughter. Another freak-out from the freak from North Carolina. She shook her head, not trusting herself to say even the simplest word for fear that she would lose it and confess that she was worried and scared and perhaps most importantly of all, still not sure that anything she was feeling was actually real.

Dr. Palmer didn't say anything for a long time, barely moved, as if she thought Claire might just need somebody to be close, another person she could trust, for the last few minutes of class. And just before the bell rang, Dr. Palmer reached out and touched the copy of *Frankenstein* Claire had sitting on the desk.

"If you need something—anything—just come by my class. No matter if there are students in here or not. Okay?"

Claire didn't make it to her next class.

Leg and God stopped her in the hallway, neither of them carrying bags or books—only their skateboards. Normally, this would be a marvel. She understood that some kids didn't care about grades, or didn't know how to care, but these two seem a different breed entirely. They took not caring to an elite level.

"Hey—how are you?" God asked.

Her mind shot back to Saturday night, lying in the snow and unable to move. They must've been the ones that had called Derrick, unless she'd truly blacked out and done it herself. All of this, now, seemed dramatic, at best, so she deflected the question.

"Have you seen Dark?" she asked.

Leg grimaced and shook his head. "No. And I guess that's not that abnormal. The dude was just suspended. But still. I was hoping to see his dumb ass this morning."

"That's the other reason we came to find you," God said. "He didn't, like, reach out to you this weekend? Anything?"

Claire shook her head and Leg swore loudly, making one of the custodians shake her head. Leg either didn't see or didn't care because he just kept talking.

"We need to find him, man. Like, right now."

God leaned against a locker and picked at a piece of dead skin on his thumb. He was trying to hide his concern, but his face, his entire body, betrayed him.

"Do you think he's okay?"

God sighed, pushing up from the locker when the late bell rang and the other students in the hallway started rushing for their classes. God and Leg didn't move.

"I haven't seen him that pissed in a long time."

"Where do you think he went?" Claire asked.

"Who knows, but we can't let him just roam the Cities," Leg said, talking to God. "Let's just ditch and go check all the usual spots. He has to be somewhere."

They looked at Claire, expecting her to join them. When she took a step toward her next class instead, God's face dropped.

"If you see him, let us know. Okay?"

Claire didn't see Dark—or God and Leg, for that matter—when she walked into the cafeteria. The room was chaotic, more so than usual. A line for the hot lunch extended out the door and into the hallway. Two girls shrieked, pointing at their phones. The entire room seemed alive.

She sat down at the table, where all of God and Leg's friends were watching Dr. Palmer's new video, which not only included the part she'd seen—they hadn't cut out Leg's desperate attempt at a prom date after all—but also the aftermath where her husband continued filming the entire police encounter, including the moment they wrapped yellow police tape around the trebuchet to wild boos from the crowd.

The only thing that could've pulled the group's attention away from the latest Storming the Castle video was the screaming.

Claire dove to the ground immediately, an action that, under normal circumstances, would've put every set of eyes on her. Instead, everybody was looking at the twenty students—younger, probably freshman—raising their fists. Yelling. Holding signs. Wearing shirts with one simple message.

FUCK GUNS.

It wasn't the same shirt Eleanor had worn, not exactly.

Since then, a savvy person had trademarked the phrase and turned it into product. And whenever another shooting happened, the slogan would pop up on T-shirts or buttons or, once, a banner ad on a website for reading television spoilers—a site she'd deemed safe before then. And every time since then, she'd been able to click the page closed or turn her head. She'd been able to escape.

A girl with a nose ring was screaming now.

"Shut *Right-Wing Report* down!"

Another girl yelled, "Fuck guns, fuck *Right-Wing Report*, save us!"

The whole room grew louder and louder as the rest of the cafeteria began to join in—*"FUCK GUNS, FUCK GUNS."*

Claire tried to crawl under the table (breathing, breathing), the same survival instincts at work a year later, but all she could do was wedge herself against the hard legs of the table. And even there, she couldn't escape the raw sound of the protest.

Run.

It came from deep inside her, cutting through the panic like a knife.

She crawled from under the table (breathing, breathing), across the floor of the cafeteria until she could stand up and start running—ignoring the security guard who told her to stop, because his words were nothing but mud in her ears.

She turned blindly into the stairwell and froze.

There was room to hide under that staircase, too.

(breathing, breathing)

But she didn't need to hide. There wasn't anyone here. Nothing was happening.

Her body screamed—*move or hide. Now.*

She took the stairs two by two, running as fast as she could, going up floor after floor, not because she had a plan, but because it was the only way she could think to avoid the storm, the Monster—whatever was behind her.

When there were no more stairs to climb and she burst out of the stairwell, she almost flattened Dr. Palmer. Claire hit the ground hard and started scrabbling across the floor, just to keep moving.

"Claire—*Claire*."

Dr. Palmer held her firmly by her shoulders, not letting her move. And instead of feeling caught, she slumped down, finally letting the tears come—tears that she'd been holding for weeks, months.

So long that she couldn't even remember all the times she'd stopped herself or why.

CHAPTER TWELVE

CLAIRE SAT IN DR. PALMER'S CLASSROOM, LISTENING AS she talked in a hushed tone on her desk phone. Claire assumed Derrick would be here soon enough and maybe the school counselor. She was still frozen by the fear of—what?

It was irrational. She knew it was irrational. Why couldn't she just see a T-shirt that said fuck guns and, you know, laugh with the rest of the cafeteria? Stand up and raise her fist high in the air because, yes, *fuck guns*. She had no problem with the sentiment or the words, because what else was there to say at this point?

And yet, she couldn't move. She could barely speak, which is what really made Dr. Palmer transition from "typical teenage drama" to "she is in trouble." And when she wouldn't say why, Dr. Palmer brought her to her classroom and sat her in a desk with a cup of water.

"Okay. Okay. Yes." She glanced at Claire. "I think so. Let me ask."

"Claire, is there an immediate threat to you?"

Claire didn't know how to answer. She shook her head. There wasn't an immediate threat. But just as quickly, her brain shot back—*how do you know?* Because wasn't that the case? They could be sitting here, just another day, and all of a sudden, the entire world might start deconstructing with the rapid sound of gunfire. Nothing was really ever safe.

It wasn't long before Derrick came rushing into the room, bending down to peer into her face. A few seconds later, both the principal of the school and the counselor were standing in the room, all of them asking the same question—*are you okay?*

When she didn't answer, the counselor asked her a different question.

"Claire, can you wiggle your toes for me?"

It seemed like a ridiculous request, one for a baby. Wiggle those toes for Mommy, darling! And yet, she did it. And her toes moved on command, which felt like a win given everything.

"Great. Now, rub your hands together for me."

Bryan Bliss

She did, another success. And then the counselor asked Claire her favorite color and she answered, "Blue" without thinking. It just spilled out, which burst the tension in the room, and everybody seemed to be able to take a step back for a moment.

"Can you identify three blue things in this room?"

One, two, three—Claire pointed them out. She could already feel the storm receding and becoming a memory. Not a real, living thing.

So when the counselor asked one more time if she was okay, Claire could finally answer.

"Yes."

The next class was beginning, so they moved the entire group, save Dr. Palmer, who gave Claire a weak smile as she was leaving, down to the social worker's office. Claire tried not to look at any of the other students as she walked out of the classroom. Of course, all of them knew something was going on—knew all about her—which only got worse when Derrick, the principal, and the counselor essentially surrounded and escorted her down the three flights of stairs like some kind of foreign dignitary.

Once they were in the office, Claire wasn't sure she could explain what had happened. Now that she was outside of the event, she could tell that she was never in any real danger. But in the moment, it felt more real than the chair she was sitting in.

"Claire, the first thing we need to do is make sure that you feel safe," the principal said. "When you started here, I was serious when I said we'd do whatever was necessary to make sure you not only got the help you might need but could also become a vital part of the Central community."

Every word was careful. She turned to Derrick, who was busy twisting his wool stocking hat in his hands and nodding slowly.

"It was the kids in the cafeteria," Claire said suddenly. "The protest."

She didn't want to say anything else, wanted to pretend the *FUCK GUNS* shirts would never show up in this school, anywhere near her again, and they could forget this had happened. But she knew it was bigger than just the T-shirt, and that made the tears come even harder.

The counselor handed her a box of tissues. Claire took one and said, "I'm sorry."

"You have nothing to be sorry about," the woman said, patting her on the knee.

"She's been . . . better," Derrick said. "Like, going out with friends. Going to the skate park without me. Just *better.*"

Bryan Bliss

Claire looked up when the counselor handed her a small package of almonds and a tiny bottle of water. Claire took both and held them on her lap as she thought about what Derrick had said. Had she been better? Or was it just a Band-Aid over a bigger wound, something they used to forget what was actually underneath? She honestly didn't know.

"Tell me about your friends," the social worker said. "Did you meet them here?"

"No," Claire said. "At the skate park."

"Where do they go to school?"

"Central."

The social worker and principal looked at Derrick, confused.

"She didn't know they went to school here," Derrick explained. "And then she came to school and the degenerates were standing at the top of the stairs and—"

Derrick looked suddenly troubled, perhaps by the perplexed looks on the faces of the other two adults in the room. He coughed and tried to explain.

"Sorry. They're not really degenerates. I just like calling them that because, you know . . ."

They did not, obviously.

"God and Leg are good kids," Derrick said. Claire could tell he was trying to summon every bit of "adult" he had in his voice. At first Claire thought it had worked. When they heard the boys' names, the principal and counselor had sat up straight as boards.

"God and Leg . . ." The principal repeated their names slowly, looking to the counselor. "So I'm going to assume that Peter is also a part of this new group of friends."

"Dark?" Derrick said. "Yeah. He's always lurking somewhere."

The image made Derrick smile, which made Claire feel momentarily better. But then she saw the principal and counselor and her stomach dropped.

"Peter has a lot of trouble in his life. And that trouble sometimes spreads to other places," the principal said. "I have no doubt that he is a good friend. The devotion of Francis and William attest to as much. But the fact remains that he is also working through a lot of things and, well, we've had concerns recently."

This time Claire sat up a little straighter. Concerns. A coded word, the kind she learned to parse out years ago when adults would try to speak over her. And *concerns* was exactly the sort of word a principal would use to express an opinion without crossing any sort of legal or privacy boundaries.

"Are you saying Dark is dangerous?" Claire asked.

Both the principal and the counselor shook their heads so

fast, she was surprised they stayed attached to their bodies.

"Peter is . . . we've had a lot of discussions with him. And while we have concerns, we would never endanger the students of this school."

That was bullshit. Claire had heard it a million times, how the kid who came into their school had never been seen as a threat. They, too, may have had *concerns* about the pictures of automatic weapons he'd posted online constantly. The lyrics, thinly veiled at best, that painted pictures of destruction, pain—horror. And after it was over, after three of Claire's schoolmates and one teacher were dead in the hallway of a school that had promised to keep them safe, the *concerns* became another piece of a puzzle that should've been solved months or maybe years before.

It was blood on their hands, even if they washed it off with every saccharine wish for unity and community strength. Claire wouldn't have it, not again. She reached down into her backpack and pulled out the two journals, holding them out to the principal and the school counselor. At first, neither of them reached for the books.

"These are Dark's—I mean, Peter's. I think you should look at them."

The school counselor took the notebooks, holding them carefully as if they might combust in her hands. She opened one, handing the other to the principal, who looked at Claire for a second before she opened hers, too.

Claire spent the next day at home, wrapped in blankets. Derrick hovered constantly, eventually giving up on trying to assuage his own guilt—*I should've known*, all that—in the form of more hot chocolate. Another batch of cookies. Now he just glanced her way every ten to fifteen minutes.

When he saw the journals, his face had gone dead white. And that was only the Monster. When they got to the more graphic ones, which turned out to bear a striking resemblance to a biology teacher who had confronted Dark only a week earlier, the entire office went into a red alert of sorts. The principal was on the phone. The counselor tried her best to smile as she encouraged Derrick to take Claire home.

And so they'd been home since then, a kind of watered-down version of those first days after the shooting, when they were too scared to leave the house, if only because the sense of normalcy and safety that had once ruled the world was now gone.

They fell back into the routine seamlessly. And this time, Claire couldn't shake the feeling that they weren't protecting themselves but were just avoiding the real problem.

Bryan Bliss

Could she go through the rest of her life simply waiting for the next surprise? The next moment that would unravel everything. She didn't know if there was another way, so she sat there with her hot chocolate and her streaming baking show, hoping for the millionth time that everything would magically fix itself.

Claire must've fallen asleep because the knock on the door jolted her awake. Before she could get out of bed, she heard Derrick answer the door—and then God's voice.

By the time she got to the living room, Derrick was leading him back to the front door. And while God wasn't being forced, Claire could tell he wasn't ready to leave. They both saw her at the same time, but God spoke first.

"Are you kidding me?"

"Man, I told you—not now," Derrick said, but God shook away from Derrick's grip and walked toward Claire.

"You know he got expelled, right? Fucking miracle that he didn't get arrested, too. But expelled. That's sure to set your life on the right track, isn't it?"

Claire was trying to figure out what to say, how to explain, but God shook his head.

"I told you. *I told you.*"

"Okay, enough." Derrick grabbed God by the shoulders

and pushed him out the door. Before he could close it, God yelled out one last thing.

"*He didn't fucking deserve that, and you know it.*"

Once he was gone, the room still felt charged. As if somebody had turned on every light in the small carriage house. When Derrick spoke, it was in his most calming voice.

"They're just mad," he said. "They'll get over it."

"Will they?" Claire asked.

Derrick rubbed the back of his neck, choosing his words. "Those pictures, Claire. They're not good. And that one with the severed head? That's a *teacher*. You did the right thing."

Claire didn't need him to say any more. Didn't want him to say anymore. He was right: the pictures had frightened her from the very moment she saw the Monster. And when she saw the others, drawn only a week before, something else clicked into place. It might've been that one moment that nobody acts on, the *see something, say something* opportunity so many people miss because they're either too oblivious or too scared.

But maybe God was right, and the pictures were nothing. That's what Claire couldn't shake.

"People don't do that sort of stuff unless they have real problems," Derrick said.

"I have real problems," Claire said.

"That's different," Derrick said.

She wanted to tell him about Dark's grandmother. Everything God and Leg had told her. How the explanations danced across her mind, making sense one moment and burying her in panic the next.

She started to cry.

"Whoa, hey. What's wrong?"

"I don't know what's right," she said, trying to stop herself from crying.

"What? I don't understand."

And that just made her cry harder because she couldn't explain it to him, the way every single moment in her life felt open to interpretation. She didn't want to tell him that she might've made a mistake, because it didn't *feel* like a mistake in the moment. It didn't *feel* like a mistake now.

But that didn't mean it wasn't one.

CHAPTER THIRTEEN

CLAIRE DIDN'T GO TO SCHOOL THE NEXT DAY AND SHE was on edge the whole time—waiting for the next knock on their door. When it didn't come, it only made her feel worse. When Derrick offered a trip to the skate park early the next morning, she hesitantly agreed.

By the time they got to the Lair, she didn't want to get out of the car and Derrick, unsure what to do, let her sit there in the warm car while she—what? Fifteen minutes later she started feeling foolish, so she grabbed the keys, her board, and pads, and walked in.

The place was empty; the only sound was the music softly playing through the PA system. Somewhere she could hear the sound of a single board hitting the ramps.

When Mark-O saw her, he gave her a nod and told her that

Derrick was already skating. And then he looked back down at the magazine he was reading.

"Is anyone else here?"

"Nope," he said, not looking up. "It's early on a Tuesday. Not exactly peak."

She walked back into the main room, taking a moment to appreciate the emptiness—the complete stillness, like a painting.

Derrick appeared at the top of the ramp and waved.

"You going to ride?"

"Yes," she said, her voice echoing in the empty room.

But she didn't move, even as Derrick dropped back into the bowl and started skating. She stood there, trying to reclaim that one moment of peace she'd found when she walked in. It was funny, because so much of what she'd originally wanted from the Lair was not stillness, but movement.

Claire eventually put her board down and crossed the park a couple of times, trying to forget the feeling of Leg's and God's guiding her around the room. Her legs felt weak, like she'd already been in the room for an hour, and when she kicked her board into her hand a couple of runs later, she was ready to lay down.

She scrambled up the ramp to the couches. Mark-O had said the room was empty, so when she saw a person wrapped in a too-small blanket, curled up and motionless, she dropped her board and nearly fell back down the ramp.

Before she could yell out for Derrick, the body shifted, and she saw his face.

"Dark," she said.

He mumbled and rolled onto his back, stretching his legs the length of the couch. She said his name again, this time a little louder. When he sat up and saw her, his eyes went narrow.

"Fuck you," he said.

"I didn't mean—"

"*Fuck you.*" He grabbed his bag, rolled his tiny blanket into a big, messy ball, then tried to shove it into a hole in the plywood wall behind the couch. It kept getting caught and he started cussing louder. Claire looked back to see if Derrick had noticed, but he was still in the bowl, oblivious.

"Are you living here?"

"Just . . . fuck you." It came weaker this time. And when the ball of belongings wouldn't go into the hole, he dropped them and fell to the couch. He sat there, staring off into the emptiness—refusing to look at Claire, to even acknowledge that she was here.

"God and Leg are really worried about you," she said.

He laughed bitterly. "Well, they won't have to worry much

longer, since I got fucking *expelled*." He looked at her then, his eyes more sad than angry. "You kept one of my journals? And then showed it to them? And now I'm officially on the fucking Most Wanted list. Or something."

"I'm sure you're not on the Most Wanted list," Claire said, unsure of what else she could say.

"Well, I'm a *threat*," he said, once again giving Claire a pointed look. "As you know."

Before Claire could say anything else, he sighed and said, "It's not like I would ever do anything. I want you to know that."

Claire hesitated, unsure of what she should say. But Dark wasn't finished.

"Why didn't you just *ask* me?" He leaned forward toward Claire. "Please, just tell me why."

Claire could feel the storm starting to rage, rising higher and higher into her throat—she could taste the bitterness in her mouth. And before it choked her completely, she spit out the first thing that came to mind. The truth, she realized.

"Who's going to admit they're dangerous? Who would ever say they're going to do something?"

Dark opened his mouth, but this time it was Claire's turn to keep talking.

"Do you know how many times I've heard somebody say

they saw the warning signs but didn't do anything? Do you know how many times the kid who shot up my school posted about guns or told people he was going to make everybody pay?"

Dark's head dropped and he turned toward her, hesitantly putting his hand on top of hers. The simple pressure, the weight of his hand, was calming. They sat there like that, like middle school kids afraid to hold hands at a dance, until Claire started to feel like she wasn't turned completely inside out.

And when she finally could, she looked at Dark and tried to say the right words.

"I know this all sounds like an excuse, but I don't know what's happening to me," she said. "And I am sorry. Really sorry."

Dark leaned back on the couch. "I guess it wouldn't have been that bad if my grandma hadn't, you know, already kicked me out of the apartment."

"Is that why you're living here?" Claire asked.

"Better than the alternatives," Dark said. "Plus, Mark-O gave me a key a couple summers back when I helped lead a camp. Leg and God don't know I have it."

He studied Claire, trying to figure out if she could keep his secret. She wasn't sure she could.

"They're really worried about you," Claire said. "And I assume even more so now, not that they'd talk to me at this point."

"They're loyal idiots, that's for sure," Dark said.

"What are you going to do?" Claire asked.

Dark shrugged. "Live off the land. Maybe grow a beard. Not sure what order those come in."

Claire laughed and, a few seconds later, so did Dark.

"Do you, like, need anything?" Claire asked.

Dark thought about it for a second. "I would love some Taco Bell."

Claire was always amused that there was a Taco Bell next to the otherwise industrial complex that housed the Lair. When she told Derrick she wanted something to eat, he paused long enough to fish a sweat-soaked twenty-dollar bill out of his pocket and hand it to her.

"Get me one of those Crunch Wraps," he said. "The Supreme kind."

"I don't think they make a non-Supreme Crunch Wrap," Claire said, smirking.

"Well, that's because the Bell has *standards*," he said, dropping back into the bowl, his laughter rising up to surround her.

She walked over to Taco Bell, hurrying through the cold, and spent the entire twenty dollars, which amounted to an absurd amount of food. When she carried it into the Lair, Mark-O eyed the bag and she was sure he was going to remind her of the strict no-outside-food policy. Instead, he smiled and let her pass.

Before she could get through the door he said, "Tell Dark to clean his shit up after he's done."

Claire spun around, shocked. Mark-O didn't look up from his magazine. "Do you really think I wouldn't know that somebody was essentially *living* here every night?"

Claire's mouth dropped open, and she stared at Mark-O, who finally looked up and smiled. "Don't tell him I know. But make sure he cleans up; I'm serious about that."

"Okay," Claire said, hurrying into the main room. Derrick was sitting on the lip of the bowl, and Claire tossed his Crunch Wrap Supreme up to him. He stared at the otherwise stuffed bag.

"Shut up, I'm hungry," she said, turning to walk back to the other side of the room. When she was out of eyesight, she climbed back up the ramp and dropped the bag of tacos on Dark's lap.

He handed her a taco and they ate silently. She was about to unwrap a second taco when Dark cleared his throat and quietly said, "What about you?"

At first Claire didn't understand. She looked at the bag, thinking that he was being Minnesota Nice, unable to take the last taco. But it was still full, and she was about to say as much when it hit her.

What about you?

She was suddenly aware of every sensation in her body. She'd felt like this before, after being called "bossy" during a middle school group project. The other kids had misinterpreted her excitement, or maybe they hadn't. But she heard their laughter—could feel the way her neck got hot with embarrassment—for weeks afterward. The same feeling of helplessness gripped her now, leaving her unable to do anything but stare at the taco growing cold in her lap.

"I'm not an expert, but I think you need help, too," Dark said.

Claire felt tears begin to well up in her eyes. She wiped at them, but they wouldn't go away. Her entire body felt like it was on fire and nothing would ever be able to mute the flames. She opened her mouth, but nothing came out.

"I. . . I don't know," Dark stammered. "Maybe that's part of, you know, all this."

Claire didn't need to see Dark to know what he meant. All

of this. The last few days. The last few weeks. Hell, the entire year—every single moment of her life since that kid walked into the high school and started shooting.

"The Monster," Claire said, looking over at Dark.

He looked confused for a second, but then he nodded.

"The Monster."

When Derrick finished skating, Claire was already sitting in the waiting area—trying to look normal. However, as soon as he saw her, he opened his mouth to ask what was wrong. Claire stopped him with a smile and, after a beat, he changed course and asked, "Got any tacos left?"

The idea that she would've eaten ten tacos was ridiculous, but she shook her head anyway.

"Finished them off," she said, forcing the words to be light. "Trying to get to my goal weight."

It made him laugh. "Okay, well. Ready to hit it?"

She stood up and glanced at Mark-O, who was still deeply invested in his magazine and ignoring them. But once Derrick was turned to the door, he looked at Claire and winked.

When they got to the car, Derrick was still in a good mood—still laughing about her comment. But every bit of energy Claire had in reserve was gone and she slumped

Bryan Bliss

against the window of the car, feeling the cold against her cheek.

Dark had struck to the heart of something she and Derrick had tried to bury, whether intentional or not. They'd convinced themselves she was getting better. That all they needed was time. Another day. Another absence from school. Another skating trip and the wound would scab over and heal and be nothing more than a light scar. Something you might not even notice if you weren't looking for it.

She didn't even realize she was crying at first, and when Derrick looked over at her, tears on her cold cheeks, he turned the radio down.

"Hey—what's happening?"

"I need help," she said.

For a few seconds, she could see him flipping through the various kinds of *help* she might need in the car before it hit him, with the same force that it had hit her, taking the air out of his stomach, the color from his face.

"We can do that." He rubbed his hand up and down his face, stopping the car just as a traffic light was turning yellow. A car honked behind them.

"God, Claire. I fucked up."

He hit the steering wheel once. He wasn't angry, just on the verge of tears, too. And so many times before, Claire would have assured him that everything was okay—attempted to walk back her own feelings, her anxieties. Not because she thought it was Derrick's fault, but because absolution was the only action she could take.

She didn't do that now. They'd both fucked up and chose to keep fucking up again and again, day after day. She looked out the window and tried to think of something they *could* do. It didn't have to be much. But maybe that first step would lead to another smaller step and, soon, they'd be halfway down the road to wherever they needed to be.

"We can do this," Derrick said, reaching over and squeezing Claire's knee. "We can do this."

Bryan Bliss

CHAPTER FOURTEEN

DERRICK FOLLOWED CLAIRE INTO THE SCHOOL, AND they waited silent and nervous in the office—a glass box right at the entrance of the school. And while Claire knew it wasn't true, it felt like every set of feet stopped when they saw her. Every pair of eyes stuck to her like she was a person of interest. See something, say something. And she could all but feel their whispers, every single accusatory word they spoke as they passed.

She told herself it wasn't true. Tried to focus. But she couldn't keep herself from looking out the windows, half expecting to see God or Leg suddenly standing outside the office, something worse than anger on their faces—indifference.

Derrick reached over and touched her on the shoulder, just as the counselor was coming to greet them.

"Hey, Claire. Derrick. Follow me back?"

Claire was surprised to find the principal already sitting in a chair in the counselor's small office. When they walked in, she stood up and greeted them warmly. After the obligatory handshakes, they all sat.

Derrick cleared his throat, but it was the principal who started talking.

"We're wondering if Claire might benefit from . . . "—she smiled, a genuine but still practiced emotion—"a more focused environment. There are a number of schools that can help Claire navigate everything she's working through."

Claire looked at Derrick, expecting him to be shaking his head. Instead, he was looking at his palms.

"I don't want to leave Central," Claire said.

It wasn't because she felt any sort of attachment to the school, or even because she *liked* it. But the idea that she would have to start over. Would have to learn all the little things—which routes to take in the hallway, which teachers would understand when she needed to just put her head down, everything that made her feel safe—made the storm, the panic, rise up.

She didn't want to feel unsafe again. And for all its faults, at least she felt mostly safe at Central.

"Claire, let's listen to what she has to say," Derrick said.

Bryan Bliss

The principal continued, handing Derrick a piece of paper.

"There are a number of schools we consider to be trauma-informed. You could take a week or even a month—however much you need—and do some more intensive services and then, maybe, start at the new school right after spring break."

Derrick nodded, taking everything in. Now Claire looked down at her hands. This is what she wanted. She wanted help. But for some reason, the idea of leaving and starting over made it seem impossible.

And maybe it was more than just not wanting to start over. Maybe she was feeling something else entirely, a loss that she hadn't expected. The loss of friendship. Of the only community she'd had since leaving her own school, even if two-thirds of that community weren't currently speaking to her.

"It sounds pretty good, Claire," Derrick said. "What do you think?"

She didn't look at Derrick as she nodded.

Claire stopped listening as the principal continued explaining the process of switching schools. The phone numbers for therapists. Treatment. Help. Everything could be buttoned up by early next week, depending on when Claire was ready.

"Can I at least say good-bye to . . ." She struggled to pull a name. In fact, she'd been a ghost to most of this school. But her struggle to name a single person must've looked more like emotion because the principal reached over to pat Claire's hand.

"Sure thing, Claire. Take as much time as you need."

Claire walked up the stairs slowly, figuring that she could stop by and make sure she hadn't left anything in the narrow locker they'd assigned her at the beginning of the year. By the time she got to the top of the stairs, she was nearly out of breath, and instead of turning to go to her locker, she walked toward Dr. Palmer's room.

Naturally, she had a class—packed with kids Claire had never seen—and they were all busy working with their heads down. At first Claire was just going to walk by but before she could get past the doorway, Dr. Palmer saw her and hurried into the hallway.

"Claire, how are you?" Dr. Palmer looked like she wanted to give her a hug, but suddenly remembered they were in school. She leaned close, almost confidentially. "We're bringing the trebuchet home tonight."

Claire couldn't hide her shock. "You're not, like, breaking it out of the impound or anything, right?"

Dr. Palmer laughed loudly and when the students in her

Bryan Bliss

classroom looked into the hallway, she said, "Back to your projects. "

She turned to Claire and said, "No. They're letting us have it as long as we promise not to fire any more watermelons onto the highway."

Claire laughed and very quickly, she started to cry. This time, Dr. Palmer didn't stop herself. She put a hand on Claire's shoulder.

"Does your brother know you're here?"

"He's downstairs. I'm—"

God, she didn't know why she couldn't bring herself to say it. Why it was affecting her so much. She didn't care about this school. The new one would be the same as this—something to endure. Something to make her way through. And yet, standing here in front of Dr. Palmer, she couldn't deny that it felt like she was losing something once again.

"I'm not coming back," she said, as fast as she could manage the words.

Dr. Palmer closed her eyes for a long moment. When she opened them up, she had tears, too. She wiped them discreetly, as if Claire hadn't seen them.

"Are you going back to North Carolina?"

"No," Claire said. "A different school. Where they can, you know, help me."

"That's good, Claire. I'm sad to see you leave, but that's really good."

Claire could hear the whispering from inside Dr. Palmer's room. And when Dr. Palmer snapped her fingers and pointed at a kid who was up and out of his seat, Claire took a deep breath and said, "I should probably let you get back in there."

Dr. Palmer nodded, but as Claire went to walk away, she stopped her.

"So, let's do this now. *Frankenstein*."

Claire wasn't sure how to break it to Dr. Palmer. "I'm not in your class anymore."

"Have you filled out the paperwork? Are you officially unenrolled?"

Claire shook her head, fighting a smile.

"So, *Frankenstein* then. The Monster. You said that he was created—that he didn't get a chance to decide how he would live in the world, right?"

Claire nodded.

"When's the last time you read the book, Claire?"

Claire's face went hot. What did it matter if she read the book now? She started to stammer out an excuse, but Dr. Palmer stopped her.

"I should've said it better—do you remember what happens to the Monster?"

Bryan Bliss

Claire had vague recollections that he disappeared, maybe was dead, in some kind of great arctic. Lost in the blowing snow.

"He died. I think."

"Before that."

"He terrorized a bunch of people."

"Did he?"

Like many of the things she'd read, Claire could pull out the highlights—a trick that made her popular with teachers. *Animal Farm*? Why, it's about fascism and here are the connections to today. It didn't help her with multiple choice tests—she was terrible at multiple choice tests—but there was never an essay she couldn't dominate.

But right now, she had nothing, and she said as much.

"The Monster becomes emotionally sentient. He *learns* to care. He *learns* to feel things. And the true horror of the story isn't some monster running around mindlessly—because who cares? That's just a popcorn movie. Instead, it's that we might forget that—no matter how scarred, how patched together, how monstrous seeming—that kind of change is possible. Do you understand?"

Claire thought about it for a second. "You're trying to tell me that I'm the Monster."

Dr. Palmer looked momentarily panicked. But then she

shrugged and worked her mouth into a smirk. "I mean, kind of!"

Claire felt like she should walk away now, before Dr. Palmer compared her to . . . who? Jack from *Lord of the Flies*? Nurse Ratched?

"Wow, thanks, Dr. Palmer."

"I guess I'm saying, we all get a chance to heal. Nothing stays broken forever. It may not look the same as it did before, but that doesn't mean it isn't strong—isn't *okay*."

Claire could feel herself getting ready to cry, so she nodded and took two quick steps toward Dr. Palmer, forgetting the rules—damning the rules—and grabbed her in a hug. It was quick and Dr. Palmer was obviously surprised, but when she let go, Claire felt better. She felt like something small had changed insider her, and that was enough.

Claire opened her locker and wasn't surprised to find it empty, save a couple of notebooks and what looked like a wrapper for a candy bar she was sure she hadn't eaten. She was about to bend down and pick up the notebooks when she heard an unmistakable voice in the hallway.

"She said *yes*," Leg said. "It's a mutually beneficial arrangement, because she's going to letter, too, and—"

When he saw Claire, he stopped talking. God nearly

Bryan Bliss

ran into him and was about to say something when he saw Claire, too. For a second they all stood there without talking. And then God hit Leg on the shoulder and nodded back in the direction they'd just come from.

"I'm not trying to get another detention; let's just go back to PE."

It was like Claire didn't exist, which was fair—expected, even. But as they turned around, it felt like something was being ripped from her body. Nothing major. Not a fundamental organ that would cause her to drop to the ground in a heap. Instead, an appendix. Something unnecessary, but still painful.

Just as they were about to turn the corner, Claire said, "Dark is staying at the Lair—he has a key."

God stopped, more of a slight pause in his step, but he didn't turn around. And just as quickly as they appeared, they were gone.

Claire closed her locker and walked down to the office, where Derrick was waiting with a single sheet of paper. He held it up with faux triumph.

"You're officially a high school dropout," he said weakly.

CHAPTER FIFTEEN

THEY SPENT THE NEXT FEW DAYS RESEARCHING THE different schools, which really meant they looked up the teachers and then looked up their various social media profiles to critique their suburban hairstyles and determine which ones were, in fact, Republicans. And when they grew tired of that—it didn't take long—they sat in the house, the way they had in the days and weeks after, and played make-believe.

Derrick pretended that this would fix everything.

And Claire pretended that she wasn't battling an entirely new emotion, something that hadn't been able to squeeze into her body with all the anxiety and pain—sadness.

It wasn't a crying sadness. Instead, her entire body ached,

draining her energy. It was the day after a long run. Two days after a particularly nasty stomach bug. And no number of streaming movies or social-media voyeurism seemed to do the trick. She woke up and felt like she hadn't slept a single minute.

They had started therapy at a small office just off the light rail line, which meant she could take herself when she felt ready—if she ever felt ready. For now, Derrick would come and sit in the waiting room as Margaret, the therapist, led her upstairs to a room that was obviously used for children of all ages. In one corner, there was a beat-up bean bag chair. In the other, a table with chairs too small for her or Margaret, but that's where they sat—moving the pieces of a board game around and talking.

Talking.

Even after the first session, she felt as if something had been taken out of her hands. It was the same feeling of having hugged Dr. Palmer. And when she told Margaret that it felt like she wasn't carrying as much, Margaret nodded and didn't say anything, which of course made Claire talk even more.

When she told Derrick, it looked like the entire world had come crashing down around him. He wouldn't look at her, wouldn't acknowledge the forgiveness that Claire had extended a hundred times since that ride home from the Lair.

"I'm sorry," Derrick had said. "I should've known."

But it wasn't entirely his fault. It had been the cost, past preconceptions about the benefits of therapy, and an irrational confidence in their ability to fix anything. They'd both been lost, stranded in some foreign and frozen place that was built in a circle, a trail that took them around and around until they were both dizzy and unsure of where they had even started walking.

This gave them a map. Or so it seemed. And that was enough for Claire. She hoped at some point it would be enough for Derrick, too. Now he was sitting on the couch, watching skating videos on his phone—which felt normal. It felt like a place they could both use as a foundation and slowly build up.

The knock on the door jolted them both, and for a moment they shared some brother-sister mental telepathy.

Should we just pretend we're not home?

They can probably see the lights.

Well, in that case, you can get the door.

Claire wrapped her blanket around herself tightly and Derrick sighed, dropping his phone onto the couch and walking to the door. Claire smiled, going back to her laptop

Bryan Bliss

and turning the volume up so she wouldn't have to hear the conversation about newspaper sales or upgrading their Internet or . . .

Derrick was staring at her, like he wasn't sure if he should say something. She pulled her earbuds out and said, "What?"

It sounded more panicked than she'd wished. She had just stood up when Dark appeared in the doorway. And then God and Leg were behind him, the three of them looking some mixture of embarrassed and nervous.

"Hey," Dark said.

"Hey . . . " She said. God and Leg were both blank, suddenly devoid of any readable emotion. "What are you guys doing here?"

Dark glanced back at God, who bit his bottom lip and stared at the ground, working up the nerve to say something.

"We're going to the park," he said. "Over by my house."

When Leg spoke, his innate excitability was too much to suppress. He pulled out his phone and held it toward Claire. "The Storm Mob is assembling! What-*what*!"

"We thought you might want to go," Dark said. "Well, it was my idea. But whatever. You should come."

God and Leg were noncommittal. Claire wanted to go, but

it was obvious the other two weren't interested in having her tag along. At least, not God, who hadn't looked at her since entering the carriage house.

"I don't know. I'm sure Derrick wants me to stick around the house. But thanks."

Derrick shrugged, which was enough for her to call the exchange settled. She was about to put her earbuds back in and force herself to forget about all of them—to be okay with being alone once again—when Derrick said, "I mean, what else are you doing?"

Leg slapped his hands together. "What-*what*!"

Dark smiled, but God only stopped staring at the floor to focus on the snow falling outside instead. Claire shook her head one last time and said, "Yeah, I'm good."

Dark paused before finally nodding and, with a smile, ducked out the door, followed by Leg and God. Claire put her earbuds in and tried to tell herself that this was better— that she'd been nearly content not ten minutes before— when Derrick popped back up and opened the door. Before Claire had her earbuds out, God was walking in and, finally, acknowledging her.

"Come with us," he said. "It's stupid for you to stay here, so you might as well go watch Dr. Palmer and her idiot husband get arrested this time."

Bryan Bliss

Claire gave him a polite smile. "You guys go. I'm fine here."

God sighed. "Listen, it's not that I don't want you around. And yeah, I was really pissed at you. Maybe I still am. But. Shit." He glanced at Derrick, a default reaction anytime there was an adult in the room, Claire guessed. When there was no reaction, he took another deep breath and said, "You fucked up. Me and Leg fucked up. Dark fucked up. So, the way I see it, we're likely to do less damage if we all look out for each other."

"Or you're one short to round out the four horsemen of the apocalypse," Derrick said, once again watching a video on his phone.

Claire couldn't stop herself from smiling, from showing every single emotion she was feeling—joy, excitement, and relief. She hurried back to her room to pull on a fleece and a warmer pair of jeans. It took less than a minute for her to be back in the living room, shouldering the heavy winter parka they'd bought after realizing their North Carolina "winter clothes" were JV in a land of varsity weather.

Once they were outside—the cold air burning Claire's lungs and stinging her cheeks—they were met with a rowdy cheer from Leg. Even Dark gave a few perfunctory claps, unable to contain his smile. And then Leg raised his hand in the air, pointing them forward with a loud *"What-what!"* that seemed to carry through the air as if it had wings.

They walked silently, the cold wind swallowing all of their words, before coming to a park Claire had never seen before, even though it was only fifteen minutes from the carriage house.

"Are you sure this is the place?" Dark asked.

Leg pointed to the trebuchet, which was in the corner of a large baseball field. "Unless St. Paul Parks and Recreation is planning to invade Minneapolis, I'd say we're in the right spot."

They trudged across the field, their steps the first in the blanket of white. The snow was deep now, almost halfway up Claire's shins. When they finally got to Dr. Palmer, she looked surprised to see them.

"Claire! Boys! I didn't think we'd have anybody show up with all this." She motioned dramatically at the snow. "But either way, the show must go on."

"The Storm Mob will *not* be denied—what-*what!*" Leg said.

"Uh, well, yes. We're not going to film this one. So, a special event."

Claire looked at the trebuchet, still as impressive and

menacing as it had been the first time she'd seen it. A quick sweep around the park confirmed there were no interstates in throwing distance, but there were still plenty of houses, cars, and other things that could be severely damaged by a flying melon.

"Um, I thought you weren't supposed to use the trebuchet. . . . "

Dr. Palmer's eyes lit up and she raised a finger. "Actually, they said we weren't allowed to throw *watermelons*."

Just then, Greg appeared. "Almost ready, Wendy. Let's get rolling. *Literally*, ha ha!"

Claire raised an eyebrow and Dr. Palmer reached down, packed a snowball, and handed it to Claire. At first Claire thought she was supposed to throw it at Greg for making some kind of joke she still didn't get.

"Oh, shit. I get it," God said, finally smiling. "Claire, hand it here."

She gave God the snowball and he put it on the ground, gingerly. And then he knelt down and just as carefully began rolling it in the snow. Claire hadn't grown up in snow—had barely built a snowman—but she understood now.

"Get down here," God said. "Leg, you and Dark start on another one."

And they started rolling, in large circles around the

trebuchet. Each time they completed a lap, they moved a few feet closer to the center, taking advantage of the fresh snow. Her jeans were soaked, her knees frozen. And the gloves she'd worn had never been regulation, not for Minnesota, so the wool was already wet and beginning to freeze to her fingers.

"Here," God said, taking off the shells of his snowboarding gloves. "You're going to lose a finger."

And then they rolled some more, almost ten minutes before either of them spoke again. This time, Claire.

"This takes way longer than you'd expect," she said, starting to breathe heavily.

"Rookie," God said, looking over at Dark and Leg, who had given up right away and were pretending to play soccer with their roughly cantaloupe-sized snowball. "But the bar is low."

"So, was Dark pissed? For telling you where he was?" Claire asked, not wanting to see God's reaction.

"No," he said. "I think, in some ways, he knew you'd tell us."

"He was pretty adamant that I not tell anyone," she said. "But maybe it's because I bought him tacos."

"I mean, the dude was living on whatever he could steal from Mark-O's snack bar. So that might be true." God sat down in the snow and started packing a snowball. He tossed it a few feet away from them and watched it land on the ground. "And even if he was, it all worked out. Plus, I've got a roommate now. So, bonus."

"Can I say I'm sorry?" Claire asked. "To you?"

This time it was God not looking at Claire. He nodded, wiped his nose, and started packing another snowball. This one, he threw at Claire. It hit her shirt and exploded.

"Apology accepted," he said, laughing. Claire started packing her own snowball, but it fell apart in her hands and the second one did the same thing. "Oh wow. Go back to North Carolina with that weak shit."

Behind them, Leg and Dark had started lobbing snowballs. They fell around her and God like meteors, disappearing into the deep snow with barely a sound. Claire tried one last time to pack a snowball and in a moment of pure luck or grace or something else otherworldly, threw it at God in one perfect motion. When it hit him right in the face she gasped, and then she laughed.

"Oh! I'm sorry!"

God wiped the snow from his face, laughing. "Like I said, this isn't my first rodeo."

"Excuse me." Dr. Palmer was staring at them, her arms out to her side like she'd just realized they were teenagers and couldn't be trusted with the important task of building snow ammo. "Are we having a snowball fight? Or are we *launching* a snowball?"

God stood up and started pushing the snowball toward Dr. Palmer. It was bigger than Claire realized, almost to her waist now. And by the time they got it back to Dr. Palmer, it looked impossibly large—something they wouldn't be able to load onto the trebuchet, let alone launch in the air.

"We should pour some water on it and make it freeze," Leg said.

Dr. Palmer's eyes lit up, but she must've had a flashback to the watermelon—new visions of a four-foot-tall ice ball hurtling through the bay window of some nice grandmother's house—so she shook her head.

"No, no. This is going to be great."

As she was talking, Greg carefully loaded the snowball onto the trebuchet, offering up random facts—he called them Storm Nuggets—as he worked.

"What made the trebuchet preferable was its ability to handle heavier projectiles," he told Leg and Dark, who humored him with enthusiastic grunts. "Your typical catapult could handle, maybe a hundred twenty pounds. But a trebuchet?" He laughed knowingly. "You're talking three hundred fifty pounds. A *disaster* for a castle under siege."

Bryan Bliss

Claire was shaking from the cold. Her wet jeans, wet hands, and increasingly freezing neck and face and, well, everything, was catching up with her. Dark came over and stood next to her. Even the small amount of body heat helped, and Claire took another step toward him.

Dr. Palmer was watching them and said, "Okay, I can't afford to lose my job, so we need to leave before any of you die from hypothermia."

"I, for one, think it would be worth it, Dr. Palmer," Leg said, his teeth chattering unintentionally.

"Thank you for that, Francis."

"Here for you, Dr. P. Storm Mob!"

God and Leg joined her and Dark; all of them were freezing. Huddled close, trying not to catch their death— something her grandmother would say. Something Claire hadn't thought about in years.

But maybe if they stood just like this, they could protect one another. Maybe they could keep just warm enough, just safe enough, to fight off whatever might come.

"Are we ready?" Greg asked.

Dr. Palmer clapped her hands and then, slowly, so did Claire—getting louder and happier than was probably warranted. And when Greg pulled the lever—when the trebuchet fired the snowball into the air—Claire took in a breath so quick, so sharp, she thought she might need to sit down.

But she didn't. She watched as the snowball launched into the air. Watched it rise up, slowly at first, and then in one rapid moment, rocket into the sky at an incredible speed.

It disappeared almost immediately. Maybe it was the snow. Or maybe it disintegrated as soon as it left the ground. But Claire wanted to believe that it was still flying, climbing higher and higher, never landing.

Bryan Bliss

If we could, we would protect you.

If we could, we'd reach out

to all of you.

To the entire world with arms

that stretch and stretch and stretch

like shadows at the end of a long afternoon.

A reminder.

After the news trucks have disappeared and all that's left is

flat grass and flat words,

what do you hear except the start of engines, the screech of tires

pulling away to the next story?

PART TWO
The Face

CHAPTER ONE

MRS. HOFFMAN, ONE OF THE TWO ORIGINAL TEACHERS Noah brought over on the ark, is carrying on about sentence structure and why "the teens" in her classroom have pretty much made a deal with the devil with all their texting and social media because now nobody cares about grammar or pretty much anything and that's when she literally, like, seriously, clutches at the pearl necklace she always wears, ready to stroke out right there in front of us.

I've seen it all before, of course, but the pure theatrics of it is always surprising.

Tyler whispers to Ben something like, *This lady could make sex boring* and a few people laugh, but not me because Hoffman is looking for any reason to pounce these days.

She pauses, and I feel Tyler tense up behind me, but Hoffman just stands there gathering herself, looking like she's one step away from raising a faltering hand to her forehead, trying to ward off a case of the vapors, just like in those Victorian novels she loves so desperately.

Nothing against the Victorians, mind you, but you get what I'm saying.

Anyway, seeing her react—that pained look on her face—reminds me of the T-shirts, and I promised myself I wouldn't think about that anymore, but it's damn near impossible as I sit there watching her get all worked up about *nothing* when she sure as hell didn't give a shit when the entire world blew up for all of us, her included.

Anyway, nobody much likes Hoffman.

And not even because she's the sort of teacher who goes to school council meetings to push Creation curriculums, even though she teaches English, because she felt it was her duty as both a Christian and a prayer warrior, to make sure all the kids who cross through Ford High School are nice and safe and, you know, saved.

Maybe Tyler can read my mind, because he repeats his winner a little louder—*She could make sex boring*—this time getting some chuckles from the people sitting around us. Loud enough to make Hoffman peer over her glasses and open her mouth to ask what was so funny. But then the bell rings and we all push out of our desks like our lives depend on getting out of that classroom as fast as possible.

When I walk past Hoffman's desk, she gives me a cursory glance, her eyes boring through the cardigan I'm wearing, not in a creepy way, but more like she's trying to access some kind of chaste superpower, an X-ray vision that would confirm everything she already thinks about me.

Nothing but trouble.

Tyler is waiting for me in the hallway, and a big smile comes across his face as he reaches to pull me close. I met him at the start of sixth grade, in PE class, when we played one on one. I was taller than him then and I'd been playing travel ball for years, so he never had a chance. Not when he checked me the ball or when he smiled at his friends, like, look at this girl, or when I hit that first shot—nothing but net—not to mention the next ten. Still, to hear him tell it, you'd think it went down to the final point. But all you have to do is ask his friends about that day. They are more than happy to remind him.

That was before I made the varsity basketball team as a freshman. Before I went All-Conference my sophomore year and All-State as a junior. Before a couple of colleges started sniffing around, talking scholarships. Before he and I got pretty serious.

"God. That lady should've retired fifty years ago," Tyler says, pausing only to kiss me on the side of my head. A mouthful of hair, mostly.

"I think she's actually been dead for the last two years," Ben confirms. "They just roll her out when school starts back every year."

They start riffing on how many other teachers might actually be dead as I watch Hoffman organize her desk until it is just so. The woman is psychotic about order, from the way she plans her lessons to the exacting way she speaks, as if every word takes a substantial effort to call forth. She believes in a world that is proper and respectful. A world that is black and white. Where there are good kids and bad kids. And I will forever be a bad kid to her now.

I made the shirt with a marker and one of Dad's old work T-shirts. Terrified and so, so angry. When I wore it to school that first day back, I didn't know the reporters would take my picture. I didn't know they'd use those tall antennas that reached from the news vans to send the picture all around the world. To make me iconic. The face of a movement.

You've seen it, of course.

Me, screaming—or was I crying?—outside the school.

Bryan Bliss

How just behind me, the front doors were open, but nobody was going inside. And of course, scrawled across my chest in a furious gospel, two words that all of us believed in that one moment.

FUCK GUNS.

Icon or not, once Hoffman and the rest of the teachers caught a whiff of that shirt, they lost their damn minds. The first day, they tried to confiscate it, but all I was wearing underneath it was my bra, so they found a smelly sweatshirt from the PE lost and found and made me wear that.

It didn't stop me.

I kept making and wearing a new one every day. Pretty soon they were waiting for me at the school doors—forcing me to change before I ever stepped inside. So I started hiding shirts in my bag, pulling one out at lunch or when we dressed for gym. Sometimes putting it on right before Hoffman's class, just to make the old bird sweat and call out an anguished prayer when she caught a glimpse of the big *FUCK* peeking out from the top of my cardigan.

They started searching my bags—which wasn't legal and, once the ACLU got wind of it, stopped immediately. But every time I opened my backpack, a teacher would appear, glancing in. The courts weren't sure if glancing violated my civil rights, but it didn't really matter. *FUCK GUNS* had become a full-on phenomenon. Suddenly the message was everywhere. If an administrator pulled one off me, another appeared in my locker or at my seat in the cafeteria. And it wasn't just at Ford. They called it a movement, and it spread across the state, across the country.

And then one day, that movement—all the screaming and crying and raging—jumped on my back like a three-hundred-pound gorilla, and it was all I could do to get out of bed in the morning, to keep moving, let alone be the face of a new generation of teenagers who would save the world, even though it was obvious that most of the adults didn't care about saving anything.

Part of it was my family. Dad hadn't gotten a construction job since I'd started wearing the shirts. He never asked me to stop, but I could hear him and Mom talking in the kitchen after I went to bed. Trying to make ends meet. To shield me from the harassment, which came from pundits and pastors and anonymous people I'd never met on websites I would soon know all too well. I became their personal devil, and they had the picture to prove it.

Part of it was Tyler and my friends, who had all healed. Ready to get back to basketball games and prom and normalcy. I could see the way they sighed when I pulled out a new T-shirt. At first, it was cathartic for me to be the lightning rod. To be the physical manifestation of our collective rage. But when they no longer needed it, when I was left standing all alone?

I stopped. Wearing the shirts. Doing interviews. All of it.

I pretended I was okay. That I wasn't always seconds away from letting loose another primal scream—from the realization that none of the people who say they care about us really do, not one bit.

"Eleanor?"

Tyler and Ben are both staring at me, the hallway nearly empty. I play it off like, "You know who else is probably dead? Mr. Young."

Ben cracks a smile and runs with it. Tyler stares at me like he doesn't believe a word I'm saying, which is probably the truth. We've known each other for too long, have learned all of the other's tells. It doesn't help that I've recently made the mistake of wondering aloud whether wearing the T-shirt made any difference whatsoever.

The bell rings and Ben cusses once and then takes off down the hallway, not waiting for Tyler even though they have the same class. Tyler reaches out to touch my arm, like I'm about to vanish right in front of him, so I give him a big smile, the one I know he likes—the one that, in my lesser moments, gets me whatever I want. Of course, it works.

"You good?" Tyler asks, his voice gentle.

Before I can say anything, Hoffman is out in the hall.

"Miss Boone? Mr. Castigan? Do you need assistance getting to your next class?"

I muster up every bit of energy, every bit of good upbringing I have inside me, to look the old bat in the eye, to smile like a good kid—hoping she believes me, hoping I can go back to the way I used to be—and say, "No ma'am."

The game was the kickoff for a week of activities meant to honor and memorialize the three students and one teacher who were killed. The girls basketball team—by far the best team in the school and maybe the whole county—would be the ambassadors, Coach Harris tells us. There will be a moment of silence and a slideshow and maybe a speaker—Coach Harris can't say for sure, but one thing is certain. We need to be ready.

"Because the game still has to be played," she says. "We still need to go out there and make our shots. Get our rebounds. Play as a team—*not* as individuals."

Normally I would be nodding my head along with everybody else, especially because this wasn't just any game. I've had this one circled on my calendar since last year when Maiden beat us, even though I'd dropped thirty-two points on them in the first three quarters, a record at the time. And I would've put another three on the board in the final seconds if I hadn't been fouled—and I was fouled, no matter what that ref had to say.

This year—my entire senior season—is supposed to be about redeeming that loss. About my plan to push, pull, or drag this team through Maiden, the whole state tournament, not stopping until a scholarship is in my hands and a banner is on these walls.

Of course, then everything changed. Which nobody wants to talk about now. Instead, we're supposed to be *Ford Strong*, a slogan the brain trusts on the school board nicked from at least two other schools. It's not that I don't believe our community is strong—it certainly is. But it speaks to a bigger problem, the idea that we are no different than the countless other schools that are having assemblies just like this one.

Ford Strong.

Kennedy Strong.

Everybody Strong, eventually.

Anyway, I'm not nodding, and Harris is giving me the laser eyes as she breaks us down.

"Okay, *Ford Strong* on me, on three."

Coach raises her hand and we all put our hands together and everybody yells "FORD STRONG" except me, because they still seem like replacement words. Words lacking conviction. Once our hands drop, I feel Coach Harris staring at me like I just kneeled during the national anthem or crossed my fingers on the Lord's Prayer—and it's a toss-up which one is worse in Hickory, North Carolina, these days.

Not that her giving me the eye was unusual. Coach Harris has been on my ass for one thing or another since I came onto varsity, which is either a great coaching strategy or a deep character flaw. Dad once said that Coach Harris could've been two things in life, and basketball coach was the one that wouldn't have gotten her a life sentence.

So, with that in my head, I try to walk off the court all casual.

"Eleanor, a word."

Coach waits for the rest of the team to file into the locker room, every single one of them laughing and whooping it up like we've already won the game. I watch them disappear one by one—Melissa Jung is the last one through the light-blue locker room door. Then I turn to face Coach Harris, girding myself with a smile she can only read as *positive*.

"I don't think I have to say this to you," she starts, reaching down to pick up a stray basketball. She holds it with both hands, a God controlling that small world. "But you

Bryan Bliss

understand that we can't have any distractions. Right?"

I nod, because I don't want to be a distraction. I want to win this game. And because I've gotten pretty damn good at pretending. But somewhere just below the surface, below this varsity smile I'm forced to trot out every single day, there's something different, a primal voice telling me to take that basketball and . . . what? Kick it across the gym? Slam it into the floor? Deflate it with the sheer power of my voice?

Because it has been an entire year and nobody has done a damn thing.

Ford Strong, indeed.

So, I smile. There will be no distractions. Nobody would even notice if there were.

"Just here to win, Coach."

God, is that true. Before I would've done anything it took to win. I would've sacrificed my body for the team, something I've heard the football coach say to his players countless times and—I have no idea what this says about me—but it just sounds *right*. Badass, yes. But more than anything, it's how I want to play the game. Living my life with skinned knees and busted elbows, a visible reminder that I will do whatever it takes, no matter what.

That's what got me up every morning to run mile after mile.

To shoot shot after shot in our dusty driveway.

To live my life with a singular focus.

And then everything splintered.

Coach Harris studies me for a long time before finally handing me the ball.

"Twenty free throws, then get out of here."

Bryan Bliss

CHAPTER TWO

THE DRIVEWAY TO OUR HOUSE IS LONG AND GRAVEL, which was an upgrade—or so Dad claims—from the dirt path I spent a lifetime riding my bike up and down, weaving around the potholes. Back then, the end of the road could've been the end of the world for all I knew or cared. If it were up to me, I'd never leave the ten acres that had been passed down to my father from his, the sole legacy of a family of tobacco farmers.

Thank God Dad can't grow a beard, let alone a patch of tobacco, because I'm not sure I'm cut out to be a farmer, either. But Dad can swing a hammer, can fix or build just about anything. Over the past twenty years, he's cobbled together a business and a reputation, ending every piece of communication—e-mail, text, sometimes a conversation at

Mt. View Bar-B-Q—with a simple reminder of "no job too small." If he believed in business cards, it would be on there, too.

Until last year he'd always worked enough in the warm months to take most of the basketball season off. He'd stand at the top of the bleachers—always stood, no matter what—and watch me play. This year he still comes to the games, but even from the court I can tell that his pacing is about more than the game.

Of course, he and Mom don't want me to worry or even know we're struggling. But I hear them whispering. I notice the way they stop talking and smile the same way I do—*Everything is fine!*—whenever I walk into the room. And of course, I noticed that Dad didn't get a call for work all summer. The traitorous looks every single person gives him, me, our entire family, whenever we leave our long gravel driveway.

When I pull up to the house, I can see them through the large bay window that Dad put in for Mom on her birthday two years ago. They're at the table, holding hands and talking. Two people who have been through a lot and still believe "no problem too big."

I walk in and they immediately turn their attention to me, not letting go of each other, which is sweet and, at times,

Bryan Bliss

the sort of thing that embarrasses the hell out of me at Food Lion. How they need to constantly be in contact. As if their bodies would stop functioning otherwise.

"How was practice?" Dad asks. "Harris still a psychopath?"

"Ronnie, please," Mom says, trying to pretend she doesn't find every word out of his mouth utterly charming. "Eleanor, I left you a plate in the fridge. Want me to heat it up?"

"Yes," I say, and fall into the chair next to Dad, leaning my head on his shoulder and closing my eyes as the smell of taco meat slowly fills the small kitchen. When the microwave dings, I open my eyes and see both Mom and Dad watching me.

"What?"

"Nothing," Dad says. "Y'all going to be ready for Maiden?"

I blow on the taco meat and shrug like what I'm about to say is no big deal.

"Yeah. I might mess around and drop fifty on them."

"Good. Those kids from Maiden were pricks even back when I was in school," Dad says.

"Ronnie . . ."

"What? Do you remember the way that one kid—they called him *Mantooth* or some shit—tried to take my knee out in the conference championship game junior year? I swear they teach those kids to be dirty from the moment they step on the court. Hell, probably when they come out of their mommas!"

That makes Mom laugh. She sits down at the table and picks up her puzzle magazine, cocking her head to the side as she reads through the different clues. My phone buzzes and before it's even out of my pocket, Dad is shaking his head.

"Tell that boy you've got a game tomorrow," he says, smiling.

"You know who wears the pants in this relationship," I tell him, and Dad laughs.

They both love Tyler but aren't like some parents, inviting boyfriends on family trips. Not that I'd ever give them any reason to think that my relationship with Tyler might throw me off the course I've been following since the first time I picked up a ball.

A scholarship. Didn't matter where. Anything that can take me away from this small town—even if I wasn't always sure I wanted to leave. It's not fear, not really. But I love living in Hickory, NC. I love how I know every back road, every stitch of this county. And I love the idea of being just down the road from my parents, with my own kids someday, piling everybody in the car for Christmas morning on the same wooden floors I opened gifts on for my entire life.

Bryan Bliss

"I'm going to my room," I tell them, looking down at my phone as I stand up.

"Make sure you don't stay up too late, okay?" Mom says.

I lean down and give her a hug, holding it long enough that she gives me a look, a quick check-in that I dismiss with a big but tired small. And then I take my buzzing phone and walk down the hallway.

It buzzes four more times before I'm in my room and I look at the messages.

How was practice?

You know, Coach Harris really likes me. I can tell.

???

...

Don't ghost me, Boone.

Instead of typing out a response, I put him on speaker phone and let it ring while I start getting my stuff ready for tomorrow's game.

"Booooooooone!"

"Mr. Castigan."

"God, you sound just like Hoffman. Please don't do that ever again unless you want my junk to shrivel up." He pauses for a second. "Holy shit, Boone, do you have me on speaker phone?"

"Yes. But I'm in my room."

"Oh, sexy. What are you wearing?"

"I'm going to hang up on you," I say.

"Okay, okay. I was just kidding."

I lay down on my bed and close my eyes. When Tyler speaks again, I jolt awake—had I been asleep?

"I'm sorry, what?"

"Boone, are you literally falling asleep while I talk to you?"

"I'm just really tired. Sorry."

"You excited about tomorrow?" he asks, his voice suddenly cautious. It's enough to make me sit up on my elbow, pretty sure I know what's about to come out of his mouth.

"Yeah, it's Maiden. I'm going to wreck them."

"And, you know, you're just going to play?"

I sigh hard and heavy, picking up my phone to make sure he can hear it. When I first wore the T-shirt, Tyler was still in shock—enough that he didn't have a strong, or at least verbal, opinion of his girlfriend suddenly finding herself on every website and social media platform. At war with nearly every teacher and administrator in the school.

But soon, he started making little comments that seemed harmless enough—*Are you going to wear your basketball shooting shirt to the pep rally tomorrow? Want to go to the mall and look at clothing?* And maybe they were harmless. He's always been a good boyfriend, especially compared to some of the Neanderthals my friends have dated. But that doesn't give him permission to decide fundamental things about my life.

So, I give him one more long sigh. Just so he remembers.

"Jesus, sorry—I'm just looking out for you," he says.

"I'm going to bed," I tell him. "If you're lucky, I'll let you see me tomorrow."

He pauses, his tone changing immediately.

"How *exactly* am I going to see you?"

"Good night."

And then I hang up the phone and turn it off—maybe for the rest of our relationship.

Dad is up drinking coffee when I walk into the kitchen the next morning. When he sees me, he kicks a chair out from the table and motions for me to sit down.

"You ready for tonight?" he asks.

"Maiden isn't as good as they were last year," I say. "They lost that girl who signed with Elon. So, yeah. I think we're going to whip them."

Dad smiles, but it's pained. I already know what's coming.

"There's going to be a lot of people there," he says. "People who might not normally show up for a girls' basketball game."

I nod, because how could I not know?

I'd only gone to one football game this year after having a group of men yell at me—calling me a snowflake, a liberal (like it was a slur), everything you could think—as the crowd, people I'd known for most of my life, laughed and clapped and gave me looks that could cut glass. I didn't give them the satisfaction of a reaction. Sat there with the same lead in my veins that had made them cheer for me in countless games. Not a whiff of emotion. Just eyes forward, clapping when the team scored and shaking my head at the refs when they deserved it.

But inside? I was, as Dad likes to say, *tore up*. I hadn't worn a shirt in months at that point and would've been happy if nobody had mentioned *FUCK GUNS* or that picture ever again. It didn't mean I was over it. Or that I wasn't still angry—because I was. I am. But I'd made a deal with Tyler and the teachers and, I thought, every other person in this town.

No more *FUCK GUNS*. We can all get back to normal.

And yet they still stood up and chanted my name, called me every other one in the book, until halftime finally came and I told Tyler and my friends that I was going to get a hot dog—smiling, smiling—and then I basically ran to my car and roared out of that parking lot faster than you could count to three.

Bryan Bliss

"It will be fine," I tell him. "It's going to be so loud in there, I probably won't be able to hear anything they say."

It must make sense to him because after a second he reaches over and messes my hair, the way he would when I was a kid and still short enough to fit just under his arm.

"Well, give them hell then. Okay?"

"What else am I going to do?" I say, but I'm not sure if he's talking about the other team or the people who, like he said, normally wouldn't give two drops of piss about a girls' basketball game.

When I walk into school, the principal, Mr. Townsend, is standing at the doors, greeting students with his slick politician smile. He doesn't see me at first, so I try to match the watts of his smile—engage backup generators!—and when his eyes catch mine, I must look like a complete psychopath, all teeth and crazy eyes.

"Miss Boone" is all he says, looking past me, to the next student who gets an enthusiastic high five.

Townsend had taken the brunt of the ACLU's attention. In all honesty, when I looked up their website and sent an e-mail on the general form, I hadn't been sure anything would come of it. I was still so angry. Maybe if anyone had just asked me *why* I was wearing the shirt, if they'd just let me wear it without making such a big fucking deal—but it *was* a big fucking deal, wasn't it?—it might've lasted a week, two at the most. And then it would've gotten buried in the back of my closet along with the rest of the news cycle.

Instead, they tried to stop me. So every single bit of muscle memory kicked in and I decided to do what I do best—fight.

Even then, enough was enough. Once I stopped wearing the shirts, once I pledged to never wear, say, or even think about anything that said *FUCK GUNS* ever again, I figured the adults would just go back to being *adults*.

But every single one of them still looks at me like I spit on Jesus's tomb, which of course just proves my point—that they care more about their guns than they do about me. About every other kid in this school.

So, fine. I let it go. I went back to the normal Eleanor that everybody loved.

The question is: why can't they?

Tyler is at my locker and my face must be telling the whole world everything I'm feeling, because he straightens up and starts apologizing immediately.

"Shit, is this about last night? I was just messing with you. I'm sorry."

"No," I say, leaning over and giving him a peck on the cheek. "It's nothing. I'll get over it."

He wraps an arm around my shoulder and pulls me close, giving my hair a kiss. He holds me that way for a couple of seconds and it's all I can do to keep myself from crying, screaming, because sometimes the anger gets watered down just enough that I can't tell which emotion I'm actually feeling.

Sometimes I just want to be held, like this, so I can remember what it's like not to feel constantly tense, constantly ready to attack.

The ball comes to me and I drive into the lane, taking a step around Katie Light, who is chasing down a missed jump shot from the other side of the court, and kiss the ball off the glass backboard. It drops into the net without a sound and I run to the three-point line, pausing, before I cut back to the top of the key and catch another pass from Coach Thompson, one of the assistants, and put it up: nothing but net.

"You've got it going tonight," Thompson tells me and she's right—I'm feeling it.

"Going for fifty," I tell her, and she smiles, passing me another ball. It's barely in my hands when I release the shot. I don't even watch it go through the net. I jog over to grab some water.

Some boys from Maiden are sitting right behind our

bench and they get started on me immediately, which isn't abnormal. Every word they say is weak, the kind of trash kids talked in grade school, and for a second I think about turning around and saying something like, "Really? Is that all you've got?" But I just drink my water and smile, shaking my head every time they say something that rises past ridiculous and gets to absurd.

When Coach Thompson comes to the bench, it takes two seconds before she turns around and just stares at them until they finally get up, laughing, and retreat to the back of the bleachers. Thompson played at NC State and is a legit six-foot-three—a woman you don't mess with.

"Jackasses" is all she says.

Coach Harris and the rest of the team come to the bench soon after that, and she gets everybody to circle up.

"There's going to be a speaker and then a quick slideshow. So we've got some time before tip-off. Keep loose. Drink water. And be ready to play as soon as the lights come up."

She gives me a quick glance, but I'm staring at the scoreboard, watching it count down. Waiting for the tip so I can get on the court—the only place where everything else disappears—and do what I've come to do.

Anyway, my focus must make Harris feel better, because she grabs a cup of water and sits on the bench just as Townsend taps a hot microphone, sending feedback through the gym. He clears his throat once before he starts talking.

"I want to thank everyone coming out tonight for what's—well, what I hope is just another example of our community having the opportunity to heal."

The crowd explodes with applause. The scoreboard has stopped counting down, which means we should throw the ball up. But Townsend keeps talking.

"When the school board came up with *Ford Strong*, it took my breath away. Because if there is one word that can be used to describe this community, it's *strong*."

More applause. Townsend waits for it to die down. He smiles, only half wattage.

"People always ask me: how do you come back from something like that? And I tell them . . . *this*. This is what we do. We come together. We don't let hate stop us. We *heal*."

People are crying now. As Townsend talks, two students bring out a projector and a large screen, setting it up under the basket by the locker room.

"It looks like Cody and Kellen have our slideshow ready, yes?"

They give him a thumbs-up and the lights drop out of the gym. Normally a few kids would hoot and holler, but nobody says a word as the projector slowly comes to life. The slideshow begins, the music being cued on a nearby iPhone, with a picture of the high school.

People clap, whistle. And from there, it's pictures of the hallways. Kids smiling. The band. The football team. A school play. A picture of Claire, taking a shot in last year's Maiden game. And then the music shifts and the slideshow fades to black before the first picture comes up.

Taylor Ann Montgomery, 15

A second passes, and then the next picture.

Kevin Anderson, 17

The third picture.

Richard Merry, 14

I can hear people crying. Some of the players on the team are doing their best to keep it together, but Coach Thompson isn't even trying to pretend. The music swells higher and everybody knows what's coming before the next slide switches over. And when I see his face, I can't help myself. I start crying, too.

Coach "O" (Owen) Faribault, 57

Coach O's weathered face stares at the crowd, his grizzled but jovial smile frozen on the screen as the music drops. I didn't know him the way a lot of kids did. He was the sort of man who would drive kids home, just happening to stop for dinner on the way. Despite being a well-known curmudgeon with a reputation that was tough as nails, there wasn't a single kid in the school who would've said a bad word about the man.

Three kids, one adult.

That's the official number—the one that was reported over and over again. And of course, everybody knows Coach O's story now.

How he put dozens of kids inside the wrestling room and, instead of staying with them, ran toward the gunshots, pushing kid after kid back toward the room—telling them to hide, too.

Pushing me under the stairs. Telling me to quiet down. That it was going to be okay.

And just as the intruder was coming down the hallway, Coach O dove on top of some kids hiding in a corner. He took six bullets right in the back, dead almost immediately, the news reports told us.

But not a single one of those kids was hurt.

The music tapers off and the lights come up suddenly. Every single person in the gym is wiping at their eyes as a local television crew eats it up, filming the crowd, the team— everyone. I wipe my eyes two times before they're finally dry.

Principal Townsend clears his throat and, his voice breaking, and said, "*Ford Strong*, indeed."

Bryan Bliss

CHAPTER THREE

I DON'T GET FIFTY, BUT FORTY-TWO IS CLOSE ENOUGH. I probably could have twenty more but Coach Harris takes me out of the game at the end of the third quarter, all smiles and high fives from the bench.

We are beating them like they stole something.

After the game Dad pushes his way through the crowd, and when I see him, his face showing none of the anxiety he's lived with for the last year, I throw my arms around him and don't let go until Tyler and Ben and the rest of their idiot friends are jumping around us, nearly knocking everyone to the floor.

And so maybe that's why I agree to go to Applebee's with Tyler and the rest of the idiots, something I never liked doing even before the entire town marked me as Liberal Enemy

#1. But in the moment, after playing undoubtedly the best basketball game of my life, the only words on my mind are *Screw it*.

So I get in the car with Tyler and I sing along with their terrible music and I order two baskets of fries and a never-ending soda because this is the first time in months, maybe the entire year, when it feels like nothing can stop me. Not that sophomore from Maiden everybody said might be something. Not the people in the booth across the restaurant, whispering and pointing. Not a single person, not a damn thing.

"I swear to *God*," Tyler says. "You shook that girl from Maiden so bad. Like, she might never play basketball ever again. You didn't just break her ankles, Eleanor. You broke her *soul*."

I laugh, because it's true. I may have ruined that girl.

"Is that how she broke you?" Ben asks, laughing as Tyler punches him.

"Nah, I let her win because that's the only way our relationship can work."

This time I punch Tyler.

"That's why he won't go near a basketball court. You've noticed that, right? Like his mom told him it was bad luck."

Tyler only smiles because he knows what's up. He pulls me

a little closer, that same smile on his face, and so I let him off the hook.

"Anyway, what did you guys think about the slideshow?" I ask.

"Ben was crying like they weren't going to make any more comic book movies," Tyler says.

"First, you know my 'no crying in public' rule. It puts the wrong message out for the ladies," Ben says. "*And* if they were going to stop making comic book movies, the ladies would understand that a few tears were necessary."

He reaches across the table and swipes one of my fries, popping it into his mouth with a satisfied grin.

"I don't even know where to start with, like, all of that," Tyler says. "And Jesus, *everybody* was crying. Did you see Townsend? He probably lost five pounds of water weight tonight."

"I mean, it was pretty emotional," I say.

I swear both of them almost break their necks the way they turn to look at me.

"Oh my God, the robot *feels*!" Ben says.

"I'm not a fucking robot," I say, unable to keep the anger out of my voice.

The anger.

I spend so much time making sure nobody ever sees this

fast blood, this fundamental and undeniable part of me—no less necessary than my heart, my lungs—that sometimes I trick myself into think that it isn't still there, lurking.

But here I am in the middle of a crowded Applebee's, giving Ben dagger eyes and not thinking twice about it.

"Guys, c'mon—it *was* pretty sad to see all those names. And then Coach O? Jesus." Tyler tries to get me to relax, but the blood is moving and I'm not sure I can control it.

"I'm just saying, Eleanor is usually so . . ." Ben swiped his hand down in front of his face, wiping all emotion. "Like, you're stone-cold on the court. Shit, I was just messing around. Sorry."

I know he's backing down, but it doesn't matter.

"Do you know what it's like tiptoeing around all the time? Do you know what it's like making sure that you *never* show any kind of emotion because people think you're about to . . . I don't know . . . start a fucking revolution when you just have your damn period?"

"Gross," Ben said.

"Dude," Tyler said. "C'mon."

I stand up and for a moment, both Ben's and Tyler's faces go white. Maybe they think I'm actually going to raise my voice, my fist in the air—I don't even know. Instead, I walk out of the restaurant and keep moving until I get to Tyler's

Bryan Bliss

car, so hot it doesn't matter that all I'm wearing is a hooded sweatshirt and a pair of track pants. I pull myself up onto the trunk and sit there watching the traffic come and go from the stoplight, trying to cool off.

Tyler comes out and leans against his car, watching the traffic, too. A few seconds later, he takes his coat off and puts it around my shoulders.

"I didn't know you felt that way," he says. "That you can't, you know, feel anything."

"I feel things," I say. "I feel things all the time."

"Don't I know it," Tyler says, smiling.

"Shut up," I say. "It's just, *damn*. I think I'm allowed to cry. To be angry."

"*Of course* you are. And I'm sorry if, you know, I kind of make you feel that way." He isn't looking at me when he adds, "Do I do that?"

Most of the time, Tyler is pretty good about tending my feelings. Or at least, making the effort to figure out what is wrong—even when I don't know, or can't explain. But at the same time, over the last year, an unspoken threat has clouded every interaction between us. He couldn't—or wouldn't—stick around if I kept choosing to go on television. To become a Twitter presence. To become the Face of a Generation.

And while I can't blame him—who wants to be second

fiddle to all that?—can you really say you care about somebody's feelings when you essentially won't engage with the most prominent thing in their life?

"Sometimes," I say, turning to face him. "And hey, listen. I get it. Everything that happened? Sometimes I feel like . . ."

I don't want to say the next part—that sometimes I feel cheated. Not that I want fame. What I want is a chance to scream and keep screaming until there's nothing left. Until I am completely empty. And then—*then*—go back to being Eleanor the basketball star. The good girl. Tyler's girlfriend.

Tyler already knows all of this, though. And he takes it on the chin, with a smile.

"You want me to take you home?"

I say yes.

The next morning I know something is wrong as soon as I walk into the living room and find Mom and Dad staring at the laptop. They snap it shut and ask me to come and sit next to them on the couch, which means it's something really bad.

"You guys aren't getting divorced, are you?"

I laugh; they don't.

"There was another post," Mom says.

I take the laptop from Dad, who hesitates a second before

Bryan Bliss

letting me have it. And when I open it, the familiar archaic site design of *Right-Wing Report* is on the screen in all its trolling red, white, and blue glory.

There's a picture of me, blown up so that it nearly fills the entire screen. I'm crying. Above it, the headline reads, "Eleanor Boone Can't Stay Away from the Spotlight." The article, which is really only a few sentences, claims the tears are manufactured—another calculated decision in my attempt to steal guns, the Constitution, and maybe even God from all the good people of this country.

I close the laptop and look at Dad.

"You can stay home from school if you want."

"It might be for the best," Mom says.

I shake my head.

I want to add, *fuck those guys* but that would change the tenor of the conversation completely and put the spotlight on me in a different and decidedly more parental way. But that's how I feel right now, nothing short of *fuck those guys*.

"The only people who read *Right-Wing Report* at school are the Future Farmers of America dudes and that one gym teacher," I say, trying to blow it off. But when their concern doesn't disappear, I try a different tact.

"I don't want anybody to think that this bullshit even registers with me," I say. "Not even a blip."

Mom clucks a bit at *bullshit*, but I can tell Dad is proud of what I just said. And it's true. While staying home does sound nice—streaming nineties sitcoms and maybe convincing Mom to take me to Carol's for breakfast—people would immediately think it was the article that kept me here.

And right or wrong, I'm not going down like that.

"I'm going to go shower and get ready," I say.

By the time I'm inside school, I'm pretty sure nobody has seen the picture except Tyler, who comes storming up to me red-faced and ready to fight the first person who mentions it.

"You're not a fighter, babe," I tell him. "And surprisingly, not a lover, either."

When it doesn't puncture his anger and frustration, I reach over and pull him toward me, the way he always does for me.

"Seriously. It reminds me of my favorite Bible verse—*And the Lord smiteth all those bitches*."

Still nothing.

"That's from the little-known Boone translation," I say. "Hugely popular in the square states."

Finally, he smiles.

"You were crying about Coach O! It's so ridiculous."

In some ways, his outrage is cute. But it's also frustrating. This is what I live with every day. Every single time I walk into a grocery store or restaurant, some gun-toting Real American is giving me the eyes. Sure, the clickbait article and picture are bad, but a day later they're usually gone. The looks and the whispers never stop. And if he hasn't noticed, what does that say about him?

The bell rings and Tyler glares up at the speaker like he's never heard the sound before.

"Hey, forget it. Just try to make it through the day without starting a fight, okay?"

By the time lunch comes and I see Tyler walking into the cafeteria with Ben, I'm certain nobody has actually seen the article and, as a result, Tyler won't end up being suspended or arrested. When they sit down, though, he's still angry—and surprisingly, so is Ben.

"Listen, I'm no Democrat," Ben says. "But that's just bullshit, okay? It makes me wish I was a hacker so I could redirect the site to, like, a picture of a person taking a giant shit. Because that's all that site is. A huge piece of shit."

"I appreciate that passionate and perhaps unnecessarily explicit defense," I say. "But honestly, it's just the same thing on a different day. If you really want to get upset, just Google my name. On second thought, don't do that. You two might combust."

"What should we do?" Tyler asks.

"Eat lunch. Never mention the site to me again," I tell them.

But it's obvious they want to keep talking about it, to work themselves up even more and, honestly, I'm too tired to care about anything the mouth-breathers from *Right-Wing Report* might have to say about me or, you know, pretty much anything.

"I'm going to shoot some baskets," I announce, not giving them a chance to respond or, hopefully, follow. Once I'm in the gym, empty and quiet, I grab a ball, strip off my hoodie, and put up maybe the prettiest jump shot that's ever been taken in the history of basketball.

From that moment on, it's just my hand on the leather, the release, and the snap of the net. Losing myself until the bell rings and, sweating and likely smelling pretty bad, I pull on my hoodie and run to my next class, not giving a damn about whether I'm late, any of it.

After practice I walk into the house and find Mom and Dad smiling like they've won the lottery, which honestly would solve a lot of problems, the more I think about it. Instead, Dad holds his hands out wide and says, "How about we go out to dinner tonight? Anywhere you like."

"Wait. *Did* you win the lottery?"

They both stare at me for a second.

"Your dad won a bid," Mom says, and this, honestly, is better than winning the lottery. I drop my bag onto the ground and run over to give Dad a hug.

"What? Oh my God! For who? Where?"

"Nothing huge," he says, downplaying his obvious excitement. "But it's solid work for the next two months and that's a start. "

He looks at Mom and they both smile and, damn, it's maybe the best thing I've seen in my entire life.

"I won't mess this up," I say.

Dad's smile drops from his face and he holds me at arm's length. "What did you say?"

"I won't mess this up," I say again. "I know all of this is my fault and I won't mess it up, I promise."

"Eleanor, it's not your fault," he says, pulling me back toward him for a hug. "It's *their* fault. This entire damn town's fault. You're a kid. A kid who went through something terrible. And instead of trying to understand it, they . . . well, they did what they did."

He squeezes me once and announces that we're going to Red Lobster, which is the height of fine dining according to my parents. Whenever it comes up, Dad always says, "They've got actual live lobsters swimming around—right there in the waiting area!" All impressed. And honestly, I still don't know if he's kidding or not, because every time I think about those poor lobsters, it all feels kind of twisted.

But once we're in the car, I'm not thinking about those lobsters one bit. I'm listening to the radio play, my parents talk, as the lights from the interstate pass above me, pulling me down, down, down until I'm asleep, just like when I was a kid on those long road trips up the coast and to the beach. I never remembered falling asleep then, only waking up—the ocean appearing outside our car like a miracle straight from God himself.

Except this time, it's the red neon lobster on the sign.

And it's just as good.

Bryan Bliss

CHAPTER FOUR

AT BASKETBALL PRACTICE THE NEXT DAY, COACH HARRIS keeps barking at me like I kicked dirt on her dog. I try to ignore her because, like my dad said, she can be a grade-A psychopath most of the time, and you can't spend too much time trying to figure out what people like that are carrying on about.

And so, I'm not surprised when practice ends and she yells for me to follow her to her office, which must've been a closet at some point, because there are no windows and no money for something better, unless you're the football team, which hasn't won a game in about two decades.

But hope springs eternal, they say.

Anyway, she's already behind her desk by the time I get in there, un-showered and still sweating. She motions to the seat in front of her desk as she crumples a piece of paper and sends it toward the garbage can, a perfect shot.

"All right, here we are." She gives me a quick smile and I already know what this is about.

"I didn't know they were going to write that article," I say. "I was crying because it was actually sad to see all those pictures."

She should know that I'm not the type of person to manufacture emotions of any kind. If I feel it, you know. My freshman year, when I challenged the lackluster leadership of a senior whose play was also lacking, I sat in this same seat and told her that I wasn't trying to make problems for the team—I was trying to make us better.

And even though our relationship from that point on seemed as hard as granite, somehow, she's forgotten. Somehow, she now thinks I'm made of less solid stuff—that I'm making myself cry to get the attention of *Right-Wing Report*.

"I was really crying," I say again, forcing myself to remain calm.

Coach Harris looks utterly confused. "I'm not sure we're talking about the same thing, Boone."

She smiles again, but this time it's different. Harris pulls out an e-mail she's printed out and hands it to me.

Bryan Bliss

I see the wolf. The bright-red logo.

"Holy shit," I say. "NC State?"

"Yep. I spoke with the coach this afternoon. They're offering you."

"That's the ACC," I say, still unable to process what I'm reading—things like "special player" and "scholarship opportunity." Before this, I'd had a few Division I schools interested, but mostly in places like Illinois or West Virginia. Not only was this closer to home, NC State regularly played on television. In the tournament.

"You've earned this," Coach Harris says, tapping her desk with a pen. "Now all you have to do is go out there, keep playing hard, and everything's going to work out."

"Can I take this?" I ask, showing her the e-mail. It's the sort of thing that will make Dad cry and Mom want to put it on the refrigerator, even though I'm how-many-years-past *great job!* stickers.

"Yes, of course. Tell your dad I said hello." She smirks and then waves me out the door. "Go shower. And hey, Eleanor . . . congratulations. You deserve this."

I don't shower—barely remember driving home—so when I burst through the front door like a maniac, Mom shrieks and Dad grabs the side of the table, which might've been due to

Mom's reaction, honestly, but they're both looking nice and panicked. Both saying the same thing.

"What's wrong?"

But I can't speak. So before they get Dr. Holston, my therapist, on the phone for an emergency session, I hand Dad the paper and watch as he reads it, finally glancing up at me with a look I've been wanting to see my entire life.

You did it.

"What is it, Ronnie?"

But now Dad can't talk, either, so he hands the paper to Mom, his smile matching mine. It takes Mom exactly three seconds to start screaming and run around the table to suffocate me with a bear hug.

"Oh my God, Eleanor! Congratulations, honey! Can you believe it, Ronnie?"

"The only thing that would've been better is if it had been Carolina," he says.

"Wow, thanks, Dad."

"I can't help it if my blood runs Carolina blue, but . . ." He reaches up to wipe away the wetness from his eyes. "I guess I could root for the Wolfpack—just don't tell my dear old and departed father."

And he comes over to hug me, too.

"Have you told Tyler yet?"

"No. I wanted you two to know first."

"That boy's about to turn in a quick application to State, I can tell you that much."

I hadn't considered this. The idea had always been for me to go to the best college I could—and that almost certainly meant leaving the state. At least, that's what I'd always told Tyler. And so he was planning on going to Appalachian State University, up in the mountains of North Carolina, because I might end up in Southern California and, well, I wouldn't let him follow me to some no-name college in the name of high school love.

"I should probably go call him," I say.

"I'm going to call your aunt Penny," Mom says, pulling her cell phone out and walking into the living room as she waits for Penny to pick up. Before I can leave the room, Dad stops me.

"Hey—congrats, kid."

When I call Tyler, he picks up on the first ring like he was sitting there waiting for me to call—an image that amuses me. But I don't get a chance to give him shit for it, because he nearly explodes into the conversation.

"Hey, so, I'm glad you called. Have you been online?"

"What? No. But wait, I have something big to tell you."

He pauses. "Okay, well, you should know that, um, something's going around."

There have been so many things.

Memes and GIFs and long-winded screeds on social media when somebody either sees the FUCK GUNS picture again or happens upon one of the other commentary pieces months later and decides to make a stink about it somewhere—only made better by the inevitability of Dad seeing it and getting in the comments, which always, always, always makes it worse.

So, I guess I'm saying I'm bombproof now.

"Just tell me," I say.

Tyler's voice breaks when he starts to answer, forcing him to stop and clear his throat a couple of times before he tries again.

"It's those fuckers at *Right-Wing Report*. They made . . . T-shirts."

I put Tyler on speaker and drop the phone on my bed as I open my laptop. I don't have *Right-Wing Report* bookmarked on principle, but I might as well at this point. While I never comment—again, Dad has given us more than enough reason to avoid that shit show—I also don't live in fear of what those basement dwellers say. Or more correctly, type. Because none of them would say a damn word to me face-to-face, that much is certain. Nothing but keyboard heroes from front to back.

When the site loads, I'm greeted by my crying face—larger than life and dancing back and forth in an animated GIF. Every couple of seconds, a red crosshair pops up on my face, freezing the image with the sound of a gunshot. Below it a large text balloon pops up that says, "Gotcha!" followed by an offer to buy T-shirts with the image for $19.99, same-day shipping included to any "God-fearing, Republican-voting" state.

I sit there, silent as the GIF plays again and again, until Tyler says, "Eleanor, are you okay?"

I want to slam my laptop against the wall so hard that it wipes the image from their server—from the mind of every person who has seen it, liked it, anything.

"No," I say, trying not to lose it on Tyler because he's the closest living, breathing thing I can attack.

I try to breathe.

"You should tell your dad," he says. But what is that going to do except start World War III?

"If he sees it, fine. If he doesn't, even better. I'm sure it will pass."

I look at the image again, which was posted only an hour ago and already had 10k likes. I tell myself there have been posts like this before. I tell myself that what they think does not matter.

"This is . . . Shit, Boone. This is different. Like, they're threatening you."

Something catches in my throat, and I can't say anything for a few seconds. Outside of one guy at the mall—fury and bravado on his face—nobody has ever confronted me in person. Before he got more than three words out, Dad had him up against the wall. Soon after that, the mall security guards had Dad pinned against a different wall and the whole thing made the local news, because back then I couldn't take a breath without it attracting attention.

But I'd never been threatened.

And while I've spent a lot of time training myself not to engage, not to care, it was hard to deny that Tyler is right. This is different.

"I think it will go away," I say. "I don't want Dad hunting those people down and going to jail forever."

Tyler laughs, puncturing the tension a bit. "I'm not going to lie, Boone. Your dad scares me."

"He's harmless."

"He's, like, six-foot-four, three hundred *hard* pounds. And a former fucking marine to boot! He's not harmless, Boone. And, worth saying again, *terrifying*."

"Well, only to people he doesn't like. So maybe you're right."

"He likes me," Tyler says.

"You sound confident."

I laugh, picturing Tyler's sudden panic, and it helps. To laugh. To feel normal. To imagine a time when my entire life wasn't determined by the whims of idiots who worshipped pieces of metal. Just a normal high school kid excited about going to college.

"Oh, shit. I almost forgot," I say. "Guess what happened?"

"You got nominated for the Presidential Medal of Freedom," Tyler says.

"Pretty close . . . NC State."

I let it sit there, no context, until he finally figures it out.

"Holy shit. Are you serious?" I can feel his excitement through the phone.

"Yes. I don't know how it happened."

Tyler doesn't hesitate. "It happened because you're awesome, Boone."

"I know. I'm glad you understand this."

Tyler laughs. "Seriously, though. That's amazing. You're going to be a part of Wolfpack Nation. God help your dad."

The next morning the school day starts with an announcement that I'm going to NC State. Even though I haven't technically signed, it's presented as fact, and that's the way most people in the class take it. There's a legitimate cheer in Mrs. Hoffman's class, which of course she hates, and I can already see the new black mark in whatever mental file she has on me.

But I don't give a single damn. Because once the announcement is made, it's like I'm flying—only a few feet over the ground, but flying is still flying—throughout the rest of the class, the rest of the morning.

And you would've thought it was Tyler who'd been offered, given the way he goes peacocking through the hallways. Not that he's trying to siphon off any attention. Instead, it's a weird sort of pride for me that, while it shouldn't be surprising, makes me want to pull him aside and hug him until he can't breathe.

"Get that Duke shirt the fuck out of here, Guthrie!" Tyler says to a thick-necked guy I don't really know, but has made the mistake of wearing a Duke shirt on the wrong day. Tyler's smiling as he says it, though, raising my hand and saying, "Wolfpack! Nation! Boooooooooooone!"

The last part he said with his nonschool voice, hands cupped and head raised to the moon. Guthrie shakes his head and pops his shirt once so we can see the grinning blue devil.

"State's better than Carolina, I guess," he says, before disappearing down a different hallway.

Bryan Bliss

This is how it goes for most of day. When I have a class with Tyler, he makes sure everybody heard the announcement and comes at me with the proper amount of respect. In the classes without him, the love and shock and awe doesn't dip much. People are legitimately excited, even the ones who had spent the better part of the last year giving me the side-eye.

So, by the time lunch comes around, I'm really soaring. I half expect the cafeteria to erupt into applause when I walk in, not that I want it to happen, but the way people are acting it wouldn't have surprised me.

Instead, a few people say, "Congrats!" but once I get my food and sit down, the excitement ends and the cafeteria goes back to business as usual. A few minutes pass before Tyler and Ben slide into the seats on either side of me, Tyler leaning over to give me a peck on the cheek, and Ben pretending that he's going to do the same.

"Kidding. I don't feel like getting my ass kicked," he says.

"That's right," Tyler says, opening his lunch bag.

"I was talking about Eleanor, but you do you, bud."

I laugh and squeeze Tyler's knee. I'm about to suggest that we all go out tonight—Keep the party going! Applebee's!—when a couple of kids start scream-laughing in the corner of the cafeteria, the typical *Oh no you didn't!* type of freshman shit that's fairly common, no matter if they're freshmen or not. At first, I ignore it, but pretty quickly people are staring at our table. It must be something to do with NC State, so I'm about to wave or stand up, *something*.

But then a few things happen all at once.

There's more laughter, louder—across the cafeteria. That same corner.

A boy emerges, laughing as his friends push him up and away from their table.

And then I see the reason.

His shirt, my face. The target superimposed on top of it. And now everybody in the entire cafeteria laughing as this kid takes a bow like he just won the blue ribbon for best pig.

Bryan Bliss

CHAPTER FIVE

TYLER TEXTS MY DAD—I DON'T WANT HIM TO, BUT HE holds me back as he hits Send—and then I swear both my parents are in the office in a matter of minutes. Dad is red-faced and slamming his hands on Mr. Townsend's desk. Mom looks just as angry.

"That shirt has to violate your precious dress code," Dad says.

Townsend smiles stiffly.

"The student is no longer wearing the shirt," he says. "And it's the district's code, Ron. Not mine."

The *dress code* was made out to be nothing short of scripture back when I was wearing the FUCK GUNS shirt. It wasn't my First Amendment rights they were violating—no, no!—but, you see, the school district's dress code ensured that all students were protected from any language that might be deemed dangerous or unsavory.

"The kid should be expelled," Dad says. "At *least*. And if I—"

Before he can finish the sentence, Mom sits forward and puts a hand on his knee.

"We're just concerned that somebody would not only make that T-shirt, but that a kid—a *kid*—in her own school would wear it."

"Yes, well, Mr. Banfield's actions were misguided and ill-timed, for sure," Townsend says. "And there will be consequences."

"Which are?" Dad says, pushing himself forward, knocking over the wooden cross on Mr. Townsend's desk, until he's nearly face-to-face with the man. "Because I want to make sure you understand that there was a *target* on my daughter's head."

Mr. Townsend readjusts his cross—it says something about wings of an eagle on the base—and clears his throat one more time before saying, "I'm not allowed to discuss the specifics of another student with you, Ron. Just like I couldn't discuss anything about Eleanor with Trevor's parents. But I've placed a call to the district office and we'll be handling it accordingly."

Dad sits down, laughing bitterly. "Well, perfect. Don't we all just feel so much safer now?"

"Ronnie . . ." Mom's tone tells me she isn't as calm as she seems. "Let's just get some specifics on next steps, and then we can take Eleanor home. Okay? Ronnie?"

Dad's still staring intently at Townsend and, to his credit, the man isn't backing down even though Dad is giving him everything he has. Townsend waits two, maybe three seconds, before finally answering Mom.

"We'll make an announcement and send an e-mail"—Mr. Townsend looks over at me briefly as he talks—"a phone call, too. Making it clear that this isn't acceptable in the Ford community."

The principal smiles again, just as stiffly.

He's obviously spent a lot of time being yelled at as an administrator, because this guy is barely sweating—barely moving. I bet if you took his pulse right now, he'd be asleep. Calm as anything.

"So you're just going to let him get away with it," Dad says. "But I'm guessing if this was Eleanor wearing a shirt, we'd be having a totally different conversation, right? Probably have the National Guard up here to make sure she didn't get out of hand."

"I'm just following the policy, Ron. It's not a personal thing. And trust me, there will be—"

"Consequences," Dad said. "I know."

When I first wore the FUCK GUNS shirt, Mr. Townsend pulled me into his office and appealed to the emotions that had brought it about in the first place. *What is this going to do to the school?* he asked. *Haven't we been through enough?* And for a second, I understood. Hell, I even agreed with him. None of us wanted these wounds.

But that's also where we differed. The shirt wasn't about causing more pain. It wasn't about shitting on some district policy I'd never had a reason to know, let alone subvert. It was a desperate attempt to actually change something, to be heard amid all the screaming and crying that still echoed in my ears, even now.

Dad turns to me. "How are you doing, kid?"

Every single word on my tongue is sharp as a dagger and ready to be thrown across the room. Because it's all a bunch of bullshit. The *Right-Wing Report* shirt existing. Some basic boy named *Trevor* wearing it. The way the principal, even if he doesn't realize it, is protecting him in the name of bureaucracy.

But I can't say any of this, because as soon as I unload, it would be the same old story.

Eleanor the troublemaker.

Eleanor the attention hound.

Eleanor *why-can't-she-just-stop!* Boone.

This, for better or worse, calms the fires. I summon my own fake smile and give Mr. Townsend a big thumbs-up, one I hope he realizes has the DNA of a completely different finger on the same hand.

"As long as he doesn't wear it again," I say. "I'm fine with whatever you think is best."

Dad looks like I've been swapped with an alien.

"Eleanor, you can tell him how you really feel," Dad says.

His words are a two-ton truck crashing into a brick wall. The cracks climb up the wall and suddenly, I can't feel any part of my body, only the sense that I'm going to start crying, which is something I do not want to do in front of Townsend, or anybody else at this school.

So instead I say the first words that come to my lips.

"Can I?"

Dad's face falls. He turns to the principal, ready to explode once again when I stop him.

"I just don't want him to wear the shirt anymore. And I don't want anybody—teachers or students—to say anything to me about it. I just want to go to my basketball game tomorrow, get through the rest of the semester, graduate, and go."

The words come out in a burst, enough that I feel like I'm gasping for breath at the end. I swallow, push back more tears, and refuse to look away from Townsend. When he speaks, all I can hear are plastic words.

"We're here for you, Eleanor. I want you to know that."

I tell Mom and Dad I'm not going home because I don't want people like Trevor Banfield to win, but also because I have practice and it will feel good to run up and down the court. To lead the break. To get buckets.

When I walk into physics and hand my pass to the teacher, Tyler looks flabbergasted.

"Why didn't you go home?" he whispers.

"I don't want to miss practice," I say. "And what am I going to do at home? Sit there until tomorrow? I might as well just stay and not get behind."

Tyler tries to figure out if there's more. If I'm hiding something from him. I reach over and pat his forearm.

"I'm good. Trust me."

But the more I sit in my desk, the more untruthful that statement becomes.

At some point, I should be able to have a bad day. Normal ups, normal downs. I shouldn't have to worry that my face will end up on a T-shirt simply because somebody needs to

Bryan Bliss

have an enemy—a place to focus the anger they've been stoking.

The bell rings and I don't move. Even though I'm pretending to look through my bag, I guess Tyler can tell something is up because he hangs back and sits on the edge of my desk.

"You look like you're about to cut somebody," he says. "Like, pull a razor out of your boot and *cut* somebody."

I laugh, but it doesn't feel right. Instead, it feels like the time I had pneumonia. A hollow cough that doesn't move a thing.

"Maybe just hand out a light beating," I say.

Tyler reaches down to carry my backpack for me. Once it's on his shoulder, he offers me his hand and pulls me up, intentionally making me bump into him, which normally might lead to some fake offense from him. *Boone,* he'd say, *I'm standing here—I'm standing here!*

Instead, he secures my backpack one more time on his shoulder and never lets go of my hand. And for a second, I can feel the anger get replaced with the sweet memories of Tyler when I first met him, when he could barely reach for my hand without blushing.

But as soon as we get back into the hallway, as soon as I see the people staring—and, hey, maybe they're not laughing at me—the sweetness curdles, churning itself back into the thick rage that I can't honestly say has disappeared, even a year later.

After basketball practice I don't want to go home. So, I drive, rolling the windows down and trying to see how long it takes me to reach for the heater. It's a game I've played with myself for years, one that forces me to endure any number of pointless tests of will—the sort of things I want to believe most people wouldn't do. Likely because it's not smart to practice, take a shower, and then drive with your windows down in forty-something-degree weather. But in my mind, it's not stupidity as much as its strength.

I'm not paying attention to where I'm going at first, but then I'm deep into the Hickory city limits, in the downtown area, where you can never fully tell if the stores are open. But there's always something or someone moving, but not the way I assume bigger cities operate—places that stay awake hour after hour. Just enough so you know it's still alive.

When I park, I don't intend to go to Dr. Holston's office.

I start out walking along the brick sidewalks, looking into storefronts that have closed or will soon. There's a pay-as-you-go jewelry store where Tyler bought me a locket freshman year—one that he might still be paying off for all I know.

A tavern that, much like the city itself, always seems to be moving, even if with only a few people at a time. And then Dr. Holston's office, on the second floor, above a mortgage company that I've never seen open.

The light is on. So I walk in.

Before, in the days and weeks after the shooting, the school hallways were filled with therapists and psychologists. Every opportunity for healing was given to us. Emotional support dogs. A few cats, for those sorts of people—even a therapy llama, which might not have actually been certified because it ended up being weirdly aggressive. In the midst of all of it, in the midst of all the FUCK GUNS attention, the school bullshit, my entire world coming apart, it was Dr. Holston who came up alongside me, even though she likely regretted it once the shit really started piling up and her name got leaked to the press, too.

But she was a rock.

In fact, we rarely—if ever—even talked about any of the attention. Every time I came into her office, she would offer me a cup of tea and asked a very simple guiding question: "How is your world today?"

And at first there wasn't a session that went by without my world being filled with napalm. Burning without end. And unlike almost every other person in my life, the entire world,

Dr. Holston said, "Okay, let's just feel that today. Let's really *feel* it."

When was the last time you were told it was okay to feel something like napalm? In most cases we're told to bury our emotions, anything that might embarrass or anger or make somebody uncomfortable. In those early sessions, for months actually, all I did was scream and cry and rage. And I never felt like I was finished. Session after session, it was like a match had already been lit and I was ready to explode.

When I knock on Dr. Holston's office door, I don't hear anything at first and wonder if she accidentally left the lights on. But then the door opens, and Dr. Holston is standing in front of me, her wild, graying hair tied down with a headband.

"Eleanor! Did I forget about a session tonight?"

"Is it okay for me to still be angry?"

Holston has an unreadable expression on her face. I'm about to apologize and leave when she says, "Why don't we go over to Drips and get a cup of something. Talk. Sound okay?"

As we walk, she calls my parents and makes sure they know where I am. As soon as she hangs up, my mom texts me.

Are you okay?

I quickly type out, Yep, don't worry. Just stopped by.

Drips is a coffee shop filled with secondhand couches, a

Bryan Bliss

small stage, and a continual collection of high school and college students dotting the tables. The windows are fogged up by the conversations, the entire shop warm and full.

Holston orders a tea and I get some caramel macchiato monstrosity, and when we sit down, she steeps her bag and waits for me to talk, which is by far the therapist's biggest trick. Holston is a master, too, always letting me guide the conversation until I somehow stumble into an answer or paint myself into a corner that, you know, ultimately leads to an answer.

"My world is pretty shitty today," I finally tell her.

It makes her laugh and she nods, her eyes closed, as if I've just solved some kind of Zen koan.

"Shitty, how?"

And so I tell her everything. About Trevor and *Right-Wing Report* and pretty soon I can feel the anger coming alive, which is the whole reason I stopped by. Because at what point does it end? At what point am I not going to be angry?

"Well, anger is a symptom, Eleanor. You know that. Everybody heals in a different way. Some of us avoid danger. Some of us weep. Some of us disconnect. And some of us scream." She considers her tea, takes a sip, and then looks at me. "Trauma is often more of a spectrum than a fixed position. Sometimes we might feel normal, but that doesn't mean our trauma ever really goes away. If we're triggered, then it's natural we might go back to the things that seem to heal us. You know?"

"I spend most of my time telling myself everything is okay," I say. "That I *shouldn't* be angry. It's been months of that. Months of pretending. And sometimes? I catch myself thinking it's real—that I'm not really, really angry."

"Or maybe you're not pretending?"

I sit back in my chair and work the handle of the coffee cup between my thumb and forefinger. Of course, Holston lets me sit there like that, wordless and clueless. Because I have no idea if I'm actually pretending. Or if this sudden flare-up of anger is normal. Or if everybody lives with a bubbling layer of hot lava under every single interaction.

"It hasn't gone away," I say. "All the anger is still there, just like it's been all year."

"Healing isn't a straight path, Eleanor. It twists and turns; it curves back in a way that, sometimes, we see where we've been. But the path is still moving forward."

"Unless it's just a big circle," I say.

Dr. Holston sits back and considers this, which is something I truly appreciate about her. As if I sometimes introduced a concept that was not only new to her, but something that might affect her life in a positive way.

She sips her tea, playing with the jade earrings she always wears. Early on I made up a story about how she'd gotten them on a trip to Antigua Guatemala in the nineties, where she'd fallen in love with a man named Arturo, who'd driven her around the country on the back of his motorcycle and, for a time, sent her gifts, including those earrings.

"Even if anger were a circle," Holston says, "that doesn't mean we aren't still moving forward. In fact, it might actually prepare us for the ups and downs, the twists and turns, of our life. If it's a circle, we've been there before. What do you think?"

"I think I'd rather be on a flat drag strip with no turns and a clear direction."

Dr. Holston laughs and says, "Wouldn't we all, dear. Wouldn't we all."

When I get home, Dad is waiting for me in the living room. I know he won't let me walk by him without at least a little bit of conversation, so I sit down on the arm of his chair and watch the basketball game he's got muted on the television.

"We could take you out of Ford," he says. "Put you in private school for the last couple of months. I don't think it would affect your scholarship."

"I don't want to change schools," I say. "Or leave my friends."

"It's could be a fresh start, you know?"

"I'm a hundred percent sure they would all know me at Piedmont Christian Academy, or wherever I went."

"Well, it would definitely not be *that* place," Dad says. "I'm pretty sure they don't have prom because dancing and chiffon offend Jesus."

I laugh and pat him on the top of his head. On the television, a player takes a three pointer and falls to the ground, despite obviously not being fouled. When he stands up, hands spread wide and face twisted into a grimace of indignation, I slide off the arm of his chair and stretch my back.

"I just want you to be safe," Dad says. "I don't want you to have to deal with all this bullshit."

"I know, Dad. But I can handle it. So don't worry, okay?"

Dad looks at me for a long second before finally saying, "Okay."

As I walk away, he pulls the handle of his chair until the leg pops out and he reclines backward, unmuting the television.

CHAPTER SIX

THE NEXT MORNING I'M RUNNING LATE TO SCHOOL, so I convince Dad to give me a handful of dollars for a little breakfast at Carol's, which is just up the road. It's only open a few hours a day, five a.m. to whenever the last furniture worker stumbles out, and the menu is simple—egg sandwiches, fried Livermush, sausage biscuits. Everything you'd ever want.

The parking lot is full of trucks and all other kinds of beaters in nearly every spot. I pull onto the grass near the side of the building, hoping I won't get blocked in like Tyler did a few weeks back. He showed up for Hoffman's class, sausage biscuit in hand, trying to explain how the county sanitation workers wouldn't move their truck no matter how much he pleaded.

But it's this or a gas station egg burrito, so I throw the

car in park and jump out, texting Tyler to see if he wants a biscuit. I'm not looking where I'm going, so when I bump into two guys, I'm apologizing before my eyes come up from my phone.

"Oh, shit. Look at this."

He's in his early twenties and wearing a Ford football T-shirt, cut off at the sleeves despite the winter temperatures, and stained with what is either mud or some kind of paint. His buddy in the Carhartt jacket smiles as he takes the last drags off a cigarette.

"You see those T-shirts? I gotta get me one of those," the first guy says, slapping his buddy on the arm.

I don't move, don't react, nothing.

Instead, I step around them, trying to get into the restaurant without a confrontation. My hand is on the door when one of them says my name—I don't know why it surprises me that they know my name—and I turn to look.

The man lifts his Ford football shirt so I can see the small handgun tucked into a holster on the side of his pants. He smiles. His friend laughs.

"You ain't *never* taking away my rights," he says, the humor dropping from his voice. "You hear me?"

"Why don't you go fuck yourself," I say, the words squeaking out. And then push the door of the restaurant open. Too hard. The door nearly takes out an ancient candy machine that still sells a handful for ten cents.

"Careful now, Eleanor!"

Carol, the owner, is a sixty-something woman with a hairstyle from when she was still in high school, tall and meticulous and, seemingly, immovable. Her strict tone softens like warmed butter almost immediately.

"Where's that good-looking boyfriend of yours?"

But I'm so angry, I can barely move, let alone chop it up with Carol, who normally wouldn't let me just stand there without another barb, maybe two. She's about to say something else when she drops the check pad she's holding and lifts the hinged counter that separates the cashier from the rest of the dining room.

"Hey, honey—what's wrong?"

I'm shaking, which makes it look like I'm about to cry, but when Carol comes to comfort me, I turn and run out of the restaurant, back into the gravel parking lot. The two men have already left, but I run all the way to the road, the tears finally coming down my face. The morning traffic is just starting to lock the only road to the interstate. I can't stop myself. I scream.

At the men, already gone. At the passing cars. The sky. The birds. I scream until it feels like my throat is going to rip apart. Eventually Carol comes up behind me, a collection of people from the restaurant congregating in the parking lot watching all of this unfold, and I let her take me by the shoulders and lead me back into the restaurant.

Still too angry to say anything.

When Dad comes into the restaurant, I still haven't said a word to Carol or anybody, even though every single one of them is watching me, their phones ready to record the next outburst. Dad is wearing his work clothes, which means he must be starting the new job today. He nods at Carol and sits across from me.

"What's up, kid?"

I shake my head. The anger isn't gone. I'm afraid if I open my mouth, the only thing that will come out is another scream. Nothing but screaming for the rest of my life, like a laser beam from my mouth.

And of course, Dad can see it all. Right after the shooting, he would come into my room and I'd be lying on my bed, nearly shaking with the rage. He held my hand. Brought me a soda. Anything to calm me down.

Except, none of it worked. Not then. Not now.

"I'm going to need you to give me a heads-up to what's happening here," he says. "Or else I'm taking you to the hospital."

I give him a look and shake my head again. Manage to croak out a single word. "No."

He leans forward to pick at the now-cold biscuit Carol gave me, popping a piece into his mouth. He leans back, studying me. Waiting for me to say more.

And the longer I sit there, the more I feel the tension in my jaw beginning to loosen. I think about Dr. Holston telling me that my anger, my rage, is actually fear and pain—a way to adapt.

It doesn't make me less angry. But it does make me talk.

"Two guys. They had a gun."

Dad is up and out of the booth immediately, going to Carol, who seems shocked. Dad is ready to tear the building down to the foundation.

"Who were they?"

"I—I don't know, Ronnie. I didn't see who she was talking to out there. You know I'd tell you."

"What did they look like, Eleanor. Be specific."

I tell him about the Ford football shirt with no sleeves, the Carhartt jacket, the smug fucking smiles.

"That's Timmy Hoke and Chris Russell," Carol says softly. "They're young and stupid, Ronnie."

"And they're about to go to jail," Dad says, tapping the counter once, calm like he'd just ordered a coffee. He walks over to me, already holding his phone to his ear.

"We're going to file a police report," he tells me. "And then we'll get you home."

I nod, unsure if I could sit long enough for the phone call, let alone for the police to actually get here. I try to breathe the way Holston taught me, in and out through my nose—a meditative trick she'd learned on a yoga retreat—but every time I suck air in through my nose, my mouth opens, as if my body is refusing to release the anger.

"Yep. Over at Carol's. Yep. Thanks, officer." Dad hangs up his phone and sits down in the booth across from me. He wipes a hand across his face and doesn't say anything until the police arrived, almost twenty minutes later.

Naturally, Carol's is busier than it has ever been at nine a.m. People refusing to leave their tables, nursing coffee cups and nibbling on the crumbs of egg sandwiches, pretending not to watch as I tell the story once again, trying to remember every detail. Trying not to seem as angry as I am.

"He had it holstered?" the police officer asks me.

"Yes. What does that have to do with anything?"

The officer ignores me. "And did he advise you that he had a permit?"

"Jesus, do you think he was trying to give me a lesson on conceal and carry?" I ask, my voice rising above the low din of the restaurant. The police officer stares at me hard before turning to Dad.

"It's not illegal to carry a weapon in the state of North Carolina if you have a permit."

"I'm pretty damn sure it's illegal for him to intimidate my daughter with it, though," Dad says.

"Until we talk to Mr. Russell, I don't feel comfortable making any assumptions about his intentions."

I laugh and everybody in the restaurant turns to look, no longer pretending.

"Sure. Of course. You wouldn't have a *Right-Wing Report* T-shirt on under your uniform, would you, officer?" I ask.

"Eleanor, I think the officer has everything he needs," Dad says, reaching for my hand. The officer makes a note on his pad as Dad walks me out of the restaurant.

Before we're out the door, the officer calls out, "We'll let you know what we find out."

Dad doesn't say a word.

Once we're out in the parking lot, I cuss loudly and kick at a can of soda that somebody had obviously thrown toward the garbage can, missing badly.

"What a joke," I say.

"Eleanor."

"Well, it is."

Dad opens his mouth, but then he shrugs. "You're right. And I'm sorry."

"Does that cop seriously think those guys were scared of me?"

"Honey, I have no idea what is going through the minds of most of the people I meet. But I'll tell you this: you have more fight in you than just about anybody I know."

"I mean, shit. Do they really think I'm going to drive up to Washington, D.C., and shred the Constitution? And God, even if I *did*, does that mean all of our rights will just disappear? Suddenly we'll go back to being a colony or some shit?"

This tickles Dad.

"Well, for what it's worth, I think you should leave the actual Constitution alone."

"I just don't get it," I say. "I'm the one who went through the shooting. I'm the one who could've died. These guys are just out here pretending like they need to carry a gun in case the government decides to . . . hell, I don't even know. And what do they think they're going to do against *tanks*, Dad? A bunch of untrained rednecks aren't doing shit."

I don't realize I'm still shaking until Dad comes over and puts his arm around me.

Bryan Bliss

"They're scared and ignorant, plain and simple. And that's a dangerous combination, especially when they encounter a person with actual integrity. So all they can do is resort to the only thing they know—intimidation."

My first year of travel basketball, a girl fouled me hard. For the rest of the game, every time she came near me, I'd pass the ball like it was a live grenade. It got so bad—I ended up with what had to be a state record for turnovers in a single game—that my coach pulled me out and made me watch from the bench.

Up until that point, I didn't know what it meant to be intimidated. I'd lived a mostly anxiety-free life. An easy life save a few skinned knees and other normal childhood mishaps. So, when this girl came at me hard, I had no idea how to respond.

And I hated it.

As I got older, I learned how to deal with aggressive players. How to use their aggression against them. But more importantly, I learned that I couldn't control every situation. Sometimes I had to respond, even if it meant going beyond my comfort zone.

But I have no idea how to respond to this. I have no idea how to use their intimidation against them.

"Can I go home?" I ask.

"Yeah. Of course. Are you good to drive? I can come back and get your car later, if you want."

I tell him I can drive and he gives me a long hug. As we're standing in the parking lot, he whispers that he loves me—so much—and, for a second, I want to believe that it's enough to wipe away the anger, if only for a couple of minutes.

Bryan Bliss

CHAPTER SEVEN

MOM IS COMPULSIVELY CLEANING THE KITCHEN WHEN I get home, and after she finishes hugging me, I go back to my room and close the door. I pull out my phone to text Tyler and realize he's sent me almost thirty text messages.

Where are you?

Everything okay?

Boone, text me back.

Please.

I type out a quick message.

Sorry. Not coming to school. Call me at lunch.

Killing me, Boone.

KILLING ME.

I drop my phone on my bed and sit there with my eyes closed, trying to calm down. It isn't hard to remember how I felt in the days and weeks after the shooting. As if every part of my body was plugged into an electrical current, every muscle simultaneously alive and constricted. Ready for a fight that had already happened.

That's how the FUCK GUNS shirt came about. A need to do *something*. To expel that energy, that anger, any way I could. And for a brief moment, it worked. It made me feel as if I was in control of my life, if only in that one small way.

I never wanted to be on the news.

I never wanted the interviews.

I just wanted to feel whole again.

I open my eyes and sit up, sliding to the floor. I reach under my bed and pull out the dusty shoebox that has been there for a little under a year now. When I open it, the smell of paint and permanent markers greet me—still strong, months later. I pull everything out. A few newspaper clippings. A dirty rag. Some stencils. And in the bottom of the box, one of the original shirts—musty and forgotten.

When I stopped wearing the shirts, I made a big show of getting rid of them for Tyler and Ben, mostly because they were starting to get worried about where it was headed, but also because I knew they'd let other people know it was finished.

And it mostly worked. I packed this box under my bed, stopped wearing the shirts, and everything got back to normal for a little while. But sitting here now, holding the T-shirt in my hands, I can't deny the simple thrill of it. What if I put it on right now and go to school? What would they do? What if I refuse to stop screaming? What if I don't let anybody forget—not ever—what happened to all of us?

But the truth is, I don't want to wear the shirt anymore. I don't want to be a target. I want it to be over. But if they aren't going to let me forget, if I am going to be forever labeled as a troublemaker, what's the point?

Mom knocks on my door and is in my room before I can get the T-shirt back into the box. When she sees it, she sucks in a quick breath and then bites her bottom lip.

I put the shirt away—hoping that will be enough for her. It isn't.

"I don't think that's going to help," she finally says.

"I wasn't going to wear it," I say. "But I wanted to see it. To touch it again. It probably sounds stupid."

Mom comes and sits on the floor next to me, picking the shirt back out of the box and holding it up so she can study it.

"Nobody will ever accuse you of being subtle," she says, folding the shirt and putting it on her lap.

"I'm sorry, Mom."

"You have nothing to be sorry about, honey. Not to me. Not to anyone. Okay?"

"Okay."

She reaches over and lifts my chin so she can see my eyes.

"I wouldn't care if you wore this shirt every day for the rest of your life. That's not it. I was so proud of you, honey. I *am* proud of you." She hesitates. "But I don't want things like what happened today to . . . well, I already worry every time you leave the house. And I know I can't stop people from being idiots. Still. "

She smooths the shirt one more time before putting it back in the box.

"I guess I'm trying to say that you can show them who you are in other ways. You don't have to be only the person they think you are."

Tyler doesn't wait for lunch.

"I already heard what happened," he says when I pick up. "Fucking *assholes*."

I don't want to know how he already knows or, honestly,

Bryan Bliss

have this conversation right now. I just want to go bed and only get up for basketball games and the occasional slice of pizza.

Tyler sighs and says, "I'm sorry. I should've asked if you are okay."

"I'm pissed," I say. "But other than that, fine."

"Good," he says. "And, uh, I saw your dad at school this morning."

"What?"

"He didn't look happy, Boone."

I have no idea why Dad was there, but his patience and tolerance of anything related to Ford has been on a steady decline since the shooting. Mom won't let him go in for parent-teacher conferences, or even to sign the most basic of permission slips because he's always on the verge of, as my grandmother might've said, *showing his ass*.

"I should probably go tell my mom," I say.

"That's right. Ronnie got banned, what, six months ago?"

"I wouldn't call it a ban, but more of a suggestion."

Tyler laughs. "Hey, do you want to do something tonight? You can't go to practice, right? So, I thought maybe we could go somewhere. Do something. A date, even."

"I don't know, Tyler. I just want to stick around the house and not see anybody."

"Like, *anybody*, including me? Or *anybody*, as in the ninety percent of this town that are insufferable rednecks who wear T-shirts with lightning bolts and wolves on them—not ironically, I might add—because they're not only fashionable, but easy to find at your local gas station?"

"I'm pretty sure there's a picture of you wearing a wolf T-shirt on the wall at your house."

"That was for the wolf sanctuary and you know it," he says, laughing.

I can practically see him leaning up against a wall in one of the quiet hallways at Ford, shielding his voice from anybody who might walk by. Keeping all of this between us, which had always been his best trait—the ability to make it seem like he was giving me the entirety of his attention whenever we were together.

"Okay, we can do something," I say. "But only if you dig out that wolf T-shirt."

"Deal. It's probably going to fit me like a crop top at this point, so warn your parents."

Tyler shows up at my house an hour after school, refusing to tell me anything except to "wear good shoes," which is kind of amusing, because it's not like I make a habit of wearing heels.

Bryan Bliss

When he walks into the house, I show him my feet—slip-on skate shoes—and the asshole actually spends a few seconds trying to decide if they're appropriate.

"I'm seriously happy to just stay home," I say, and that ends his deliberations.

"It should be fine" is all he says before grabbing my hand and practically dragging me out the door. I could probably physically stop him from moving me if I really wanted to, but I let him pull me out the door and across the driveway. When we get to his car, I refuse to get in without some kind of explanation.

"We're losing daylight."

"We're losing daylight?"

Tyler looks up at the sky and then back at me, a mischievous smile on his lips.

"Trust me, Boone. When have I ever steered you wrong?"

"Uh, sophomore year for starters. The Carowinds Incident."

I do air quotes because I know it will piss him off.

"You literally ate nachos before you went on that ride! What are you even talking about, Boone?!"

"Still, I blame you."

He looks positively flummoxed by the idea that I might've secretly been harboring a grudge from a theme park date two years ago. He shakes his head and opens his door.

"Fine, blame me. But get in the car because—"

"Yeah, yeah—daylight."

We drive to the other side of the county, where the roads are narrow and they cross back and forth over one another as the hills begin to turn into mountains. The radio is turned down low, but neither of us is talking. The sun is slowly dying, a few inches lower every time it reappears from behind the trees that line both sides of the road.

I can feel my eyes closing. It's the soft murmur of the road beneath us, the warm sunlight.

"Are you falling asleep?"

"I don't sleep," I say, smiling.

When I was younger, as the story goes, I would refuse to acknowledge or admit that I ever slept. Every morning I'd wake up and my mom would ask, "How did you sleep?" And I would respond with something to the effect of, "I don't sleep." Every morning, the same thing—Mom asking a normal question and me answering bizarrely, and with conviction.

I think Mom and Dad thought I was being precocious, and as an only child I was certainly guilty of turning the spotlight on myself more than once. But that wasn't the case with this. I honestly didn't remember sleeping. The days ran together in one continuous stream, which maybe sounds horribly tedious—but it wasn't. If anything, it was a testament to my desire to stuff every minute of my day with *something*.

When Tyler parks the car, he says, "We're here."

Outside, I see a sixty-something-year-old man wearing what looks like an oversize Boy Scout uniform—brown shirt, brown shorts, hiking boots. He's even got a floppy sun hat.

He smiles and waves, stretching as he stands up.

"Where are we?"

"Bakers Mountain," Tyler says, waving to the park ranger. "C'mon."

He opens the door and greets the ranger by name, which of course makes me wonder if he's living some kind of double life because we've never been to this park once and suddenly he's on first name basis with Ranger Rick, whose name is actually Dean.

"Dean runs the trails every morning before the park opens," Tyler tells me. I look up at the mountain, which is admittedly small when compared to, say, the Rockies or even the Smokies, but it's still a serious grade, so I must look skeptical because Dean nods.

"Cheaper than a gym membership," he says, patting his nonexistent gut. "And from what I hear, you could probably give me a run for my money."

"I'm not much for running. But my friend Claire might be willing."

Dean laughs, knowingly. "Tell her to come up here sometime and we'll see what she's made of."

My body tenses at the thought of Claire, who might as well have disappeared. Ten years of friendship, of basketball tournaments and laughter, and then, poof—gone. Not that I didn't understand. Didn't dream about my own escape, usually at moments just like this, when somebody is about to dispense with expected pleasantries and show me who they really are—how they really feel.

Instead, Dean smiles—an actual warm and genuine smile—and hands me a map.

"We just cut out a new trail here." He points to a place on the map near the peak. "It's not on the map yet, but it's ready and I think you two will like it. Very private."

He winks and Tyler blushes, which makes me really wonder what in the hell is happening here.

"Yeah. Anyway," Tyler says, moving toward the trailhead a little too quickly. I kind of want to give him some shit, to press Dean for more information. But he's moving so fast I have to jog to catch up with him.

"I have so many questions," I say, and all he does is smile, taking the map from my hands and acting like he needs to do some serious orienteering or whatever, anything to avoid this conversation.

We're the only people on the trails, which is nice. And even though we have the entire mountain to ourselves, we don't talk—just walk. Up, up, up, winding around a mountain that, according to my dad, used to be the place to escape your parents, and sometimes the police, so you could camp out, smoke some weed, and generally escape your life.

I never asked any more questions whenever he mentioned Bakers Mountain, but it strikes me this still is the perfect place to escape. The tree cover blocks out the entire sky on certain parts of the trail, and the only sound is the birds or the occasional hidden critter scrambling through the fallen leaves.

After one final climb, we come to the peak and the entire city of Hickory, my entire life, is spread out below us like a child's puzzle. I can see the road leading to my house. Ford High School. The start of the real mountains just west of us.

Tyler puts his arm around me and then just as quickly steps away.

"Oh, gross. You're all sweaty."

I punch him once in the ribs and he laughs, pulling me close to him. He kisses the side of my head and we stand there together, watching everything. The whole world looks manageable from up here. As if I could move the pieces whenever and wherever I needed them. Maybe it's the complete silence, Tyler's arm around me—simple biology— or just the mountain air, but I feel like I can breathe. I close my eyes and take another breath, a third.

And then I punch Tyler again, hard.

"What the hell, Boone!"

But he's laughing.

"*You're all sweaty.* I should push your ass off this mountain."

"You know I was kidding." He rubs his ribs gingerly. "Have you ever thought about going into MMA? If the whole basketball thing doesn't work out? Because, Jesus, Boone. You hit like a truck."

"Thank you," I say. "Not about the punching, although I do consider that a compliment. Thank you for bringing me up here."

Tyler nods and then looks down into the valley. "I thought you could use a break. And this is where I like to go when I need a break."

"To hang out with your buddy Dean."

"That, too. Yes."

I lean my head against his shoulder and take another long, deep breath.

"I love you," I say.

"Me, too, Boone. Me, too."

CHAPTER EIGHT

THE NEXT MORNING I'M UP HOURS BEFORE I NEED TO be, still floating after the hike with Tyler. I walk into the kitchen and find Dad at the table, coffee in hand, checking the news on his phone.

"Is the world ending yet?" I ask him.

"Just about, kid. You want some eggs?"

"I'm not that hungry. But thanks."

He puts his phone down. "So I went up to the school yesterday. I assume Tyler told you."

"Yeah. He did."

"The little traitor," he says, smiling weakly. "Anyway, I went up there and let Mr. Townsend know what happened."

I shouldn't be angry—and until this moment, I wasn't. If anything, last night had been one of the best nights in the past year. The first time I could unplug from all the anger, all the bullshit. And while I know that Dad was just trying to protect me, I'm still hot.

"They didn't need to know," I say. "They could've just thought I was sick."

"Well, the T-shirts and then this . . . Eleanor, it feels like there's a trend. And I want to make sure you're safe."

"Safe? I'm never *safe*. I'm always ready to run. And it really never ends, not when I'm at home, on the court, or even asleep. I never feel safe, Dad!"

Mom comes rushing into the kitchen, but I can't stop myself even though I know I should.

"I need everybody to stop trying to protect me and realize that you can't!"

"Eleanor, honey, calm down," Mom says.

But I shake my head. I want to run out the door the way I would in middle school, when my only defense against perceived injustice was to slam the screen door as hard as I could, trying to bust the hinges.

But I'm scared that if I get in my car and drive away right now, something will happen. I don't know what, or whether the anxiety is credible. But fear presses down against me like an elephant, seven tons pushing me back into the chair I had risen out of in such glorious righteousness.

It's the moment after a tornado, when the birds start singing and everybody wonders how they didn't get blown away. Dad looks at Mom and then picks up his phone, dialing a number which turns out to be Dr. Holston, who says she can stop over before school, no problem.

Dr. Holston comes with her own tea, maybe because she knows my parents drink single-cup brewed coffee. Or maybe she was on her way to yoga—she's dressed for it—or maybe she was just sitting at home enjoying her morning, expecting to do anything but show up once again to fix whatever is wrong with me.

"So, how's your world today, Eleanor?"

"Nonexistent," I say. "My world doesn't start before eight thirty a.m. at the earliest."

She doesn't smile at my joke, just stares at me until I give in.

"It's not good. I guess."

"What do you mean by 'not good'?"

This time I stare at her because we both know what she's doing—she already knows that I freaked out on my parents for no reason. Because I've been *not good* for a year.

"I'm pissed off. And scared. And exhausted. And now I'm hungry, too."

"Do you want to talk about what happened at Carol's?"

I shake my head. She opens her tea and takes a sip, content to sit here in complete silence because she's some kind of psychopath who is more than happy to just "be in the moment" or whatever it is she's always saying.

"Do you remember when you told me that anger was a second emotion?" I ask.

"Mmm. Yes."

"Well, I don't understand it," I say. "And maybe that's why I'm not good."

This time she smiles.

"Anger often masks our pain. Our trauma. It doesn't make it less"—she thinks for a second—"valid, perhaps. But whenever I'm angry, I often ask myself, *why?*"

"I'm angry because that asshole wanted me to be scared," I blurt out. "That's the only reason he showed the gun to me! Because he wanted to scare me."

"Yes, I'm pretty sure that's exactly what he was trying to do. And guess what? Your reaction is a hundred percent normal. If somebody threatened me with a gun, I'm not sure how I would react. But I can tell you that, afterward, I would be angry and terrified and confused—just like you are right now."

She reaches over and puts her hand on top of mine.

"Eleanor, I want you to know that it's okay to be upset. To be angry. That anger is an expected and normal response to this. But I think I hear you saying that you can't seem to pull the plane back up. That you're stuck in a nosedive."

That was more true than I wanted it to be. But what if I've always been in a nosedive? What if nobody has realized it and they thought we were just flying and not falling? And perhaps scarier, what if I *want* to be in the nosedive?

"What if I like being angry?" I ask her.

Holston barely blinks an eye. She drinks her tea and watches me, swallowing two sips before putting the cup back on the table and speaking.

"Well, I think it's a good recipe for tearing yourself apart if you can never throttle back."

But I have throttled back. I tried not being angry. And what changed? People still tell lies on social media and make T-shirts and, now, rednecks show me guns tucked under their waistbands because they think it will make me stop—which it never, ever will.

At the same time, I can feel the hundreds of tiny cuts, the tears of countless barbs and attacks, in every bone of my body. None of them are fatal, but they've slowed me down in ways I can't begin to explain.

So what if I can't be angry and I can't hide? Am I just supposed to pretend? Forever?

I try to smile. I nod and shrug and generally play the part I've been playing for the last nine months of my life. The one that screams out—Happy! Happy!—that everything is fine. Nothing to see here.

But it's failing and everyone can see it.

"I just want to be okay," I finally say.

When I get to school, Tyler is waiting for me in the parking lot with an iced mocha and a big smile. I decide to play my part with him, too, not to let him know anything about this morning or how I'm still seething.

I take the mocha, which is undeniably good and I think, maybe, this is what Holston is talking about—the ability to enjoy something simple. To not let my hot anger turn it into a bubbling mess.

Tyler waves a hand in my face. "You with me, Boone?"

"Yeah, sorry. Hey, thanks for the drink."

Thankfully, the bell rings and even though we've been late to Hoffman's class a hundred different times, I tell him I don't want to be late and start walking. And of course, he sees that I'm doing everything I can to avoid him—everything I'm feeling—so he jumps in front of me.

"Did I make you mad? Was it something last night?"

I shake my head and try to move around him, to join the rest of the students as they make their way to their classes, every single one of them seemingly happy. Unaffected. As if they don't remember every single second of that day.

"Hey, hey—what's up with you?"

"Nothing," I say. And then, because I can't stop myself, "It's not like you want to hear it."

He flinches like I hit him with an elbow.

"Whoa. What does that mean?"

"Nothing. Never mind."

I try to step around him again, but he's too quick for me—a first. I push him into the lockers, which makes him laugh at first. But when I start walking away, not playing one bit, he runs to catch up with me.

"What the hell, Eleanor?"

"Just leave me alone, okay? I want to be left alone."

"What's going on? Talk to me. Please."

This was probably the first time I've ever been happy to see Mrs. Hoffman, standing in the hallway, watching all of this unfold, disapproval curling across her lips.

"Mr. Castigan. Miss Boone. Are we coming to class today?"

"Yes ma'am," I say, ignoring every instinct telling me to feel indignant with her tone—we aren't even late yet. But with her standing in the doorway, there's only room for me to squeeze through, so Tyler has to wait for Hoffman to move at her crawling pace before he can follow me inside.

As soon as I sit down, my phone buzzes. I ignore it and it buzzes a second time. A third. I make a show of putting it in my bag and Tyler cusses behind me, which Hoffman also hears.

"Mr. Castigan. Do you have a problem?"

"Maybe," he says, his voice angry. It breaks through the wall I've built up. I want to turn around and tell him to calm down—that we'll talk afterward. I'll explain.

"Excuse me?"

"I said, *Maybe*. Are you deaf?"

This time, I do turn around, along with the rest of the class. Anticipation hangs in the air as Hoffman tries to get her pearls rearranged after such an outrageous show of disrespect.

"Mr. Castigan. To the office."

Tyler doesn't break his stare with her at first. Doesn't move. Then he finally stands up and snatches his backpack from the ground. Just before he's about to leave the room, he turns and glares at me for a long second.

And then he's gone.

As soon as class ends, I pull out my phone and text Tyler immediately.

I'm sorry.

I can explain.

I wait for the little dots to pop up, to show that he's about to respond. When we first started dating, we'd spend hours texting back and forth. Stupid messages that skirted around my feelings, intense and embarrassingly earnest. And while our text conversations are more practical—Come pick me up—these days, I keep screenshots of some of those original messages on my phone. Sometimes, when I'm feeling down or I just want to remember those early days, I'll open the folder and enjoy how goofy and ridiculous and wonderful he really is.

Text me back.

Please.

I wait for the dots. But it just sits there on my phone, unread and killing me.

I don't see him until lunch. And when he walks into the cafeteria with Ben, I'm worried they're headed to a completely different table. Instead, Ben peels off and gets in the lunch line, while Tyler heads right for me. He doesn't sit down, and I start to apologize, but he stops me.

"Are you okay?" he asks.

I nod, biting my lip so I don't start crying in front of everybody.

"Okay. That's all I need to know."

"I'm sorry," I say.

He looks back to Ben, still standing in line, and sits down across from me, rubbing his hands over his face.

"Can you, like, explain it? I mean, if I did something wrong, just tell me. And if I didn't . . ."

He shrugs and it breaks me. I want to reach across the table, grab him and hold him and promise that I will never treat him that way again. Instead, I fumble with the words that are both what he wants to hear and what he doesn't.

"I'm just—everything that's happening has me all messed up. And I'm so angry. Like, *really angry*. And I don't want to be. But then again, I do want to be angry. I want to scream and hit things and just lose my shit because I'm so *fucking tired*."

I stop to breathe. Tyler doesn't move, an unreadable look on his face.

"And I'm really afraid that you're not going to want to be with me," I finally say.

Finally, a reaction.

"C'mon, Eleanor."

"Are you saying you weren't over me wearing the shirts? All the attention?"

He can't answer, because we both know it's true. He

Bryan Bliss

wanted me to stop. Everybody wanted me to stop. And while I understand it, I want him to acknowledge that it didn't end for me when I took off the shirt.

"I never stop thinking about it," I say. "Like, ever."

"I know," he says. "I can tell."

"And I tried, Tyler. I will keep trying. But——"

He shakes his head.

"You don't have to explain. And . . ." He clears his throat, looks back to Ben who is paying for his lunch. As he steps out of the line, Tyler turns back to me.

"I think about it every day, too. I dream about it. Not every night. But sometimes. A lot."

When Ben gets to the table, we must look like emotional zombies or something because he doesn't sit down. He stands there with his tray looking very nervous that one or both of us is about to break down into tears in front of the whole cafeteria.

"Just sit down, idiot," Tyler says.

Through the smile, I see something different in Tyler. I was so consumed after the shooting—with my own anger, my own pain and sadness—that I never considered his. I never thought that every time I screamed, it might rip apart something inside him, too.

Once Ben is sitting down, he launches into his impression

of Tyler's moment of disobedience in Hoffman's class.

"She looked like she was going to legit explode," he says, laughing his ass off.

The whole time, even though we're both smiling and laughing, Tyler and I keep checking in with each other. Quick glances. Little smiles. All of it making sure that everything was cool, that we were fine, and life could go on like normal.

Or as normal as it has been.

CHAPTER NINE

WHEN I FINALLY GET TO BASKETBALL PRACTICE, I'M so exhausted I'm not sure I'll be able to get a shot up, let alone spend the next two hours running up and down the court. Surprisingly, as soon as my feet touch the hardwood, it's like my energy meter immediately recharges.

I'm winning windsprints. I'm jumping out of the gym for rebounds. And I'm pushing the break so fast Coach Harris laughs and asks what's gotten into me. The only answer I give her is another bucket.

After practice, Coach Harris breaks us down—"one, two, three, *Ford*"—and I feel completely empty, which is weirdly perfect. There's a difference between being drained by somebody else and giving everything you have in pursuit of a goal—something you want.

I sit on the court, unlacing my shoes so I don't have to bend down and do it in the locker room. Trying to imagine tomorrow's game, the points I'll drop on them. The way the scout will look when she sees my performance—a perfect night.

I'm smiling when Tyler walks in and sits down next to me. He doesn't say anything, just uses his finger to trace a line of sweat on my knee until it starts to tickle, and I suddenly feel every drop of sweat on my body.

"Looks like you were really killing it," he says.

"So, you were out there creeping again?"

"That's the first time I've waited for you to finish practice in, like, three years," he says.

Freshman year he would sit outside the gym, waiting for me. Even though he was just sitting there, it freaked out a lot of the older girls on the team, all of whom ended that season and graduated from high school thinking Tyler was nothing more than a freshman pervert. Later I found out that he was worried they would pull me into their junior and senior stratosphere, leaving him behind.

Still, I like to give him shit.

"Remember when Connie Shilson—"

"God. Stop. Please."

"You don't remember?" I lean over and nudge him with

my shoulder. "She went to Coach Harris and made, like, a formal complaint against you?"

"For one, it wasn't a *formal* complaint. It was a request that I not 'watch' practice," Tyler says, fighting a smile. "Which I wasn't doing. I was doing homework. And the way it was explained to me was it had more to do with competitive advantage and less about, you know . . ."

"Being a creeper?"

He laughs, but I can tell he didn't come in here to joke around. He stayed at school, hours past when he would normally leave, so he could catch me at this exact moment to say something very specific.

"Okay, so out with it."

"What?"

I stare at him and he eventually rolls his eyes, both because I can read him like a book, and he doesn't ever like to admit that I know exactly what he's thinking most of the time.

"I heard something. About the game tomorrow."

I take a breath, pull my first shoe off. "Yeah?"

He shifts uncomfortably and then grabs my hand and holds on to me like he's about to fall of the side of building. I forget my second shoe and turn to face him. His expression is nothing short of stricken.

"Fucking Trevor Banfield," he says, and my heart feels ready to stop beating. "He's not doing it, of course. But he got the rest of those assholes thinking, and now there's, like, this whole *thing* happening."

"Tyler. What are you talking about?"

"They're going to wear the shirts to the game tomorrow night," he says.

If my heart has already stopped beating, this is where it falls completely out of my chest.

"Okay," I say, trying to rationalize. To make a plan. To fight the fury that is rattling toward me like a runaway train. "Okay."

"I already told that little fucker Trevor he needs to put an end to this. Immediately. But then his brother—the dude with the epic mullet that runs the cash register over at the Wilco—kind of got in my face, so who knows if the message was received."

He takes a deep breath. "Maybe you should skip the game."

"What? No. The scout from NC State is going to be there."

"Right. I know. But, like, she could probably come a different time? Because . . ."

He stops talking, probably at the exact right time. Because even though I want him to finish the sentence, I don't need to hear the words to know what was coming next.

"You're afraid I'm going to lose it," I say.

"What? Eleanor. No. I'm worried that something's going to happen to you."

And while I don't doubt his sincerity, I can't help but let the anger take over. The thought of all those boys showing up at the game for no other reason than to get a reaction out of me. To hurt me. It's the same *boys-will-be-boys* bullshit that I've dealt with my entire life, the exact same shit.

"We have to tell your parents," Tyler says.

"They won't let me play," I say.

I can already hear the conversation—how it won't be safe. How we shouldn't give those boys the satisfaction. I know every single word that will come out of their mouths, all of them meant to protect me from a threat that is impossible to see until it's staring you in the face.

"Maybe that's for the best," Tyler says, and I nod, not because I agree but because I just want time to think.

"I should probably go tell Coach Harris," I say, pushing myself up.

Tyler stands up too and reaches for a hug.

Then he asks, "Do you want me to come home with you?"

"No, I got this."

And then I walk away from him, across the court, which now seems impossibly large.

· · ·

Coach Harris is at her desk, watching a video on her phone. When I walk into her office, I must scare her because she nearly drops the phone and stares at me like I've just jumped from behind a closed door.

"Boone. You nearly gave me a heart attack. What are you still doing here?"

"So, I guess there are some guys who are planning to do something at the game," I say.

I have no idea why I'm dancing around it. Coach Harris, if anybody, has always told me—the entire team—that you couldn't go through life scared and meek. Speak up, be a leader, and all that same rah-rah shit that never seems like it matters until it does. Until a moment like right now. But standing here, I'm worried she doesn't actually believe any of it. I'm scared that when I tell her, I'll get the same disapproving look I've been trying to avoid for months.

I do it quick, Band-Aid style.

"They're planning on wearing those T-shirts to the game tomorrow," I say. "The ones with my face on them."

Harris doesn't blink and, at first, I think everything is going to be okay. But then she speaks.

"You can't be a distraction," she says. "That was our agreement."

"I don't want to be a distraction," I say. "And it's not like I asked them to do this—it's not like I *asked* for any of this."

Harris's eyes go wide and then she sits back in her chair, considering me.

"Sometimes our actions speak louder than our words."

"What? What is that supposed to mean?"

"Eleanor . . ." Her tone shifts midway through saying my name, becoming softer. Like she is about to give me some long-awaited advice. "You *chose* to wear that shirt. And now you have to accept that there will be consequences."

"It's been almost nine months."

"Sometimes consequences have longer tails than we might expect."

I stand there, stunned. As much as I want to scream, to let the rage take over, I suddenly feel remarkably calm. One question rises up out of all of it and hangs there.

"How long?"

Maybe I should soften my tone and be more polite, put to use all the lessons I've been taught over and over again.

Instead, I say it one more time, "How long?"

"All right, that's enough, Boone."

This is where I would normally blow up. But I feel like a bit of life has been drained out of me.

"I thought I was doing the right thing," I say. "And I won't be a distraction tomorrow. Don't worry."

And then I walk out of her office.

Tyler is waiting for me, and when he sees my face he doesn't need to ask. He follows me back to my house, and as I'm getting out of the car, a soft rain starts falling. I don't want to move. I just want to stand here in the cold rain, letting it slowly soak me to my bones. But Tyler pulls up the driveway, wraps me up in his arms, and walks me to the house.

My parents aren't home. Tyler starts a fire and I turn on the television. There's a sports talk show on and it drones in the background as the house grows darker and darker. I let myself relax. At first it feels reckless, as if I've put a bag down and walked away from it. But the longer I sit there in the dark with Tyler, the more I never want to move again.

The television show changes—two men sitting across from each other, debating a ticker tape of topics—just as Dad walks into the house. He must think he's stumbled onto us making out, or worse, because he starts stammering and turning on lights like it might blind him long enough for us to button up our shirts—whatever he's thinking we need to do. I stand up and stretch, my entire body sore from sitting on the couch and basketball practice, the entire last year.

Before Dad or Tyler can speak, I tell him everything. About

the T-shirts, the conversation with Coach, and my plan to pretend like nothing is happening.

Dad takes it all in without responding.

Then he says, "I think we should still call the school."

And now I'm so worn out and exhausted, I don't care if he calls the school or uses a megaphone to get Townsend's attention.

"Let them do what they want," I say. "I'm not going to say another word until graduation. Silent Eleanor. The end."

Dad stares at me and it looks like he's about to cry, which I don't understand. As we're standing there, Mom comes into the house holding two bags of groceries. She looks at me and then Dad and without putting the bags down says, "What happened?"

"Some idiots at her school are planning a protest for the game tomorrow night," Dad says, still watching me with his sad eyes. "I'll call the school tomorrow and, well, that will be that, hopefully."

Mom seems satisfied with this answer. She puts the groceries on the kitchen counter and quickly recruits Tyler for the job of shredding cheese as she starts cooking the pasta for baked ziti. I wash some lettuce for a salad, trying not to look at Dad. When I sneak a glance at him, he's fiddling with the stove. He catches my eye and gives me a smile, the kind usually reserved for weddings and funerals. A smile like a mirror, designed to reflect however I'm feeling.

When Dad walks out of the kitchen to grab some sodas from our basement refrigerator, I follow him down. I sit on the stairs, waiting for him. When he sees me, he nearly drops the cans.

"About gave me a heart attack, kid. I swear."

When I was actually a kid, I would lie in wait throughout the house, in the backyard, hoping to catch him unaware. I'd jump out and he'd jump up, cussing loud enough to wake the dead. I don't know why I found it so funny. Why I kept doing it even into middle school.

Now he sets the cans on one of the steps in between us and looks up at me, that sadness back on his face.

"Are you mad at me?" I ask.

Dad looks surprised. He hops over the cans of soda, climbing the stairs until he is right in front of me.

"Eleanor, no. Of course not."

"Okay," I say.

"Hey—I'm not mad. Not at all. Why would you think that?"

"I don't know," I say. While it sounds like a cop-out, it's the only answer.

I don't know if he's mad at me for taking a stand. For all

the subsequent problems, the headaches. All the moments that have robbed our family of any normalcy. Or maybe he's mad because I took a stand, and now I'm tired and ready to give it all up.

"I don't know," I say again, and he takes my head in his hands.

"What you did? What you continue to do? I've never seen anything so courageous in my entire life. You understand?"

"I don't know why everybody still hates me," I say. "I stopped. I tried to make them happy."

"Most people have no idea what it means to be courageous," Dad says. "They think it's climbing a flagpole to fix a flag or lifting a car off an injured person. But true courage requires risk. Because you aren't thinking about yourself, when any normal person would be. And when most of us run into a truly courageous person, we don't know how to respond. Because it's like looking into a mirror and seeing that we don't measure up. And the way we respond? That's the true test of our character."

"I don't feel courageous," I say. "I feel tired."

Dad puts a hand on my knee and squeezes. "You know what I see when I look at you?"

Even though my parents' love has been drilled into me again and again, for a brief second, I wonder what he's going to say. I wonder if it's possible that he could be just like everybody else—could see something completely different from what I feel. Who I think I am.

I start to pull away, but he won't let me.

He forces me to look him in the eyes as he says, "I see everything I wanted to be, but never could. And I see the strongest person I know."

Bryan Bliss

CHAPTER TEN

THE NEXT MORNING DAD GIVES ME A SMILE WHEN I SEE him in the hallway. He's dressed and ready to leave for work.

"How you doing this morning?"

"Good," I say. "I feel better."

Last night, after our talk on the stairs, I spent the rest of the evening—the baked ziti, the movie Mom convinced Dad to rent, even though there was a game on—trying to put on the same unaffected face as always. Every so often I'd catch Dad looking at me and I'd smile, attempting to assure him that everything was fine. That I was going to be fine.

Tyler hadn't stopped texting me since he left my house, and when I checked my phone this morning there were ten more messages, all of them sweet and concerned and, ultimately, unanswered.

Dad leans against the wall, popping his newspaper against his leg. "I have to work, but I'll be done before tip-off. And I'll give the school a call on my way this morning. To let them know about everything."

"Okay. I'm just going to stick around after school and put up shots in the gym until the game starts," I tell him.

He nods. I watch him hesitate, decide something, and then say, "Go show them who you are, kid."

I pull into the school parking lot expecting a crowd of teen boys wearing those red T-shirts, chanting or doing whatever they think passes as activism. Yelling about dying ideas. Or maybe it will be adults, waiting to usher me from the school, once again fearful that I'm going to disrupt everything they hold sacred.

Instead, it's just the normal parking lot with the normal kids, milling around and waiting for the first bell to ring. I pop out of my car, trying to focus on the game tonight. Imagining myself releasing the ball, watching it go through the hoop, all that superstition, when somebody says my name—like they've known me my entire life.

I turn around and it's a boy I barely recognize. He's wearing boots and pressed Levi's. His jacket is unzipped just enough for me to know what he's wearing, before I even seen the top of my head.

"Good luck tonight," he says, laughing and slapping his friends on the shoulder as they walk away.

I stand there, unsure if I'm shocked or angry. A few people are watching me, phones out and waiting for me to—what? Charge the guy down and beat the living shit out of him? As good as that would feel, the only thing it would do is keep me off the court, so I started walking to the door when another guy—this one I actually have known my entire life—says my name.

"What do you want, Carter?"

I'd been in school with Carter Nelson since kindergarten, and he'd always been a sniveling douche. My ferocity—I can already see the red shirt peeking out from underneath his hoodie—takes him by surprise.

But he quickly rallies and says, "Good luck tonight."

I push past him and his laughing friends. Once I get inside, I don't even look at the next guy who says my name or respond to their laughter when they realize I'm ignoring their game. I rush toward Mrs. Hoffman room like the hallway is on fire.

When I get there, I'm the only student. Hoffman looks up at me briefly and then goes back to her lesson plan without saying a word. I stare at my desk as the classroom slowly starts to fill up. Around me, kids are chatting and laughing and maybe it's about me, but I don't look up until Ben slides into the desk behind me and says my name.

"You good?" he asks.

"Where's Tyler?" I ask.

When Ben doesn't answer, I finally look up.

"The office. He saw somebody wearing one of those shirts and he went to report him."

As soon as he says it, the speaker crackles to life and the office attendant's voice comes streaming into the classroom.

"Mrs. Hoffman, Eleanor Boone to the office, please."

Hoffman looks annoyed, even though class hasn't started, and half the kids are still in the hallway. When she says my name, she sounds tired.

"Miss Boone, to the office. And bring a pass back with you."

In the hallway I dodge other students, trying to simultaneously keep my eyes on the ground and somehow make sure I don't run into anyone. I only get a few steps before somebody says my name and it takes every single bit of strength I have not to look—not to give them every bit of my hot rage. Instead, I focus on the office, which is just around the next corner.

Two steps away. A boy jumps in front of the door and begins unzipping his hooded sweatshirt. Before he even gets

Bryan Bliss

it an inch down his chest, I shove past him, which might be a mistake but still feels so, so good.

"Miss Boone!" The office assistant is a woman named Alice who's about my mom's age and gossips more than most freshmen. The type of adult who wants kids to like her, no matter how it makes her look to everybody else.

She's up from her desk and rushing past me to see if the kid I just shoved aside is okay. When she turns back, her eyes are narrow and her hands are on her hips.

"You just shoved that boy. What do you have to say for yourself?"

Nothing. I give her nothing. She plops back down in her chair and, after taking a second to collect herself, tells me Mr. Townsend will be out in just a second.

"Eleanor, hello."

Townsend is standing with one foot out his office door, smiling.

"Why don't you come on in here for a few minutes," he says.

As I walk, I'm surprised to see not only Tyler, but also my parents. I can't move, just stand there like my shoes have been filled with a hundred pounds of lead.

"Hey, honey, why don't you sit down," Mom says.

When I still don't move, Dad stands up and helps me

into the chair he was just in. He leans against the wall and everybody looks at Townsend, who seems genuinely concerned.

"Well, Eleanor, there's no need to beat around the bush," he says. "Given everything I'm hearing, I think it might be best if you didn't play in the game tonight."

"What?" I turn around and look at Dad, who grimaces but doesn't say anything. "I'm not going to sit out. No way."

"Eleanor, listen," Tyler says. "It's best to just ignore these idiots. Let them get it out of their system and then play in the next game."

Mr. Townsend cuts in. "Well, to be clear, we're going to make sure every single one of those shirts is confiscated. You have my word on that."

Dad steps forward and puts a hand on my shoulder. "We all want to make sure you're safe."

"They're just a bunch of morons wearing T-shirts," I say. "I'm not missing the game."

Everybody shares a look and it pisses me off, how they all met without me. How they all think they can protect me. And suddenly, I don't want to be around any of them. I stand up and start toward the door. Mr. Townsend clears his throat.

"We can't officially stop you from playing," he says. "But even if we keep them from wearing the shirts, I'm afraid that we can't control how they respond to you."

Townsend pauses. He looks the same way he did at the assembly, as if every ounce of spirit has been drained out of him. For a second I wonder how this changed him. I wonder what comes to him at night, when everything is quiet and he, too, remembers everything that's happened here—everything we've lost.

"You should know there are other kids struggling. Other kids who might not be able to handle something like this right now."

I understand. Sometimes I even see it, brief glimpses of the fear—the anger—still inside me. But does that mean we should be quiet? Does it mean we should never stand up and fight?

"So, I'm just supposed to let them do whatever they want," I say. "It doesn't matter how I feel or what I want or what I have planned. My entire life is now at the whim of a bunch of high school boys?"

I look around the room, half expecting Dad to tell me this conversation was over—that it was decided before I walked in the room. Instead, I catch him smiling. Though it disappears quickly when Mom turns, also expecting him to say something. To stop me.

When he doesn't, I muster more indignation.

"Do you realize that this happens to me every single day? And it's not just students. It's adults—teachers, sometimes. People I've never met in my life who glare at me in restaurants, the grocery store. People on the Internet. *Everybody*."

What could twenty or thirty high school boys do to me that hasn't already been done? What could they possibly say that hasn't already been said? I shake my head, not wanting to be here a second longer.

"I'm playing."

Mom, Dad, and Tyler follow me out of the office. The period is about to end and there's already a few people milling around in the hallway. I let all three of them have it.

"Not play the game. Are you serious?"

"Eleanor, please." Mom tries to touch me, but I won't let her.

"No. If I don't play, the NC State scout will know that they got to me, and so will everybody else. It means they win."

"Do you understand how many kids are planning on doing this?" Tyler asks me.

"Do you understand that I don't care?" I shoot back, knowing it will hurt him. But damn. "I've already had, like, four guys come up to me wearing that damn shirt."

"Wait. What?" Dad asks, looking around the hallway like

he might spot one camouflaged against the wall. "It's already started?"

"It never stopped," I say. "And it's never going to stop—not while I'm still here. So, yeah. There's no way I'm not playing in that game tonight."

Dad doesn't respond right away, but eventually he nods and both Mom and Tyler look at him like he's betrayed them.

"Ronnie, no," Mom says.

Dad turns to her.

"I'm sorry, but she's right," he says. "Don't get me wrong. I think she should miss the game—but she is right. Even if she doesn't show up tonight, it won't stop them."

"So, she goes to the game and . . . what?" Tyler asks.

"I go, I play, and I show them that there isn't anything they can do that will rattle me," I say. "I show them that they don't register. They don't mean a damn thing to me."

CHAPTER ELEVEN

TYLER FOLLOWS ME TO MY NEXT CLASS, EVEN THOUGH he has to be on the other side of the school in a matter of minutes. He hasn't said anything since I walked away from my parents and even now, as we stand outside Mr. Bruns's classroom, he won't talk. Before I can say anything, a kid walks right between us—like we aren't even there—staring at the bathroom next to the classroom with a weird fascination.

For a second I almost don't recognize him—he's a year older, longer hair. Thinner. He's so focused on the bathroom, he might not even acknowledge me if I went up and tapped him on the shoulder.

And what would I say?

I'm still staring at the kid when Tyler exhales loudly. It

breaks the trance and when I face him, I can't read the expression on his face.

"You're mad at me," I say, a best guess.

He doesn't respond as the bell rings above us. Bruns comes out of the classroom and snaps his fingers at me, but I played AAU with his daughter my freshman year and, despite being a bit of a hard-ass to freshman and sophomore boys taking his econ class, he lets me get away with murder.

I hold up a finger and he shakes his head and says, "Disappointing, Boone. Disappointing."

I turn back to Tyler.

"So?"

"I'm not mad," he says. "I'm worried."

"Why?" He gives me a look and I concede. "What's the worst that could happen?"

"One of them gets the idea that they should run on the court and hurt you? Or they wait until after the game? Or tomorrow? Or next week? You're not exactly subtle on the court—you *feed* off people being pissed and frustrated."

It's true. My best games always had hostile crowds or been against teams that people thought we couldn't beat. Five-star recruits. State champions. Aggressive gun bros wearing T-shirts with my face on them. I'll go at every single one of them.

Still.

"Nothing's going to happen."

"But you don't know that and . . ." Now I can tell that he's not worried, but scared. And so I give him a hug. As soon as I do it, Bruns yells my name and says, "If you're going to be a meaningful member of society and not just another member of the bourgeois elite, I need you in my classroom. Now."

It's Bruns's typical rant, but with enough teeth to take seriously.

"I need to go to government, or else Bruns is going to have a stroke." I give him one final squeeze before I pull away. "It's going to be fine. Fuck those guys. Right?"

"Maybe you could write that on a T-shirt for the game tonight," Tyler says.

"Oh, shit! Good idea!" And as I'm walking into the classroom, I turn around and whisper, "Find me a marker."

It gets a smile and that's enough to get me through government, all the way to lunch, until I see him again. When he and Ben walk into the cafeteria, he looks better—normal. As soon as they get to the table, Ben starts talking immediately.

"Your boy is about to fight the whole school," he says, laughing.

"What?"

Bryan Bliss

"Some guys with those fucking T-shirts," Tyler says. "Telling me to tell you good luck tonight."

"Ignore them," I say.

"That's what I told you," Ben says.

"Yeah, super helpful. Thanks so much."

"It's just who I am," Ben says. "Now, I'm about to see the lunch lady about some pizza."

When Ben leaves, I look at Tyler and he looks to the lunch line, because he already knows what I'm going to say.

"Are you going to be able to handle being at the game tonight?"

Tyler finally looks back at me. "I figure your dad and I will just keep each other company."

"God, that sounds like a terrible idea. Should I find another chaperone to make sure you both don't start punching people?"

Tyler laughs once and shakes his head. "Hey, so. I did something yesterday."

"You *did something* yesterday? What does that mean?"

"I . . ." He laughs again, a different sort of anxiety or nervousness on his face. "I put in my application to NC State. I don't know that I'll get in. And even if I do, I don't have to go if you don't want me there. But, you know, I figured I should. Or would."

My instinct is to sit there and make him sweat a bit. To let him believe that I might have a problem with him following me to Raleigh, if that even happens. But either I've gotten nicer over the last year or I'm just too tired. So, I lean across the table and give him a kiss.

Ben drops his plate on the table and sits down.

"God, get a room."

We're walking out of the cafeteria when I hear my name and, forgetting everything for a second because I'm happy and holding Tyler's hand—listening to Ben's story about a girl he met on some website dedicated to tabletop gaming. A group of boys, all of them wearing the red T-shirt.

"Good luck tonight," they say in unison.

Reflexively, I pull Tyler an inch closer to me. And then I can't help myself.

"I plan on putting on a show for you and the NC State scout who's there to watch me play basketball. But you boys have fun with your little . . . things."

I motion at the T-shirts. And then I pull Tyler away as Ben laughs his ass off.

Before Tyler lets go of my hand and we go our separate ways for the rest of the afternoon, he leans close and says, "Just be careful. Please."

"What's going to happen?" I ask. And even though it felt innocent when it came out of my mouth, just being in this school is a reminder of what can happen. Still, these boys are literal sophomores. Literally members of the JV team.

"I'll see you after school. Okay?"

And then I hurry to my next class, ignoring the next person who says my name—going on autopilot until the final bell rings and I walk down to the locker room, which is still full of girls who had PE last period and are taking their time getting to the busses. I drop my bag and pull out my basketball uniform. Before I'm dressed, the locker room is empty and I sit on the wooden bench and close my eyes, enjoying the silence for a few seconds.

I open my eyes, grab a ball from my bag, and head into the gym. When I was younger, I would shoot for hours. Imagining the moment when the ball was in my hands and the clock was ticking down. Shouting *three . . . two . . . one* and launching the shot at the rim, making it or missing it, it didn't matter, and then pushing myself to a different part of the court. A second chance to win the game. To be a hero.

Today I put up a shot and watch it fall through the net, nearly soundless. I grab the ball, jump out to the three-point line, and put up a second shot. Nothing but net. The third, fourth—I begin to lose count—all drop with barely a sound, barely a movement of the net. By the time the rest of my team begins to show up, I'm sweating and ready. I haven't missed once.

Coach Harris walks into the gym and blows her whistle, calling us to her. When we're all standing around her, she smiles.

"Big night. Big game." She looks at each one of us individually, pausing a second longer when she comes to me. "Forget the distractions. When you step on this court tonight, I want you to support one another. I want you to be a machine. Everyone working together, playing smart basketball. Let's do what we came here to do—are you with me?"

There's some clapping, some general rah-rah, and Coach Harris waves a hand to quiet everybody down.

"Okay, let's get suited up and ready."

She raises her hand and we count down from three, all of us yelling *"Win!"* together. I run off before Coach Harris can grab me for another one of her not-so-motivational talks and go back into the locker room and put my earbuds in until I can pretty much feel the building begin to move with all the people. The energy. And while it isn't that different from any other big game, I can't help but feel some of the madness leech into my bloodstream, designing butterflies—something

I haven't felt since my first game on varsity.

I try to push them away, try to drown them in the confidence I've had since the first moment I picked up a basketball. A feeling that, no matter what, I could control this one thing.

When I look up, half of the team is staring at me and the other half is staring at Coach Harris, who looks like she's just swallowed a bug. I pop my earbuds out and am about to say "What?" when I hear my name.

In the gym, it sounds like thousands of people—and I know it can't be thousands, but it's so loud, how could it be any less?—chanting my name, followed by some words that, at first, I can't make out.

Elllllll-aaaaaah-nooooor . . .

We! Want!

Elllllll-aaaaaah-nooooor . . .

There's a knock on the door and Coach Harris gives me a look before she turns and opens it only enough for her voice, tight and nervous, to slip out.

"Yes?"

"Uh, Coach Harris?"

It's Dad. I stand up and walk over. Coach Harris holds a hand out to stop me, as if Dad is some kind of Trojan horse for the mouth breathers in the stands.

"Yes, Mr. Boone. What do you need?"

Dad clears his throat as the crowd continues chanting my name over and over again.

"I'm wondering if I can speak to Eleanor for just a minute. Before you go out for warm-ups."

Coach Harris nods and lets me slip out. We're not ten feet from the gym, just inside the tunnel that, for the boys' games, they fill with strobing lights and a smoke machine that makes it seem as if they're coming through the mouth of a dragon. For our team, it's just us walking onto the court, even though the boys haven't won a conference title, let alone state, since most of us were born.

From here, the noise from the stands is almost overwhelming. How is it possible to create such a sound? Dad steps in front of me.

"Pretty rough out there, kid." He raises his eyebrows as he talks, the way he would when I was a girl and I'd done something wrong. I start shaking my head immediately.

"I'm not sitting out," I say. Dad tries to say something else and I cut him off immediately. "I don't care if I have to wear earplugs while I play, I'm not going to let them intimidate me. I already told you."

I'm ready to push past him. To go to mid-court and stand there, arms spread wide, letting them try their best. Give me everything they've got. And maybe Dad can see it in my eyes, because he puts both hands on my shoulders and, surprisingly, laughs.

"Eleanor, I'm not trying to get you to sit out," he says. "I came back here to make sure you were okay and to tell you . . ."

He starts to choke up, wiping his eyes and coughing a few times. When he looks at me again, he smiles even bigger.

"I wanted to tell you to go out there and shut their mouths. You hear me? *Shut their mouths.*"

I nod. I've never been more ready for anything in my entire life. Behind me, the door to the locker room opens. Coach Harris, the entire team—people I've cried and bled and fought with and for—look just as nervous, just as scared, to walk out into the gym that has been our home for years.

"You ready for this?" Coach Harris asks.

I don't have to answer her because she can see it in my eyes. I turn around and push my way through the door, onto the court—ready for anything, everything.

Whatever they can bring.

We hear the songs that lift up steel and pain over every one of us.

Songs sung loudly, painted with the colors of flags.

Songs that matter more than the cries of children and the tears of mothers and fathers.

Tears of an entire generation that dry too quickly— a week, two if we're lucky—

We can hear them singing now.

Thoughts and prayers.

Thoughts and prayers.

Thoughts and prayers.

A song for nobody but themselves.

PART THREE
The Warrior

CHAPTER ONE

BREZZEN KNEW THE RULES, BUT THEY WERE REALLY INTO some shit now and he wasn't sure how else to handle it, so he picked up his d20.

"Roll for initiative," Brezzen said, rolling as he spoke—a natural twenty.

Iaophos tilted her head slightly and smiled.

"Are you being attacked?"

Brezzen shook his head.

"So, do we need to roll for initiative?"

"Better than just sitting here doing nothing," Brezzen said, immediately regretting it.

He knew better. You didn't argue with the Game Master. Not unless you wanted to face the consequences, which—depending on the GM—might involve a dragon, skeleton hordes, or, once, when the Great Mandolini's weird cousin from Florida was leading a campaign, a randy minotaur. The GM made the rules. The GM was God. Even the greenest Wizards & Warriors adventurer knew enough not to push their luck.

Still.

"Fine. Detect magic."

"No magic."

Brezzen sighed heavily and stared at Iaophos hard. She looked away only to write something down on the pad of paper she always had whenever they were playing their solo campaign.

Brezzen looked down at the d20, polished and black—a beautiful piece of geometry that slipped from his hand like silk. His old set had been a mishmash of different-colored rollers, cobbled together from various friends and relatives. This was decidedly nicer, a gift from his parents when he started this campaign with Iaophos nearly a year ago.

"Tools for the journey," his dad told him.

Iaophos, however, was being unreasonable. He'd rolled a legit twenty and now she wouldn't let him use it. So, he sat there, staring at the d20 and waiting for her to change her mind.

Instead, she changed the rules.

Bryan Bliss

"Can you tell me why you rolled for initiative, Brendan?"

Brezzen grabbed his player's manual, his d20, and started packing.

When he first became a warrior, Brezzen's friends gave him all kinds of shit. They were rogues and wizards and dark elves capable of shockingly complex and devastating attacks, spells that could leave a lesser adventurer on the verge of death. And then you had Brezzen. The dolt. The meat shield. The person whose sole purpose was to rush into battle with nothing but brute strength, a big-ass weapon, and the sort of irrational courage that only a warrior can summon.

Yes, they gave him shit and called him basic. They howled with laughter whenever he failed to roll a simple intelligence check and somehow got mind-controlled by a low-level NPC. But Brezzen didn't care. There was something pure about rushing toward a fight without a second thought. About the courage needed to put your own health and well-being at risk for the party—for your friends. So Brezzen let them laugh. He let them have their fun because he knew if—no, *when*— they got into some shit, they always changed their tune.

They needed his ax, his strength, his courage. They needed him to be Brezzen.

"Hey, *Brezzen*, we forgot to do your loot. Let's do that before you go."

Brezzen didn't move.

Iaophos was clever, and she'd been playing this game for a long time. She knew how to direct him into battles he didn't necessarily want to fight. Steer him toward the sort of shit that any normal player would avoid quicker than a legendary dragon peacefully minding its own business. He *knew* this. And he knew that she had some other motive for getting him back in the chair a bit longer, one that he'd probably dread once he figured it out.

But, loot.

He sat down.

Iaophos smiled and opened her Game Master manual, running her finger down a list of supplies, gold, and the occasional epic item that he could use in this campaign. A few weeks back, he'd received an invisibility cloak that had no cooldown period. You could simply throw it on whenever you needed to escape and—*poof*—you were gone. His friends, the Great Mandolini and Bork, would never let him get away with using it if they ever got back to their weekly campaign, but he still enjoyed the spoils.

"Twenty-five gold," she said as Brezzen fished out his character sheet and began writing. "An antique dagger with a mysterious inscription that you can't read . . . yet. Two lengths of rope. And . . ."

Iaophos paused, which Brezzen knew would lead to one of the overpowered items that he simultaneously scoffed at and took great pleasure in receiving.

"The candle of aims and purposes."

Brezzen dropped his pencil and leaned back in the chair. A candle? In the past he'd gotten the cloak, elven boots of flight, and a broken shield that could detect the presence of most magical creatures, not even accounting for the straight-up, no-frills, ass-kicking weapons that he could equip.

A candle.

"What's wrong?"

"Nothing, I guess. It's just . . ." Brezzen wasn't exactly sure how to put this. "Candles are weak. Like, *weak*."

Iaophos chuckled and spun the manual around so he could read the description, a slight break in procedure that made Brezzen pause for a second. But when she pushed it a little closer toward him, he read the item's description.

Candle of Aims and Purposes

Lighting the candle gives the user the abililty to determine the alignment and intentions of any person or creature. The candle, oddly, burns without heat or noticeable light (to enemies). Must be used with a true heart.

Brezzen looked up, wondering if Iaophos was trying to trick him. This was a candle, yes, but it seemed like something a player of his level probably shouldn't have—or at least, should have to really go through some shit to obtain.

So, he told her, "I should've probably been through some shit to get this."

"You've been through some shit," Iaophos said, but he hadn't, at least not in the campaign, and they were only allowed to talk about the campaign, because those were the rules.

When Brezzen didn't say anything else she said, "Are you saying you don't want it?"

"What? No. Are you kidding? This thing is *way* overpowered. Do you realize what I can do with it?"

"Yes," Iaophos said.

"I'm going to use it. I don't want you telling me I can't use it later, because I'm going to use it. None of those GM tricks you like to pull."

"Fair enough," Iaophos said, laughing.

Brezzen waited for the catch, because items like this always had a catch. Maybe you didn't realize that it needed to be put out after each use and, slowly, it drove you mad. Or maybe you lit it, only to find out that it called forth some kind of demon—the candlemaker, or some shit—who would seriously mess up your campaign in the usual, annoying ways.

Bryan Bliss

Iaophos could see the wheels spinning in his head.

"Just use it honestly."

"What does that mean?" Brezzen asked.

"Look at the last line of the description. '*Must be used with a true heart.*'"

"Or?"

Brezzen suddenly had visions of a campaign he'd led his friends on years ago. It started out normal enough. And then they found a mysterious elixir that clearly said it would offset *all* damage they would take, forever. *What's the catch?* The Great Mandolini had screamed, because it seemed too good to be true. And it was, of course. The elixir did eliminate damage. But it was also slowly turning them into vampiric were-beasts—wombats, specifically, which still made Brezzen laugh. It could be reversed by finding—and drinking—the anti-elixir, which meant really getting into some shit.

So, there was always an *or . . .*

"There's no consequence to using the candle," Iaophos said. "If it doesn't work, it simply doesn't work. Next item."

This made sense. Swords broke. Enchanted items misfired. You were at the mercy of the d20. One bad roll and even the most badass candle was just a stick of wax.

Iaophos smiled. "Just use it without assumption, okay? Let the candle do its job."

No player worth their salt used anything without assumption. Danger was everywhere, in everything. You only had to be attacked by one enchanted book to know that much.

Still, he wrote the candle down on his player sheet.

Brezzen ran to the car, his bag flapping behind him wildly, enough that he almost stopped to make sure his player manual, character sheet, and dice hadn't fallen out. He could see his dad, singing to the radio with the windows open— loudly, so Brezzen could barely hear the actual song on the radio.

When he got in the front seat, his dad turned the radio down. His hair was messy, sticking up like a monster clawing its way from the earth. He had a deep southern accent, a holdover from his roots in the Appalachian Mountains that he carried with pride.

"How'd it go today? You kick some ass in there?"

Brezzen chuckled, because you didn't really "kick ass" at Wizards & Warriors. Still.

"Yes."

"Get anything good?"

"A candle," Brezzen said.

His dad shot him a confused look as they pulled out of the

Bryan Bliss

parking lot. Wizards & Warriors was relatively new for him; he'd never played or even thought about playing when he was Brezzen's age. It had been all football and basketball and baseball and, during the summers, any combination of the three that he could put together with his friends. Even today, his father's buddies would show up to watch football games, drinking beer and laughing until the sun fell away.

But from the very beginning, he'd encouraged Brezzen's interest in everything not sports. If anything, his dad was flat-out enamored with the idea of sitting around with your friends and pretending to slay vicious beasts and best power-hungry warlocks. He always wanted to hear the details, the lore—and the man was a fiend for loot.

"The candle tells you if a person is good or bad. Or if what they're saying or doing is good or bad."

His dad thought about this for a moment. "Huh. Could you use it on, like, a dragon?"

"Yeah, sure. But dragons are quite independent and can be both good and bad in a single moment, so it might not be worth it."

"Hmm. Well, I can honestly say I'd never thought of that before."

His dad spent the rest of the drive home pondering dragons and magical candles, occasionally turning the radio down to ask Brezzen a clarifying question. When they pulled into the driveway of the house he'd lived in his entire life, Brezzen gathered his things and followed his dad through the front door.

The house was warm and had been decorated for Christmas since just after Halloween, because his mother didn't consider Thanksgiving a decorating holiday—who liked turkeys enough to put them around your house? Now that it was February, they were beginning to have the first conversations about, maybe, taking everything down.

Brezzen said hello to his mother and started walking back to what used to be a TV room, a space he had taken over and claimed nearly three years ago. The room was large—larger than his parents' bedroom—and had become a de facto hangout spot for him and his friends, whether that meant watching movies or playing Wizards & Warriors or simply sitting around waiting for something to happen.

"Hey, B. Hold up a second." His mom was pulling a baking dish out of the oven for dinner. She set it on the counter and pulled the oven mitts from her hands. "Tony, can you come in here, too?"

His dad lumbered into the kitchen and gave his mother a kiss. They'd been high school sweethearts, paired together on the first day of school in what might've been the most

Bryan Bliss

successful get-to-know-you icebreaker of all time.

Brezzen stood there, aware the mood was shifting. His father suddenly looked nervous. His mother seemed determined. It was the same way they looked when they told him that Santa Claus wasn't real, years later than most of his friends—days before fourth grade started. The way they looked when his grandmother had died.

He reached into his pocket and palmed his d20.

"So, it's been a year, bud," his father said.

"Do you remember the deal we made?" His mother's voice was gentle, almost encouraging.

Brezzen didn't say anything and his parents shared a look. His father spoke first, his normally fluid voice creaky with nerves.

"Bud, we think . . . well, we think it might be good to get you back in school."

"Honey, Dr. Ivy—"

"*Iaophos*," his father cut in, "agrees."

It was a sneak attack, made worse in that it had come from within Brezzen's own party. There weren't rules for this, not officially, because no player he knew would join up with a party that allowed for intergroup backstabbing. Such disregard for the dignity of a campaign. No matter your alignment, you just didn't do it.

He pulled out his d20 and his mother went to stop him.

"Honey, that's not going to fix this. The decision has already been made."

Still, Brezzen rolled for initiative—a one.

The d20 didn't lie. It was both random and yet absolute. When nothing else in the world made sense, when everything else was a storm of chaos, you could trust an honest roll.

And this one told him everything he needed to know, even before his father came around the kitchen island and gave him a long hug.

"It's time, bud. It's time."

CHAPTER TWO

BREZZEN WOKE UP WITH A START, SCRAMBLING ACROSS his bed until he slammed into the headboard. He looked around the room wildly, but whatever had been chasing him was not there—it had been a dream. He reached to his nightstand and pulled out his *Creature Guide*, turning pages until he reached the one he was looking for.

The Medusa, 5th Class Creature

Similar to the mythological creature of the same name, the Medusa is an aberration of the highest order. Its platelike skin and long, razor-sharp teeth alone make it a formidable enemy. However, experienced adventurers know to be wary of the Medusa's real threat—six tentacles, each with a menacing eye capable of nullifying an adventurer in numerous foul ways, including paralysis, mind control, charm, fear, and of course, death. Avoid at all cost. And pray to your gods you never encounter one alone.

He first started dreaming about the Medusa nearly a year ago. Every dream was the same: the Medusa appearing without warning, the sudden feeling of dread trapping his body, and a scream he could never vocalize. He woke up sweating, terrified, sprinting for his parents' room. He could never properly explain why the Medusa terrified him so much, why he would still be shaking long after his parents fell back asleep.

He'd encountered plenty of Medusas in his various campaigns and, for the most part, they weren't unbeatable, no matter what the Creature Guide said. Annoying, yes. An inconvenience, for sure. They usually showed up after you'd spent half a campaign fighting a camp of barbarians, appearing from the depths of an abandoned temple the GM had assured the party was not important.

Freaking GMs.

Still, if you had enough experience, if you could accept that you were going to really get into some shit once the Medusa appeared, you could beat it. And yet, here he was, almost a year after that first dream, the terror just as thick as it had ever been.

For a second Brezzen considered running into his parents' room and playing up the terror—which was real enough—to push them into a corner. Force a new wrinkle into this whole going-back-to-school plan.

He picked up his d20 and rolled.

A weak and completely bullshit six stared up at him from the bedside table.

He took a deep breath and closed his eyes, remembering past adventures—how he and his friends had battled through various dungeons, torture pits, and every other hellish environment you could imagine. None of it had ever scared him. He always walked in first. He always walked in strong. He always *walked in*.

But this was different. Until two months ago, he asked his parents not to drive past the school, forcing them to go nearly ten minutes out of their way anytime they left the house. Even now, Brezzen couldn't look at the school straight on. It was an eclipse, a bright burning fire. But apparently even the hottest sun was safe if you waited long enough.

When his mom came into his room two hours later, presumably to wake him up, she seemed surprised to see him already dressed and sitting on his bed with his colored pencils spread out across his comforter.

"Hey, you're up early."

She said it like he'd turned a corner. As if he had somehow healed in the last eight hours.

"I'm preparing," he said, which made his mom's smile falter a bit.

She came up behind him and looked down at the map he'd created. He could hear her breath catch, could feel her body tense as she forced herself to smile again and motion down to the map.

"Is this Ford?"

She spoke carefully. As if drawing a map of the school was a sign of some bigger problem. Brezzen nodded, holding it out to show her the pertinent features.

"This is the science wing. The gym, which I took some liberties with." He smiled, tapping the middle of the map, which looked remarkably like a medieval torture pit. "Math. English. That's the entrance."

In the bottom right-hand corner, where the legend would normally be, Brezzen had jotted down a quick dungeon rating. His best guess put this one at intermediate, something he could probably solo, but caution would be essential.

In the corner, which neither he nor his mother mentioned— Brezzen tried not to even look at it—was a rough sketch of the Medusa, peeking out just behind the doors at the end of

Bryan Bliss

the hallway on the west side of the school.

"Is this going to help you, honey?" his mom asked.

"I just want to be prepared," he said, carefully folding it into his pocket, next to his d20. For a moment his mother looked as if she might say something—break ranks with his father and tell him to get back in bed. That he wasn't going to school today, tomorrow, or maybe ever.

Instead, she reached out and straightened his T-shirt, pulling at both sleeves, as if that would erase the wrinkles. Erase her fear. When she realized both were unwinnable battles, she simply put her hands on his shoulders and smiled.

"You're going to be okay. I promise this is going to be good for you."

Brezzen nodded, even though he wasn't sure it was the case. But he wanted her to believe that he believed it.

Any GM worth their dice would call for a charisma check at this moment, not that Brezzen would succeed. He was never known for his diplomacy, couldn't sweet talk a low-level shop keep, let alone somebody as advanced as his mother.

Where was an elf when you actually needed one?

Still, you rolled. And if you failed, you tried something different. Something creative. You played to your strengths, which even the most cynical GM would reward.

And for a warrior, that meant an all-out assault.

Brezzen walked toward the kitchen, moving with the sort of feigned determination that, if you didn't know better, smelled a lot like confidence. He dropped a couple Pop-Tarts into the toaster and waited for his mom to stop him—to call his bluff. But she didn't. Instead, she started unloading the dishwasher and, when she wasn't looking, he pulled out his d20 and did a quick roll for initiative.

Thirteen.

It could go either way.

His mother walked on one side of him and his father on the other as they made their way through the parking lot to the front doors of the school, which opened and closed like the jaws of a dragon, swallowing all the students who entered.

Brezzen stopped in front of the doors, trying to think.

There was no telling what was on the other side—what kind of magic, dark or light, might be waiting for him. All of a sudden, he felt unprepared. A level-one player walking into a dungeon he had no business sniffing, let alone attempting to solo. Even that wasn't right. A level-one adventurer wouldn't *know* they were walking into a trap. But Brezzen did.

"I need to roll," he said.

His mom and dad looked at each other, negotiating which

one would tell him that it wasn't the best idea to pull out his d20 and roll right here in the middle of the bustling parking lot.

"Buddy, it's going to be fine," his dad said.

Brezzen looked at the mouth of the school and felt the d20 in his pocket. You always rolled before going into a dungeon. Detect magic, at the very least. It was about as basic a rule as there was, on the same scale as "check the shelves" and "don't touch the magical-looking cup that may or may not have just caused your adventuring partner to seize up like she'd been hit with a thousand volts of elder fire."

He shook his head. There was no way he would walk into that school without some kind of ability check. His dad must've seen the determination—or maybe it was desperation—on Brezzen's face, because he cupped his hands and held them close. Brezzen wasn't sure what was happening at first.

"Roll," his dad said quietly, moving his hands even closer.

Brezzen pulled the d20 out and dropped it into his dad's hands—seventeen.

"See?" He handed the die back to Brezzen. "You've got this."

Brezzen looked at the door one more time. Most of the other students were already inside without much fanfare or consequence, which of course meant nothing. There could be any number of things waiting on the other side of that door. Monsters and traps that would only be triggered once *he* set foot inside.

But the d20 never lied. Especially on an ability check. So he nodded, adjusted his backpack, and took a step forward.

They sat in the principal's office. His dad signed the paperwork that would reenroll Brezzen into the school he'd left almost one year ago. His mother held his hand tightly, as if he might disappear or stand up and go sprinting out of the school. In fact, Brezzen was running over a mental checklist—his map, his dice—telling himself he was prepared for this.

"First let me say that I'm here to help with anything you might need," Mr. Townsend said. "And I want to acknowledge the amazing amount of courage it takes to come back—not all of our students have been able to come back yet. So kudos to you, Brendan."

Brezzen didn't respond, and his mother cleared her throat.

"I can't imagine how hard that is," his mother said.

"It's a process," he admitted. "And every kid in this school is at a different place, so we meet them where they're at. But the important thing is that we're doing it together. As a community."

Mr. Townsend turned to Brezzen.

"So, Brendan. What do you need from me?"

Brezzen almost laughed. This wasn't his first campaign.

He didn't know this man, his alignment, nothing. Just that his parents trusted him blindly, which was a classic blunder. Brezzen would pretend; he'd nod and smile and not trouble the water in any way if they were going to force him to be here. But he wasn't going to offer up any information until Brezzen knew more about Mr. Townsend and this dungeon he was leading.

"We'll make sure we stay in contact," his mother finally said.

"Sounds like a plan!" Mr. Townsend stood up, walking over to the door. "And now I've got a little surprise for you, Brendan."

He called out into the office and Alice, the woman who answered the phone and handed out tardy slips—she'd once fussed at Brezzen for being "too weird" in the hallway—said, "Okay, you can go in now."

At first Brezzen didn't recognize the Great Mandolini—a name everybody in their party hated but that still made them laugh nonetheless—when he walked into the office. He was taller, the sort of growth that's only evident when you haven't seen a person in months, years. His hair was shorter, maybe even styled. He glanced at Brezzen and then gave everybody else a quick wave.

"Ah, great. Theo. Thank you for being here. I'm sure you're happy to see your friend Brendan."

The Great Mandolini mumbled, "Hey."

Brezzen had known the Great Mandolini since second grade, when they both had Mrs. Burleson, perhaps the meanest person ever licensed to teach seven-year-olds, and bonded over a shared sense of humor which, at that point, meant drawing pictures of old Burleson getting chased by various monsters and other delights.

But Brezzen hadn't seen him in seven or eight months, and if the Great Mandolini's visible discomfort was any indication, they weren't about to slip back into a familiar routine anytime soon.

"I thought it might be nice for you to have a friend with you on your first day back," Mr. Townsend said. "And Theo here agreed to be your guide."

Your guide.

Brezzen looked up to see if it had registered with the Great Mandolini, too.

In eighth grade they'd played through a campaign called The Guide, and it was the first time the Great Mandolini rolled with his multi-class bard/cleric. More importantly, they'd spent the entire year, into the summer, following the winding trails of what they convinced themselves was an epic adventure—the sort of thing that would pay off in a big way.

Turned out, the GM—a kid from Granite Falls who'd put a flyer up at the comic book store, guaranteeing a "masterful Wizards & Warriors experience"—actually didn't have an ending to the campaign. Every week, they'd show up, thinking this kid was some sort of savant, a master storyteller on the level of Stephen King, and it turned out he couldn't land the plane.

Every week he'd say the same thing, which is what Brezzen said to the Great Mandolini now.

"I look forward to the adventure."

The briefest flicker of recognition passed across the Great Mandolini's face—the smallest of smiles—and Mr. Townsend clapped his hands together.

"Great. Well, that settles it, then. Let's get these two to class and we can spend some time chatting as adults, okay?"

Brezzen's parents nodded, standing to give him a hug one at a time. And then in a surprise move, his mom hugged the Great Mandolini, who went stiff, but gave her a quick pat on the shoulder.

"It's wonderful to see you, Theo," she said, ignoring all of the awkwardness. "I hope you come over sometime soon. We've missed you."

She looked at Brezzen quickly and smiled one last time.

"It's going to be a good day," she said, patting him on the shoulder, too. As if she were imparting a spell of protection— one last gift before sending him off.

Brezzen followed the Great Mandolini through the hallway, neither of them talking. It felt strange to be in this building again, almost claustrophobic, as if the walls would slowly start closing in on him. He looked up to the blinking exit sign above a door probably a hundred feet from where they were standing.

"So, how have you been?" the Great Mandolini asked him. "I was surprised to hear you were coming back."

"And I was surprised to see the Great Mandolini," Brezzen said.

The Great Mandolini cocked his head to the side and stared down the hallway, as if he were trying to remember a story he'd forgotten.

"'Now that's a name I've not heard in a lonnnng time,'" he said.

Brezzen quickly apologized. The Great Mandolini laughed.

"Dude. Obi-Wan. *Star Wars?* C'mon, Bren, you're slipping!"

"Oh, yeah. I haven't seen it in a while," Brezzen said.

"Well, we should watch it. For old time's sake."

The last year had been necessary—everybody agreed. And for the most part, Brezzen would've been happy never to have set foot back in this school. To have spent the next two years learning on the computer, doing "directed studies," which somehow translated to high school credit through homeschooling magic.

Brezzen had cloistered himself in the house, leaving only to meet with Iaophos and, when forced, to fulfill the few social expectations his parents had—grocery stores, eating out, the rare trip to visit relatives who weren't a stone's throw from their house.

But whether he had intentionally separated himself from his friends—or maybe they had separated from him— Brezzen didn't know. Those first few months were locked in an impenetrable fog that pervaded every single part of his body and mind. Even now he had only vague memories of the first meetings with Iaophos, before they started their campaign, when he would sit in her office nearly catatonic. When he came out of the fog, months had passed and he and his parents operated as if their house was a fortress.

Still, the idea of watching *Star Wars* with the Great Mandolini sounded like something he wanted to do.

"And I generally go by Theo at school," the Great Mandolini said carefully. Brezzen nodded one more time.

"I understand."

The Great Mandolini stopped them in front of a classroom but didn't move toward the door. He hesitated and then leaned close to Brezzen, like he wanted to tell a secret.

"So, are you okay?"

"Okay?"

"Like, with everything. It's been a long time, and I was just wondering if, you know, you're . . . okay?"

Brezzen thought about the temporary nature of the word *okay*. How you could be *okay* one moment and then suddenly, without warning, not *okay* the next. It could be anything. You could be reading a book and, with the turn of a page, get white-hot pain on your finger from a paper cut. And the stakes just increased from there.

At this moment, he felt okay. At this moment, he felt strong and courageous. But with the simplest of missteps or a bad roll, the whole world could turn to shit. Brezzen had spent the last year trying to cope with that one simple fact.

"Hey—still with me?"

Brezzen shook his thoughts away. "Yes. I'm sorry. Is this my class?"

"Our class, actually," the Great Mandolini said, sighing.

Bryan Bliss

"Econ with Mr. Bruns. This guy is certifiable. Just wait."

He opened the door and Brezzen followed him inside.

There was a momentary pause in the classroom, from the teacher to the students, and everybody stared at Brezzen as if he'd suddenly sprouted a second head, which, in one notable instance, had happened to an NPC traveling partner and, despite the GM's pleading, they solved the matter by simply killing the bard rather than hearing him sing out of two mouths the rest of the campaign.

Brezzen smiled and the teacher thought it was for him, so he smiled back hesitantly.

"Brendan. Welcome. Your temporary desk is next to Theo, there in the back, but seeing how this school works, let's just assume that it will also be your permanent desk, shall we?"

And then, just as quickly as it stopped, the entire classroom started up again. Kids whispered and Mr. Bruns ignored them, turning back to his smart board and saying, "So, like I said, every one of you has been told a lie when it comes to the story of how the U.S. economy works."

Brezzen sat in the chair, aware of everything that was happening around him. Every time a kid dropped a pen, it was a test of willpower not to react—not to jump. And when the Great Mandolini leaned over and asked him if he was okay once again, it took everything Brezzen had to make his breathing go even, to ignore his thumping heart, and nod once.

Mr. Bruns looked at them briefly. The Great Mandolini sat back and began dutifully taking notes. Once Mr. Bruns looked away again, a folded piece of paper dropped onto Brezzen's desk.

He looked at the note, wondering if he needed to roll before opening it. He tried to remember the Great Mandolini's alignment. He remembered him being good, which was rare for most players their age—the desire to actually follow the rules.

Still.

He fished the d20 out of his pocket and tried to roll as quietly as possible, which failed on two counts. First he threw a catastrophe—one—and then Mr. Bruns called his name, asking what the hell he thought he was doing, a question he couldn't answer. So he sat there, hoping the moment would pass.

It did not.

Mr. Bruns strode to Brezzen's desk and before Brezzen could stop him, the teacher had the d20 in his hands. He held it up to the light, the way a jeweler studies a precious stone.

"Well, this isn't going to help you learn about how trickle-down economics has mortgaged the future of the lower class for generations, is it?"

Bryan Bliss

Brezzen didn't respond. Didn't move. Mr. Bruns gave the d20 one more look. For a moment he thought the teacher would give it back, a lesson learned. Instead, he pocketed it and picked up the note, drawing a groan from the Great Mandolini.

Mr. Bruns unfolded the piece of paper and read it for the entire class.

"'I don't think I have your cell anymore, but you should come to my house this afternoon. Are you sure you're okay?'"

A couple of guys hooted and hollered across the classroom and, for a moment, Mr. Bruns forgot the note and gave them a long, hard stare.

"Mr. Masterson," he said to the Great Mandolini. "You know the rules. No games. No phones. And, I'm going all the way back to nineteen ninety-five for this rule: *no notes*. Instruct your friend."

One of those same boys whispered, "*Boyfriend . . .*" and people laughed, which was enough to finally get Mr. Bruns away from Brezzen and to the front of the room again.

"Really? That's the extent of your humor, Mr. Matthews? It's lacking. Now, go see if Vice Principal Gallagher finds your witty repartee amusing."

"Are you serious?"

But Mr. Bruns was already back to teaching, the pivot

happening at a speed that Brezzen—nobody in that room—saw coming.

"Okay, so President Ronald Reagan. American hero or modern manifestation of Mephistopheles? Discuss."

Brezzen was a statue for the rest of class, but it didn't mean he wasn't panicking inside. Every time Mr. Bruns moved, the d20 bounced in his shirt pocket. Brezzen's anxiety rose with every passing second. He had two other dice—a six-side and a ten-side—and he could pretend they worked the same. Could figure out the calculations for comparable rolls, if necessary. But there was always a chance that he was one or two points shy of what he needed. And one or two points on a roll could mean the difference between a crit and a big old whiff.

When the bell rang, the Great Mandolini stood up and waited for Brezzen.

"He's not giving it back to you," he said. "The guy is a psychopath."

Brezzen nodded. "I understand."

But the panic had gripped something inside his brain, reaching down to his feet and now he was having trouble standing up. As other kids started coming into the classroom, he forced himself to stand.

Mr. Bruns said his name before he reached the door.

"Are we going to have a problem?" he asked.

Brezzen shook his head, stepping forward to avoid a group of kids who weren't paying attention. Mr. Bruns gave them a tired look and then turned back to Brezzen.

"What edition do you play?"

The question surprised Brezzen. He wished he had his d20, so he could roll to see what Bruns might be playing at. However, if the Great Mandolini was to be believed, this guy was certainly chaotic evil, the kind of loose cannon that nobody wanted to spend a few hours with and, in Brezzen's experience, was only played by actual psychopaths.

Bruns was staring at him, ignoring the room full of students, waiting for an answer.

"Fifth edition. But first, sometimes, when we're feeling nostalgic."

The briefest hint of a smile crossed Mr. Bruns's lips. "Nostalgic."

He reached into his pocket and pulled the d20 out, once again giving it a long, hard look. When he turned back to Brezzen, he didn't say anything at first. Just put the die on his desk.

Then he said, "Don't roll that thing in my classroom anymore. There aren't any monsters here."

CHAPTER THREE

BREZZEN DIDN'T ROLL FOR INITIATIVE IN HIS NEXT two classes, mostly because they blew past him at a speed he could barely comprehend. He hadn't exactly been studious in his homeschooling, figuring out way after way to study only things he wanted to study—the velocity of Iron Man's flying (math), the possibility of mutants (science), and reading various graphic novels, which was better than anything he'd done in a language arts class in years.

Of course, everyone else had been in school for months at this point, so some catch-up time was expected. But it wasn't just the information. It was the timing of everything around him. Knowing when a teacher was going to speak or expected him to speak. Interpreting the smiles of the people he'd known for years but who acted like they'd never seen him before.

As the day progressed, he retreated into himself until he was barely nodding when somebody said hello. So when the Great Mandolini walked them to their next class, which turned out to be an empty computer lab, Brezzen's entire body relaxed.

"So, technically we're TA's for Mr. Childers, the computer science teacher," he explained. "But we can use this time to basically do whatever we want. Homework. Sleep. Or—"

Before the Great Mandolini could finish his sentence, the door flew open and Brezzen nearly jumped out of his skin.

"Brendan! Holy crap! What's *up*, man!"

Brezzen had pushed himself back against the bank of computers at first, but now that he saw Bork, an orc who had eschewed his culture's warmongering in favor of living the life of a monk, intent on using his considerable brain power to heal, he took a step forward.

"Bork. A pleasure."

Bork looked at the Great Mandolini, who just shrugged and shook his head—go with it, he was saying.

"Well, uh, it's great to see you. Are you in this class?"

The Great Mandolini answered for him. "Yes. I was telling him he could do homework or sleep or play a little . . ."

At this point, both Bork and the Great Mandolini sang out the same word together.

"Interdiction!"

They gave each other a high five and then Bork went to work booting up three computers while the Great Mandolini explained.

"So, you fly across the map on a transport plane and at a certain point, the game just pushes you out—you don't get to choose where you land."

Brezzen watched the screens come to life behind the Great Mandolini. He'd played video games, of course, but they'd never been the primary source of entertainment for any of them. There were just too many RPGs, too many tabletop games that required so much more thought, strategy, and teamwork than simply turning on a computer and pushing random keys over and over again.

"And once you land, you learn your mission. You might be on the rebels. Or you might be on the interdiction team. So you have to figure out where you're at, what supplies you need, and how to link up with the rest of your team."

"Basically, it's brilliant," Bork said.

"Everybody is playing," added the Great Mandolini. "Like, even the guys who used to give us shit for playing Wizards & Warriors. They're *all* into this game and I want to be like, 'Oh, you're not too good for this?' But I don't, because, you know."

"They're all built like an elder titan?" Bork said, laughing at his joke—a joke Brezzen actually understood. "Do you remember the time we were all stuck in that dungeon and Brendan put the elder titan figure down onto the map, all casual like it wasn't a big deal?"

"Yeah," the Great Mandolini said. "You stood up and said, 'Nope.' And then you left. Like, left the whole house."

Brezzen was laughing with them.

The campaigns had gotten them through middle school. And nearly the first year of high school, until the shooting. Brezzen wasn't against the idea of playing *Interdiction*, but would it ever yield the same sort of story three years later? The kind of thing that could break through all the shit and make them laugh together?

"He got in trouble," Brezzen said.

"What?" the Great Mandolini said, still laughing.

"He got in trouble because he went to the park," Brezzen clarified. "After curfew."

"Oh, *shit*. That's right!" The Great Mandolini was laughing even harder now. "Who gets taken home by the police for riding swings at eleven p.m.?"

"Me, I guess." Bork typed a password into the last computer. "Anyway, I just set you up an account, B. So you can play with us."

And just like that, both the Great Mandolini and Bork sat down and started typing. They laughed at the same time, and that's when Bork leaned over to Brezzen and pointed out the chat window.

"We obviously can't use mics at school, so most of the action happens in the chat window. It's hard to keep up with at first, but you'll get it eventually."

The computer screen went dark and then came back to life, asking for a screen name.

Brezzen, he typed.

And then the screen went dark again.

This time, when it came back, Brezzen was on a plane.

He wasn't wearing any clothes, just a nondescript pair of black briefs, which was momentarily embarrassing until he saw the other players lined up on all sides of him. There was a clown. A soldier straight from an eighties' action movie with tall hair, bulging muscles, and a cigar poking from his snarled lips. In the far corner of the plane, a yellow cat holding a piece of cake waved at him. Brezzen looked above the cat's head and saw *TheGreatMandolini_69*. Across the plane, Bork—it said *That_Borkin_Man* above his head—gave him a thumbs-up. Before Brezzen could respond, Bork disappeared. When he looked for an explanation from the Great Mandolini, he was gone, too.

Bryan Bliss

One by one, the other people on the plane disappeared—pop, pop, pop—and when Brezzen tried to move, he couldn't. His hand was attached to a piece of green webbing on the plane's ceiling.

He felt it in his stomach first, the distinct feeling that the insides of his body were being pulled through his mouth. A flash of light. A quick ringing. And then complete darkness.

Brezzen landed in the jungle, and every breath was flooded by the humidity. His eyes blinked into the heavy sun. All around him towered trees and vines.

He started running.

There was a map, but it was useless. Just a random circle with a collection of blue and red dots moving in different directions. Ahead of him, something glowed bright like fire and he ran toward it. As soon as he was close, the item—a comically large, nickel-plated revolver—flew toward him and he felt the weight of it in his hand.

Behind him, he heard gunfire.

The whiz of bullets shot past his body.

Plants and trees exploded all around him as he ran, harder than he'd ever run before. This time there was no place to hide. No staircase to get thrown under and wait for the screaming and the shooting to end.

He turned and saw the dopey yellow cat firing a large rifle

at a group of people below him. Brezzen realized they were standing on a ridge, that there was an entirely different biome below them—desert, with a lush forest in the distance—and for a moment he stopped running and just stood there, staring.

The Great Mandolini fired his rifle indiscriminately. Brezzen felt every shot echo in his chest. When the players below returned fire, Brezzen jumped to the side and, in his haste, fell off the cliff.

"Oh, shit," Bork yelled from the other computer. "Did you really fall off the cliff and die?"

"Noob," the Great Mandolini said, smiling at Brezzen quickly before going back to his own screen.

"Did you even fire a shot?" Bork asked.

Brezzen's fingers were still on the keyboard, and he probably looked like everything was fine, but he couldn't catch his breath. He couldn't get the humidity out of his lungs or get his body to release the fear that clenched every muscle like a vise. He wanted to get up and run, to hide, but he couldn't move, and even if he could, where would he go this time?

"Shit." Bork said. "*Shit.*"

Bork threw his hands off the keyboard and watched the Great Mandolini finish the round. When the Great Mandolini hit the computer table in frustration, it broke whatever trance Brezzen was in and he looked at both of them, his eyes wild with panic.

His friends misinterpreted the terror as fascination.

"One more match," Bork said.

"We probably don't have time," the Great Mandolini said. "Especially because I need to make sure Brendan gets to his next class on time. Meet the teacher. All that."

Brezzen nodded, wanting to get out of the room as quickly as he could.

"Well, tomorrow," Bork said, standing up. The Great Mandolini stood, too, and they both looked down at Brezzen, who joined them, purely an act of muscle memory, because his legs were nothing but dead logs underneath his body.

"Hey," Bork reached out and put a hand on Brezzen's shoulder. "It was good to see you, man. I'm glad you're back."

Both of his parents were waiting in the parking lot when he walked through the doors of the school and into the afternoon sunlight. As soon as he was in the car, they wanted to know everything.

The last three classes had been challenging, at best. He desperately needed to roll, but every time he would pull the d20 from his pocket there would be a teacher, or the Great Mandolini—somebody—staring at him. The entire school was a building of eyes and ears. So he went to the classes and kept every emotion under wraps until that exact moment.

And then he lost it, right in the backseat of his parents' car.

"I can't go back," he said, the tears he didn't know he was holding back, finally coming out.

"Dr. Ivy said this would happen," his dad said. "It's normal to have a period of readjustment."

Brezzen shook his head. He pulled out his d20 to roll, hoping it would help him convince his parents and Iaophos—everybody—that going back was not a good idea. He could just stay home until he was ready, no matter how many years it took. No matter if it was the rest of his life. What was wrong with feeling safe and being happy?

He rolled a three and it made him cuss. His mom and dad gave him a look, but he didn't care. There was nothing else to do but sit in the backseat and resign himself to a fate that seemed to be sealed.

Iaophos said she knew he'd be in a world of shit when he got done with school, but it didn't make Brezzen feel any better as he sat there, holding his d20 and trying to pay attention to what she was saying.

Bryan Bliss

"You've run into trouble before," Iaophos said. "You're, what, a level fifteen now?"

"I'm level eighteen. C'mon."

Iaophos laughed and held up her hands. "Yes, of course. I forgot. What I'm saying is, you've spent a lot time preparing. But that doesn't mean you won't run into tricky encounters. It also means that you're stronger than you think you are."

Brezzen looked at the map of the school he'd drawn, which Iaophos had asked to see and was now flattened out on the table in front of them. They would get to the campaign soon enough. Iaophos always liked to have little chats beforehand. When he would GM, he'd sometimes give Bork and the Great Mandolini a brief background story—something to really whet their appetites. To let them know the stakes. As he stared at his map, he realized he'd significantly underestimated the stakes.

Most dungeons were two-dimensional, something you played top-down, able to see the scope—even if you weren't exactly sure what you were looking at in the start. Today had been an entirely different experience. Every class turned out to be a mini dungeon, a relentless test of strength, endurance, and mental agility that was not only impossible to solve but started over every time the bell rang.

Even the lunchroom was too much, forcing him to sit in

the hallway with the Great Mandolini, who was obviously uncomfortable with the way he kept rolling his d20 on the polished school floors over and over again.

Brezzen dropped his d20 onto Iaophos's desk and hit a natural twenty, a straight crit roll that had to mean something. He stared at it as she asked him if anything specific had triggered him.

"All of it," he said without thinking. "I think it would be better if I could just stay home and come here and meet with you."

"Better?"

"Yes," Brezzen said, with as much confidence as he could muster.

"Hmm." Iaophos pulled out her GM guide and paged through the book until she found something she liked, something Brezzen was certain would also make his life immeasurably more difficult.

"Roll for initiative."

Brezzen pointed at the twenty sitting on her desk, and she actually laughed.

"I'm not accepting that cheat roll."

"Cheat roll?!"

"You heard me. Roll again."

Brezzen grumbled for a second, suddenly wishing he'd taken

the path of a mage or some kind of mind-controlling wizard. Something that would allow him to tap into a deep well of mana and make Iaophos reconsider what had obviously been a fully legal roll—even if he'd made it before she asked him for initiative.

Or maybe he could wave his fingers casually across the air. A Jedi mind trick. The sort of power move he and his friends would spend countless hours debating—weighing the pros and cons of its real-world application.

"There are no *cons*," the Great Mandolini had said. "Unless it's a con that nobody would ever be able to say shit to you because you have the Force!"

"What do you want me to say?" Brezzen said. "I have ethical concerns."

"Ethical concerns?" The Great Mandolini was incredulous and borderline offended. "It's the *Force*."

"No way, bro." Bork spoke through a mouthful of Cheetos. "Nobody wants to be around a guy who can, like, make you dance like a chicken in front of the whole school . . . with *his mind*. It's just too much."

"Exactly! You could call into school because '*The Force isn't with me today*' and what are they going to say? Nothing! Because they know you can choke their ass right through the phone."

"Just like Vader," Bork said, making them all laugh.

Brezzen thought about Jedi mind tricks as he stared at Iaophos one last time before picking up his d20 and rolling—twelve.

"Bullshit," he said, and Iaophos chuckled to herself before marking an X on the map below him. Right at the front doors of the school.

"This is where you start your journey," she said. "What's in your inventory?"

Brezzen didn't rattle off the usual supplies, because this wasn't the campaign.

"What about the regular campaign?" he asked.

Iaophos didn't hesitate. "You made this map. I think we should explore it a little bit. So, what's in your inventory?"

Brezzen stared at her for a second before finally listing the standard dungeon necessities. He didn't even get to the end of the list; Iaophos stopped him.

"Your high school isn't a dungeon," she said.

Brezzen could go either way with that statement.

"You won't need rope or gold for this sort of campaign," she said. "You're going to need to think about this in a completely different way. Because there's no minotaur in the middle of this labyrinth."

"Technically, Wizards and Warriors retired minotaurs as a

Bryan Bliss

creature in the third edition," Brezzen said.

Iaophos gave him a pointed look—always dangerous with a GM—and so he conceded the point because the last thing he needed was Iaophos getting worked up and taking it out on him in the form of undead skeletons, which definitely were not retired.

"But anyway," he said, looking down at the map.

If it was a typical dungeon, there's no way any GM would let him go through a side entrance and effectively skip whatever trap had been set. The whole point of dungeon raids was how they grew and escalated. The way they built, room by room, until you reached the final boss. The big bad. So the front entrance wasn't the problem. It might be trapped, but once you went through it the first time, you knew what to expect.

"Well, I already made it through the door," Brezzen said, tapping the map. "So technically I don't have to roll for initiative for a move I've already made. Twice, actually."

Iaophos paused for a moment.

"Hmm, yes. That's right. So you walk into the school and you're staring at a line of lockers and a wide hallway with a polished floor."

"Check the lockers," Brezzen said immediately.

"They're full of books and jackets, none of which seem

particularly special. Just ordinary belongings."

Brezzen thought about potential tricks. So many times "ordinary" objects turned out to be the single trinket some old-ass rogue wizard needed to set off a cataclysmic series of events that usually ended up with him having to fight a dragon or some kind of giant worm.

"Detect magic," he said.

"No magic."

Brezzen stared at Iaophos, wondering what she was playing at. He picked up his d20, certain there would be some kind of action in the near future.

"I equip my shield and sprint down the hallway, hitting every locker with my battle-ax—just to see what happens."

Iaophos gave him a little smile. "Roll."

Brezzen landed a respectable sixteen. He sat back in his chair and smiled. Now they were getting into some shit.

"You run down the hallway and find nothing," Iaophos said. "But your ears do hurt from all the racket you made."

"What? Are you kidding me? I rolled a sixteen!"

"And you found nothing," she said simply.

Brezzen muttered to himself. What was the point of putting him in a hallway where nothing happened? He looked at the map, trying to figure out what he was missing.

"Perception check," he said, rolling. Another twenty. He

Bryan Bliss

was killing it. He'd been on heaters before, the sort of rolling streak that defied logic or odds. He looked up at Iaophos, not even trying to hide his satisfaction.

"Congratulations, you see a normal high school hallway."

"Oh, c'mon."

"I don't know what you want me to say. It's just a normal hallway."

"So there's no traps. No monsters. And no loot. Great. Awesome. I'm so happy we stopped playing our normal campaign so we could walk around a *normal high school hallway*."

Iaophos waited for him to finish. Brezzen picked up his d20 and juggled it in his hand, trying to avoid her judgment. After a few painful seconds, she cleared her throat.

"I never said there wasn't loot."

"I did a perception check and didn't find anything," Brezzen said.

"And what is your intelligence again?" Iaophos smirked.

"I can't remember it offhand," he said.

"Four. Your intelligence is four." That same smirk. "So you didn't notice the faint glow coming from under the bathroom door."

Brezzen looked down at the map. At the end of the hallway, right across from Mr. Bruns's room, was a bathroom he'd barely noticed today. As he was staring at it, Iaophos reached down and drew an impressive chest that was already unlocked and, seemingly, overflowing with weapons, coins, and other treasures.

"Detect magic."

"No magic."

Brezzen studied the map, thinking. The chest was open, which never happened. Anybody could come and pick it up. And if there wasn't magic, it wasn't trapped—which only made him more suspicious.

"I investigate the treasure chest," he said.

"Roll."

A sixteen.

"The chest seems to be stuck into the wall and, perhaps, invisible to those who haven't been deemed worthy."

Iaophos paused here, perhaps waiting for one of Brezzen's famous *Actually* . . . comments. But he'd never heard of such a thing and was fascinated.

Iaophos took off her glasses, folded them, and said, "You reach into the chest and pull out . . . what?"

Brezzen didn't understand.

"What?"

"You pull something out. What is it?"

Brezzen wondered if he'd missed something. "What are you

Bryan Bliss

talking about? You haven't told me what I pulled out."

"It's up to you," Iaophos said, which at first confused Brezzen. And then, just as quickly, he became very, very excited. He knew what this was.

Repeating Chest

A repeating chest is a rare—some would say mythical—occurrence that has been known to drive even the most stalwart adventurers mad. What do you need? Speak the words and it is yours. Simple? Yes. Treacherous? More than you might think. Adventurers have been known to spend the rest of their lives guarding a chest, too afraid to ask for what their heart truly desires, for the risk that it might draw their attention away from the chest itself. Proceed with the utmost caution.

"Repeating chests are *super* dangerous," Brezzen said.

"If you aren't careful, yes."

People had lost characters—characters they've played for decades, as the stories went—because they didn't phrase their request exactly right. Maybe you need to find a way out of the dungeon, so you ask and the GM rolls. Guess what! You got your way out! It's called death. And even if your GM isn't sadistic, even if she just rolls poorly, the phrasing matters. All you wanted was a new piece of armor and suddenly you've got a wild morlock sucking on your head.

"You said it was invisible," Brezzen said carefully. "Is it permanent repeating or a single apparition?"

"Roll."

Brezzen exhaled slowly.

This was the sort of roll that won entire campaigns. The sort of thing people would talk about for years after it had happened—like you'd hit the winning shot in a basketball game. But unlike some sports story, this *mattered*. Brezzen didn't want to just drop his d20 all willy-nilly when a permanent repeating chest was at stake.

He studied the map one last time. He thought about any possible tricks. And then, giving Iaophos one more look— her face was stone—he tossed his d20 onto the table.

"*Shit, yes.*"

A beautiful, natural twenty.

"You discover that it is, in fact, a permanent repeating chest. *Your* permanent repeating chest."

The possibilities were endless and fraught with danger, but mostly he was excited by the opportunity to pillage a chest that could literally give him everything he would ever want or need.

"Just so you know," Brezzen said. "I'm offended that you brought up my intelligence."

"Famed warriors who are also great intellectuals? Pretty rare."

It was true, of course. They mostly went by names like "Boromear the Great" or "Wildfire" and had exceptional hair that inevitably became a liability. (Once a dragon had grabbed one such warrior by his hair and carried him off, much to the delight of the entire party.) And this didn't even mention the standard, marblelike physique that, annoyingly, solved more problems than you'd think.

Of course, it was easy enough to build a character that could swing an ax *and* string together two words—you just had to build your skills tree intentionally. Spread your experience evenly and not rush toward the ability to single-handedly crush any creature who stepped in your path.

Easier said than done, Brezzen thought.

"Still. I'm offended."

Iaophos turned the GM guide around so he could see the description of the repeating chest. The artwork in the fifth edition had been updated from the original illustration and was now in full color. Iaophos tapped the picture once.

"So, this chest—it provides everything an adventurer might need for a campaign. It's a tool you can search out when you need it. When things start to feel like they're a little too much and you need some extra help."

"If you trust it," Brezzen said.

Iaophos looked at Brezzen strangely, as if she were trying to solve a puzzle. But there was no double meaning to his words; he'd meant exactly what he'd said.

You had to trust something like a permanent repeating chest. You had to truly believe that it wouldn't let you pull out the wrong tool at the wrong time. And while it could be debated that the chest did not respond to the player in that way—that it was just an inanimate object—Brezzen wasn't so sure.

"So how can you start to trust it?" Iaophos asked.

"I don't know," Brezzen admitted.

Iaophos wrote something down in her notebook. When she was finished, she looked up and folded her hands on her lap.

"If you need it, use it," she told Brezzen. "Okay?"

Bryan Bliss

CHAPTER FOUR

THE NEXT DAY BREZZEN WOKE UP WITH AN IRON FIST for a stomach. When he stood up, the pain he anticipated—perhaps hoped for—did not appear. Instead, it transformed into something much more troublesome—doubt.

He'd left Iaophos confident and ready for the next school day. He'd told his parents as much and they'd smiled at each other and, when they thought he wasn't listening, called and spoke with Iaophos, their voices light and hopeful.

But now, standing in the middle of his room in his underwear, Brezzen knew he wasn't ready.

He picked up his d20 and rolled—seventeen.

When they first started playing, he and his friends would sometimes let each other reroll particularly heinous turns, especially if it meant an early end of the campaign. As they grew older and more snobbish about the rules, the idea of rerolling might get you kicked out of the party. If you rolled a one, you lived with it. You leaned on the other members of your team. You laughed, grumbled, wept uncontrollably, but you never, ever, rerolled.

Brezzen stared at the seventeen on his bedside table, he wondered if the same rules applied for rerolling and hoping for a lower number.

Because he didn't have the energy to spend another day decoding every movement of every person, student, and teacher. And even though there was a repeating chest waiting for him—guaranteeing he'd have any tool he needed—he couldn't escape the simple fact that yesterday had nearly broken him. And now, any bravado or residual courage he'd taken from Iaophos's office had slipped away.

His mom knocked on his door.

"Hey, honey, are you ready for school?"

He looked down at that bastard seventeen one more time.

"Almost," he said

He put his clothes on, dropped the d20 into his pocket, and walked downstairs to breakfast, which was already on the table. His dad ate slowly. His mom hovered around Brezzen as he poured a glass of orange juice, just trying to be available in case he needed something.

Bryan Bliss

His dad spoke first.

"So, today's going to be a good day."

His mother nodded and Brezzen reached into his pocket and pulled out the d20, throwing it on the table.

Eighteen. Of course. He let d20 be his answer, because what else could he do?

As he was eating, his mom opened her mouth but she didn't say whatever had come to mind, which was probably another ultra-positive comment. "*Carpe diem* and all that fancy Latin shit," as Bork had once said right before rushing into a horde of what turned out to be giant bloodsucking frogs.

The thought made Brezzen grin, which his dad must've taken as an opening.

"Hey, bud," his dad said. "So maybe you could leave the dice at home today?"

Brezzen stopped smiling.

The dice had never been a problem. If anything, they helped him avoid and solve problems. He needed them in the same way he needed Iaophos's campaign. For a brief moment, he considered rolling and letting the d20 give them their answer. Instead, he ignored the comment, hoping his silence would be the end of it.

"Dr. Ivy said you didn't need them," his mother said.

"So? What do you think?" his dad asked.

Brezzen couldn't imagine a day at the school without the ability to roll for initiative. To walk through the hallways completely blind and unprepared. And just like the time the Great Mandolini had accidentally led them into a nasty patch of tendril vines that, just for kicks, also made it impossible for them to communicate verbally, he shook his head, picked up the d20, and placed it in his pocket.

The ride to the school was quiet except for the radio, turned down to barely a murmur, and the sound of his parents shifting back and forth in the front seats of the car, occasionally turning to check on Brezzen. He stared out the window, not making eye contact.

When they arrived at the school, the Great Mandolini was waiting for him at the front entrance. As soon as he saw Brezzen, he waved and hopped down the front steps, two at a time, giving him a big smile.

"What up, Brendan? You good?"

Brezzen nodded, looking at the front door.

You've solved this already, he told himself, and followed the Great Mandolini up the stairs and into the school. As soon as he was inside, he caught himself holding his breath. He'd taken karate for two weeks—a trial run at a trial rate— and while, now, he couldn't have performed a front kick to save his life, he had remembered one thing.

Never hold your breath. Breath through your problems. Focus.

So he monitored his breathing as they walked, and counted the lockers until they came to the bathroom across from Mr. Bruns's classroom.

Brezzen was standing in the middle of the hallway, staring, when the Great Mandolini touched him on the arm.

"Uh . . . you gotta go?"

The Great Mandolini would be equally enamored with a permanent repeating chest, but Brezzen wasn't sure how to bring it up—especially with all the other kids pushing past them in the hallway. There was so much backstory involved. He'd have to explain about Iaophos and their campaign. Brezzen wasn't sure how the Great Mandolini would react, so instead he gave the bathroom one more glance before shaking his head and following him into the classroom.

Mr. Bruns was sitting at his desk, reading a magazine and squeezing a small purple stress ball with one hand. He didn't look up from the magazine as he spoke to Brezzen.

"Did you bring any d20s with you today?"

Brezzen was momentarily silent. "Yes."

Mr. Bruns looked up, almost amused, and dropped his

magazine on the desk. It was a catalog for collector statues. The Great Mandolini glanced down at the page—figures for a popular online MMORPG—but before he could speak, Mr. Bruns quickly swept the magazine into a desk drawer and eyed both Brezzen and the Great Mandolini.

"So, you brought a d20. Into my class. Again."

"Yes."

Brezzen wasn't sure if he should lie or not. Mr. Bruns sat up straight.

"And . . . do you plan on *using* said d20 during my class?"

Brezzen had a sudden desire to pull the die out and roll, just to know how he should answer. Instead, he went with the honest truth.

"No."

Mr. Bruns considered him for a long time before finally reaching into the desk drawer to pull out his magazine. "Okay, then. Stop bothering me during my personal time."

Brezzen looked at the Great Mandolini, who nodded back to their desks. When they were only a few steps away from Mr. Bruns, he said, "I told you. A complete psycho."

For the rest of class, Mr. Bruns prowled the front of the classroom, asking questions nobody knew the answers to and, when he realized nobody knew the answers, proceeding with esoteric but vaguely insulting things like, *"Of course*

Bryan Bliss

you side with the capitalists. High school is just one big factory of cool." None of it made sense to Brezzen, but at least he wasn't alone. Based on their reactions, nobody else in the classroom knew what in the hell was happening.

The bell rang, and a familiar muscle memory took hold of Brezzen. He jumped up and joined the line of students leaving the classroom. As soon as they were in the hallway, he saw Bork sprinting toward them. Brezzen froze for a moment, fully expecting to see the hallway explode with movement. To hear gunfire, screaming.

Instead, it was just Bork—huffing and puffing.

When he could speak, he said, "Boys. I have a big surprise for TA period. But that's all I can say. So don't be late! I'm serious! Okay, now I've got to run back to the other side of the school and make it to precalc."

And then he was gone again, running down the hallway like a person who'd failed PE in eighth grade. Like a person whose father had looked at him incredulously—who fails PE?

Bork did.

"He probably figured out a way to access porn on the school computers," the Great Mandolini joked.

Brezzen knew he should have a response—something quick and witty—but his brain couldn't manage it. He was still frozen by the visual of Bork running toward them. His inability to read the facial expression—was it fear or excitement? How quickly his body accepted the panic back into his body.

Brezzen took a deep breath and tried to ignore how the Great Mandolini looked at that moment. Deeply embarrassed.

Brezzen tilted his head at the bathroom across from Mr. Bruns's classroom. "I need to go," he said quickly, trying to mask his panic.

The Great Mandolini checked his phone.

"We'll be late," he said.

"You go ahead. I remember where the classroom is," Brezzen said. He almost pulled out the map but once again wasn't sure how the Great Mandolini might react. "I can catch up with you."

The Great Mandolini hesitated and then looked at his phone again.

"Okay. We have a quiz—well, I do. I'm not sure that Hoffman will make you take it. But I'd like to look at the information one last time. Dickinson poems. You know."

Brezzen nodded like he did.

Once the Great Mandolini was gone, Brezzen stood and stared at the bathroom—thinking. He should roll, of course, but there wasn't a good place. Two people were standing right behind him, talking intently. And every few seconds, a kid would come running by—late and annoyed that Brezzen was standing in the middle of the hallway.

He took a deep breath, walked to the door, and opened it.

Brezzen was greeted by the faint smell of weed, mixed with a rather potent disinfectant, the combination of which made him momentarily woozy. Once he had his bearings, he looked around the bathroom. It was standard. A sink with a cracked mirror hanging above it, the corners tagged with graffiti. Two urinals. Three stalls.

A couple of older guys came into the bathroom, looking perplexed that Brezzen was standing there and not, presumably, holding a lighter or a cigarette. They stared at him until he walked over to the last stall, opened the door, and then locked it behind him. He barely moved as they chatted about nothing for what seemed like an eternity, well after the bell rang.

Once they were gone, Brezzen pulled out his d20 and rolled it carefully into his palm.

Sixteen.

He sat there, trying to breathe. Trying to find what he needed.

If he were GM'ing right now, he'd have set this encounter up with a line that sounded prophetic and would lead to loot—you will sit on a throne before the day is out—and make it seem like they were really about to get into some shit, pun most certainly intended.

Levity was as much a part of Wizards & Warriors as magic and swords. There were always hard chargers, players who couldn't enjoy the subtle jokes a GM would introduce in situations like this—situations where the player didn't yet know the stakes. And Brezzen was as guilty of this as anyone. His ax never needed a warm-up to recharge, like the unhelpful spells the wizards and clerics relied on. He was always ready to go.

But sometimes patience was rewarded. Sometimes the players who didn't run headlong into a cave that was glowing suspiciously didn't get turned into a chicken or zapped with damage that put you on the ground for the entire fight, as all your friends laughed their asses off around the table.

Sometimes it paid to look around, take stock, and find what you needed.

Brezzen sat there, waiting—maybe for longer than he realized—because he nearly fell off the toilet when he heard the knock on the door—the two voices.

The first was the Great Mandolini's. The second was Principal Townsend.

"Brendan—you in here, man?"

Bryan Bliss

"Is everything okay, Brendan?"

Brezzen stood up too quickly, accidentally knocking his backpack, the map, and the d20 all onto the floor. The die skittered under the stall door. Brezzen reached down and picked up the map, nearly falling over his backpack in the process. By the time he emerged from the stall, Mr. Townsend and the Great Mandolini both looked ready to call his parents, the paramedics—maybe the National Guard.

"We were worried about you, Brendan."

Townsend's eyes moved around the bathroom as he spoke, like he was taking a mental picture of the space. The broken mirror. The faded paint. The Great Mandolini bending down and picking up the d20. Brezzen, clutching the map of the school to his chest.

The principal smiled.

"We just wanted to make sure everything was okay."

"I'm fine," Brezzen answered quickly. "Everything's fine."

A kid Brezzen recognized from middle school walked into the bathroom and—seeing Townsend and two sophomores seemingly just hanging out—promptly turned around and walked back out the door.

After he'd left, Mr. Townsend turned to face Brezzen once again.

"Maybe we should call your parents," he said.

And for a second, Brezzen thought: yes.

That's how you get out of this dungeon, this school, for good. There were rarely escape hatches. And when you found one, they almost always led to a bigger, more complicated fight. Maybe this was different. Maybe he could pull the lever and go back to his life.

But he shook his head.

"I'm fine. Better now."

Mr. Townsend didn't seem convinced. He studied Brezzen for a long moment, only breaking his stare when the Great Mandolini started talking.

"It was probably that school lunch yesterday," he said with a believable smile. "It's hard to get your stomach back, uh, in the game, so to speak."

"Perhaps, Theo. Perhaps."

Mr. Townsend's expression had changed when he turned back to face Brezzen. He no longer looked angry, or even annoyed that a student had basically skipped an entire class to sit in the bathroom. Instead, he put a hand on top of Brezzen's shoulder and leaned down to meet his eyes.

"I promise you're safe here."

He said it low, as if he didn't want the Great Mandolini to hear. And in the process, his voice had transformed from its usual, booming friendliness to something softer, almost

Bryan Bliss

knowing. The voice of someone who knew all too well what Brezzen was going through. A person who had been here a year ago—had lost something, too.

Brezzen nodded, just as the bell rang. But either Townsend needed him to say the words, or he didn't care about the bell—if they missed the rest of the school day—because he didn't break eye contact.

"I'm going to be okay," Brezzen finally said. "Thank you."

His answer worked. Mr. Townsend stood up straight and cleared his throat once before returning to his regular, painfully official, voice.

"We're not going to worry about a pass. I'll make sure your teachers know. Just get to class, both of you. Please."

The hallways were almost empty as they walked to their geometry class. Before the final turn into the math hallway, the Great Mandolini stopped Brezzen and fished something out of his pocket—the d20.

"Here. You might need this."

"Thank you," Brezzen said, starting to walk again.

"Hold up a second, B." The Great Mandolini looked like every word that came from his mouth was painful. "So, what were you doing in the bathroom for that long?"

Brezzen clutched the d20 and tried to think.

Before, whether they were playing or not, there was an

ease to his friendship with the Great Mandolini and Bork. It was safe, organic. Something forged across countless tables playing countless campaigns. And while the world wasn't full of dancing goblins or tricksy elves intent on getting you into some shit—he never doubted that his friends had his back.

But that ease was gone now, and Brezzen had no idea what to say to the Great Mandolini or how to explain his confusion. Every person he encountered moved without thinking, without a hint of hesitation. All Brezzen wanted was the right way to ask *how*. How did they not live in that single moment again and again, every minute of the day?

"It was my stomach, like you said."

Brezzen didn't need to roll to see the Great Mandolini's disappointment. He waited one more second, then shrugged his shoulders and started walking down the hallway.

"If that's the story, then I guess that's the story."

The Great Mandolini barely spoke to Brezzen until they were sitting in front of the computers and Bork was gleefully punching letters and numbers onto both of their computers.

"It's a cheat code," he said. "Auto shot. We can't lose!"

"Yeah, we'll just get banned," the Great Mandolini deadpanned.

Brezzen was staring at his screen, the blinking cursor

Bryan Bliss

asking him to type in his screen name once again. He had no desire to get back into that plane, to face the shower of bullets he knew was coming once the screen went black.

"And besides, why do we need auto shot? Isn't the fun in trying to win on your own?" the Great Mandolini said, glancing at Brezzen momentarily. Bork dropped his head back and groaned loudly.

"Are you, like, forty years old? Because that sounds like something a forty-year-old dad would say. 'The point isn't winning, son, but having fun doing a good job and all that happy shit!'"

When the Great Mandolini didn't answer, Bork took it as assent and finished typing the code into the final computer.

The monitors flashed and they both typed their screen names. Brezzen didn't move, and Bork started barking about how Brezzen was going to get put on a different server. Brezzen entered his screen name quickly and within seconds was back on the plane.

This time he could see with hyper focus. As if every direction he turned, there was a laser pointer tracking each movement, every single speck that crossed his vision. And if he looked in one direction for too long, the laser pointer would begin drawing him closer to the object with that same otherworldly focus.

He was too distracted to notice the coming jerk, the feeling of having his body pulled through his mouth. In that second or two of disorientation, he landed on the ground—in the desert—and he started running.

This time the bullets came immediately.

There was no place to hide. He tried to duck behind a cactus, but it exploded, all the pieces floating around him for a moment, before there were more bullets. More tiny explosions going off all around his feet.

Bork was running next to him, laughing maniacally as he fired his gun indiscriminately, each shot miraculously taking out a different player. When he got to Brezzen, he started dancing around one of the bodies, smiling like a fool, and then took off running—yelling for Brezzen to follow.

Brezzen ran out of habit and fear. There weren't any bullets now. And anytime somebody got close, Bork took them out with that same cheating shot. When they got to the cliff, Bork grabbed a pulley that appeared magically in front of them. In an instant he was gone—flying up into the sky, to the top of the cliff. When the pulley appeared a second time, Brezzen wasn't sure what to do. Just as he was about to reach out and grab it, a spray of bullets tattooed the ground around him.

Bryan Bliss

He spun around just in time to see the gun being raised to his head.

"Shit, Brendan. Grab the pulley! Go!"

Before Brezzen could move, there was a flash. A sudden explosion. And then his entire body felt like it was being dragged to the ground.

Brezzen could barely breathe as Bork started yelling.

"Seriously? You just *stood there*. What are you doing, man?"

"Dude, calm down," the Great Mandolini said without taking his eyes off the screen. "He just started. He doesn't know how to play yet."

They kept arguing and Brezzen, still unable to breathe, stood up. Bork gave him a quick but dirty look. The last thing he heard before he walked out of the room was the Great Mandolini's voice, telling him to come back.

Brezzen was blind with panic, nearly running down the hallway without a plan or direction. He just needed to move—to get away from the computer lab. But when Mr. Bruns appeared outside of his classroom and stopped him, Brezzen felt a piano fall on his shoulders. All of his fight was gone.

"Where are you headed?"

"I don't know," he said quickly, reaching into his pocket

and pulling out the d20. He could roll for initiative right now and maybe it would get in front of the panic. The fear. He just needed a good roll, and everything would get back on track.

"Do you have a pass?" Bruns asked.

He did not, of course. Brezzen just stood there, unable to move or speak, waiting for some kind of instruction—a clue as to what he should do next.

"Come into my classroom," Mr. Bruns said. When Brezzen still didn't move, he leaned close and said, "Listen, it's my classroom or the office. If I was you, I'd pick my classroom. Less chance you have to talk to that sycophant Alice."

Without waiting for Mr. Bruns, Brezzen rushed into his room and rolled once—a fifteen, thank God.

When he turned around, Mr. Bruns was giving him a strange look.

"You just rolled that d20 on my desk. Why?"

Brezzen looked at Mr. Bruns and then down to the d20 in his hand. "Initiative."

To his surprise, Mr. Bruns laughed. Brezzen wasn't sure how to react, so when Mr. Bruns motioned to the chair next to his desk, he sat down and watched as the teacher unwrapped a sandwich.

"So you're rolling for initiative on my desk," he said,

looking up to the ceiling as he ate his sandwich. "Weirdly, that makes sense to me. I can't tell you why."

He took another bite of his sandwich and said, "My friends and I used to play Wizards and Warriors underneath the bleachers at our high school. We were supposed to be in gym class. Playing basketball. Or something? Like gym has ever been the linchpin of any academic institution."

He laughed at his own joke and, in a single bite, finished his sandwich. He leaned forward and looked Brezzen in the eye.

"So what are you fighting?"

"I'm not fighting anything," Brezzen said.

"So it wasn't initiative—it was a saving throw."

Brezzen hesitated, because Bruns was right.

He'd spent the first year of playing trying never to be in a position to need a saving throw, which of course made the GM try all the harder to put him in a corner. It was a stupid goal, honestly, because everybody gets knocked down at some point. And the saving throw was a chance to get back up. To start fighting again.

"Once my friends and I were in this really nasty dungeon—a level fifty campaign—and my friend Tommy started yelling, 'Saving throw! Saving throw!' And none of us had any idea what he was talking about, because nothing had happened.

We were in a hallway! Turns out, a spider had crawled up his leg in real life and he was, shall we say, using his words."

Mr. Bruns laughed.

"Did he make the roll?" Brezzen asked.

Mr. Bruns gave Brezzen a look that very clearly asked, *What in the hell is your problem?*

"Well, no. Because he pulled his pants off in the middle of the comic book shop to try to kill the spider. It was . . . well, let's just stay he still hears that story whenever we get together."

Mr. Bruns wiped the crumbs off his desk and shoved the sandwich bag into a drawer. He stood up and gave Brezzen another long look.

"The bell's about to ring, so time to roll," he said.

"For what?" Brezzen asked.

Bruns motioned toward the hallway, which was calm at the moment. But soon enough, it would be clogged with students and teachers, all of them trying to push in a different direction.

"You're safe now. So you need to do an ability check." Bruns put his hands behind his head and leaned back. "I mean, it's up to you—but I like to know what I'm up against."

Brezzen rolled. An eighteen. Bruns grunted his approval.

"Looks like you're going to make it."

Bryan Bliss

The bell rang. Brezzen grabbed his d20 and, before he walked out into the hallway, which was quickly filling with students, Mr. Bruns stopped him.

"I prefer to spend my planning periods alone," he said. "But you know where to find me if you need me."

CHAPTER FIVE

BREZZEN WASN'T TWO STEPS OUT OF MR. BRUNS'S ROOM when he realized he had no idea where his next class was or where he was going. Rationally, he knew he should just go to the office, but the idea of having to actually talk to another person right now, polite or not, was too much.

So he started walking toward the gym, away from Mr. Bruns's class, hoping that the simple act of movement would kick something loose in his memory.

The hallways were unusually busy, to the point that Brezzen wondered if he'd somehow missed the last couple of periods and everyone else was leaving for the day. But the more he walked, the more he couldn't focus on his anxiety. He needed every spark of brain power to avoid the clumps of students that formed next to lockers, in front of vending machines.

Seeing a break in the bodies, he moved too quickly and ran straight into a group of seniors. Before he could stop it from happening, one of them had his map.

"What the hell?" The guy was big and wore a T-shirt with FORD STRONG WRESTLING across his wide chest. He looked at the map and then to Brezzen, completely amused. "What's with the map, Dora?"

Brezzen reached for the map, but the kid held it high above his head, his eyes moving furiously across the page, smiling even bigger.

"Oh my God. What the hell is this? Are you, like, on a scavenger hunt?"

His friends laughed as the kid held Brezzen back at arm's length with no effort and continued on.

"Look, everybody, there's a treasure chest over on that side of the school. And some skeletons in the gym. And some kind of terrible-looking monster right down the hallway from here, so watch out!"

More laughter and a few people looked down the hallway to the doors. Immediately Brezzen forgot about the map. The staircase was just a couple feet away from him. The long hallway. The doors, sunlight spilling through the glass windows.

The wrestlers kept laughing as one of them picked up the

d20 and proceeded to roll it across the hallway, cheering even though it was a five. But Brezzen didn't care about the d20 one bit. His eyes were locked on the staircase. His ears filled with gunfire. The sound of people running and falling. The screaming.

The two girls, he didn't know either of them before. But he'd seen the picture of Eleanor, unable to avoid it even from the fortress of his house. The way she seemed to be screaming, crying. Had he seen her since he'd been back? Or the other girl? Would he even recognize either of them? Could he ever see them as anything except two girls, screaming and crying forever in his mind?

Though the others were still laughing, the kid in the Ford Strong T-shirt was staring at Brezzen like he could see the nightmares playing out in his mind.

"You okay, kid?" He tried to hand the map back, but Brezzen couldn't move his arms to take it. Just then, the Great Mandolini appeared and grabbed him by the elbow, pulling him to the side of the hallway.

"Dude. What the hell?"

Brezzen looked at the Great Mandolini. He was visibly angry, his eyes wide and his mouth moving like he was chewing gravel. His hand might as well have been welded on Brezzen's elbow, too. He pulled Brezzen even closer to the

Bryan Bliss

staircase, only stopping when the guy pushed the map into his hands.

"He's, like, having a seizure or something," the wrestler said. "We were just fucking around. I don't even know what this thing is."

The Great Mandolini let go of his arm and stared at the map for a second. Then he looked up at Brezzen.

"Is this a Wizards and Warriors map?" he asked, thoroughly confused.

Brezzen didn't answer. He was still staring at the staircase, which had been painted in the last year—made to look new, spot-free.

"Shit. Is this . . . Ford? Why do you have a map of the school, Brendan?"

When Brezzen didn't answer, panicked words rushed from the Great Mandolini's mouth. "You're not, like, planning something, are you?"

This broke Brezzen's trance. The wrestler and his friends also stopped talking. Everybody in the hallway waited for him to answer.

"What? No."

The Great Mandolini didn't believe him and it made a different—a new—emotion flare up deep inside him, something he hadn't felt in close to a year.

Anger.

"*No,*" he said again.

The Great Mandolini didn't back down.

"Okay. But, like, you just went running out the door and now this map. And, like, we've all been through this shit." The wrestlers, the other kids—everybody looked as if they suddenly couldn't breathe. "And I'm supposed to be watching you. But I can't do that if you don't let me know what's happening."

"Watching me?"

Brezzen hadn't needed to be "watched" since he was a kid.

"I don't need you to watch me."

Brezzen was on the verge of tears, hot and angry. He wanted to grab the Great Mandolini and—what? He didn't even know. But he needed to expel all of this anger and sadness and fear somehow.

When one of the wrestler's friends made a crack about Brezzen, how he was shaking—with fury or maybe it was fear—the wrestler turned and stared his friend down until he dropped his head and muttered an apology. The wrestler went to the now-forgotten d20, picked it up, and handed it to Brezzen.

"I'm sorry, man. My name is Chris. If you need anything, let me know. Okay?"

Bryan Bliss

He gave Brezzen one last look before pushing his friends down the hallway. And then it was just Brezzen and the Great Mandolini, standing there as people pushed past them, turning onto the staircase like it was nothing more than a way to get up to the second floor.

Brezzen expected the Great Mandolini to usher him the same way—to their next class. Instead, he followed Brezzen's eyes to the staircase. He looked down at the map, and then back to Brezzen.

His entire face dropped.

"This is the place, isn't it?"

"Yes."

The Great Mandolini paled like he hadn't wanted to be right. And for a moment, Brezzen finally felt like somebody else understood how he was feeling. Alone. Scared. Disconnected from every single moment that went whizzing by him. When he saw the fear and sadness on the Great Mandolini's face, he got a glimpse of how he must look. A glimpse of the same fear and sadness the Great Mandolini still felt. How that morning had affected everybody, even if they hadn't needed an entire year off from school to recover, even if some were inclined to forget, to pretend.

The Great Mandolini held the map up to Brezzen.

"This isn't your best work, by the way. And what the hell is up with this treasure chest? That thing is . . . I don't know. Like something from a cereal box. Terrible, man."

Brezzen couldn't argue—it *was* pretty awful. He suddenly wanted to tell the Great Mandolini about Iaophos, about the campaign they'd been running for the past year. But all that came out was a curt nod.

"It's actually a permanent repeating chest," he said.

The Great Mandolini did a double take.

"Shit, dude. *Be careful.*"

"That's exactly what I told Iaophos," Brezzen said. "She's my GM."

Above them the bell rang, and a few kids cursed and then took off running toward whatever class they were about to miss. The Great Mandolini didn't seem worried about a tardy slip.

"Shit, I miss playing with you guys. Maybe we could run a campaign during TA period. Kenny won't be happy, of course. He loves *Interdiction.* But, honestly, it gets boring pretty quickly. I think Bork, the Great Mandolini, and Brezzen need to ride again. What do you think?"

Brezzen nodded. "It would be my honor."

"Hell yeah. *Hell yeah.* I'll get Kenny's ass on board, too." The Great Mandolini handed Brezzen the map and smiled.

"Dude, you know I love you, so take this how I mean it—this is the shittiest Wizards and Warriors map I've ever seen. Like, ever. Show me some of those old-school Brezzen skills, what do you say?"

He didn't need to say another word.

After school Brezzen was fired up.

At first his parents were confused—he'd never been an extrovert even on his best days—but today, he wanted to tell them everything. His classes. And of course, the coming campaign.

"We'll run it in the TA class," he explained. "So we'll have to do short encounters. Like, in-and-out monster battles. Or maybe run the whole dungeon room by room and just realize that, hey, it might be weeks before we move out of a specific chamber."

His mom smiled and his dad reached into the backseat of the car and rubbed his knee. Brezzen sat back and watched the country turn to city as they headed to Iaophos's office, where he came in just as worked up.

"Well, look at you!" she said, brightening the same way his mom and dad had. "This sounds so wonderful, Brendan."

"And who knows, maybe we can sneak you in to be a guest GM at some point," he said.

Iaophos chuckled. "Well, we'll have to see."

Brezzen pulled out the map and laid it on the table, smoothing the edges until it was mostly flat. Now that he was looking at it, it definitely wasn't quality. It had been functional, but hurried—a childish and messy attempt. The realization didn't dampen his excitement.

"Anyway, I made it into the bathroom with the repeating chest," he said. "And I went here, here, and here."

His finger was all over the map, tracing his day in the pencil-drawn hallways. When he came to the stairway, Iaophos raised her eyebrows but he didn't stop talking—he was fine now. But Iaophos was no fool and when Brezzen finally ran out of steam, she leaned close, elbows on her knees, and touched the Medusa.

"Tell me about this."

Brezzen took a deep breath, feeling his energy slowly turn into anxiety.

How many other times had he stared into the face of monsters—flayers, the undead, any number of nameless bloodsuckers—without a hitch. Ran in, hero style, with the sort of reckless abandon that made for viral social media videos. He always came out unscathed. Always followed the siren's voice home, back to whatever pub or inn they'd started the adventure in, ready to pick up his loot.

This wasn't any different, he told himself.

"It was fine," Brezzen said, reaching into his pocket for his d20. Iaophos stopped him.

"Nothing to roll for yet."

"Initiative," Brezzen said simply.

"You already have initiative. In everything you do, Brendan."

Brezzen cleared his throat. "Initiative isn't assumed."

"Let's just say it is."

Brezzen shook his head. The whole point of initiative was to make sure the game wasn't rigged. If you assumed initiative, you assumed that nothing could ever go wrong. That you would always be able to act first—always able to protect yourself.

But it wasn't true. And Iaophos knew it.

"This is the first time you've come into my office and been excited about, well, anything," she said. "This is the first time I've seen *you*."

"I'm here every day," Brezzen said.

Iaophos gazed at him, not speaking. Usually, she would break her stare and change the subject. But this time it lingered, boring deep inside him. And when she turned her attention back to the table, which normally delighted Brezzen, it felt like she pulled a piece of him out with her.

"So you've explored the map. You've got your bearings. What happens next?"

This time it was Brezzen's turn to study Iaophos. Normally the GM was the one who would answer that question. The players, while definitely blessed with some agency, didn't decide what happened on the map. Now, if they were really skilled—or, in most cases, really stupid—their actions could shift the GM's priorities. But this was a question Brezzen couldn't, or wouldn't, normally answer.

"I don't know what you mean."

"I mean, what do you think you need to do next? Where does this story go now?"

Brezzen was still confused, but he looked down at the map. He guessed he could move toward the gym tomorrow. Or maybe down one of the other corridors that wrapped around the school, mostly filled with classrooms and kids who were older than him.

He sat back, frustrated.

"You're supposed to tell me where to go next. Or maybe, you know, have a monster pop out and force me to act."

Iaophos shrugged and it made Brezzen madder. If he couldn't roll for initiative and if she wasn't going to play her part and give him the next encounter, he would just sit down on the ground and wait.

That sounded amazing, great.

Iaophos reached into her bag and pulled out the GM guide. Brezzen almost made a crack—something like, "Do you need me to tell you what page, too?" But not only was it not nice, she was already paging through the book in search of something.

"Maybe you need something to help you see your path," Iaophos said.

Brezzen shook his head immediately.

"I haven't done anything. You can't get loot by just standing around!"

Iaophos didn't back down. "But sometimes you don't have to work for things. Sometimes good things actually do just happen."

Brezzen wasn't sure. Iaophos closed the book and once again leaned close to Brezzen.

"Brendan, there isn't always a reason or an agenda for every moment in your life. Sometimes really terrible things happen to us. But that's not the end. We get opportunities to reclaim what was taken from us. We get opportunities to heal. Do you understand what I'm saying?"

Brezzen nodded.

In the game it was as easy as drinking a potion or, if you were lucky enough to have a cleric in your party, asking them to perform a simple healing spell. But he wasn't sure how you did it in the real world. He wasn't sure how he could keep moving forward.

"What's going on?" Iaophos said, tapping the side of her head. "Up here?"

Brezzen shook his head and smiled. "Just thinking about that loot."

Iaophos turned the GM guide around and pointed to the bottom right-hand side of the page.

Archivist Glasses

The archivist is not a god per se, but as close as one can be without having the ability to bend space and time. A part of the archivist suite—bag, pen, and staff— the glasses are unassuming upon first glance. The numerous lenses can help an adventurer track animals, determine traps, discover mimics, and various other abilities that are unlocked as an adventurer increases in experience.

Brezzen picked up the GM guide and looked at the picture. They looked like normal reading glasses, the sort his mother wore, except for a tiny lever on the side of the right lens, which manipulated a series of increasingly smaller lenses. It

Bryan Bliss

was undeniably cool and, as Iaophos likely planned, highly useful.

Still.

"What does a warrior need with something like that? Probably better for a rogue."

She took the book from him and closed it.

"They will help you find the path."

CHAPTER SIX

BREZZEN HAD HIS PARENTS DROP HIM OFF AT SCHOOL early the next morning, almost an hour before the first bell would ring. They smiled to each other like teenagers on a date, taking it as a good sign that Brezzen would piece together two good days in a row. When they pulled away, he imagined them giving each other a high five and cranking up the radio, the perfect song coming on at just the right time.

And it was true: he had a reason for being early. But it wasn't to make any connections with teachers or to stoke the fires of burgeoning friendships. He just wanted time to have the school mostly to himself.

He walked through the doors and started down the hallway. When he first passed the bathroom, he paused—but only briefly—before he started walking down the north hallway, toward the gymnasium.

When he opened the door, the creaking hinges echoed throughout the dark and cavernous room. There was nothing but darkness save, in the distance, a flickering exit sign above the locker room doors.

He went down the east hallway, the south, and didn't see anything. Yes, he specifically avoided the west side of the school, the staircase and the long hallway that led to the side door, but he had been there yesterday, so what was the point?

After he made it around the entire school twice, unscathed and still able to breathe normally, he found a spot in the library and settled in. There was almost forty-five minutes before the first bell would ring—more than enough time.

He worked quickly, designing a new map. The lines were crisper, more certain. And he didn't let his point of view skew the layout. This was an accurate representation of the school, complete with nods to some of the more intriguing places—Mr. Bruns's room, the principal's office, and of course the bathroom. They'd have to really get into some shit before the repeating chest would be revealed, though.

Brezzen sat back and appreciated his work. He followed the lines of the map with his eyes, carefully erasing a corner that didn't look exactly right. The only thing that finally drew his attention from the map was two girls he'd known in elementary school telling him the bell had rung.

He was only the second student in Mr. Bruns's class, and he gave Mr. Bruns a nod as he passed, which the teacher more or less ignored.

As the room started to fill up, Brezzen watched the other people in his class sit down and chat with one another, showing pictures on their phones—the whole room moved with an energy Brezzen had once known, even if he had never fully participated in it.

In some respects, his existence in the school wasn't much different from the way he'd been before. Mostly ignored. Sometimes targeted. Happy to hang out with his friends and otherwise keep his head down.

"Hey."

A girl was waving cautiously, like he'd absently forgotten a coffee on top of his car. Brezzen coughed once and shifted in his seat, trying to work up the nerve to speak.

"Hello," Brezzen said, giving her a little wave back that he hadn't meant to be funny, but made her laugh all the same.

"You're Brendan, right? We went to Mountain View Elementary together. Mrs. Tate was the teacher. I'm Alaina, in case you forgot."

Brezzen nodded slowly, remembering Mrs. Tate. Her claim to fame was being able to throw a football farther and better than any other teacher in the school, maybe in the whole state. She'd played softball at Tennessee, a fact that seemed to impress nearly all of his other classmates.

But the biggest thing Brezzen remembered about her was that she was kind.

"Well, cool. I just wanted to say. . ." She looked back at Mr. Bruns, who had stood up and was stretching his back—getting ready for the day. "I'm glad you're back. It's nice to see you. You know?"

Brezzen nodded again, even though he knew it was the wrong move. The weirdo move. It didn't help that his entire body was suddenly hot, every muscle tied in a knot. Before he could say something, though—*Thanks! I remember you! How nice!*—the Great Mandolini came running into the classroom, just as the bell rang. Of course, Mr. Bruns stopped him in front of the class.

"Masterson. Are you training for Pamplona?"

"What?"

His confusion was only tempered by the relief he felt when he saw Brezzen sitting at his desk. But Brezzen, like the rest of the class, was more concerned about how Mr. Bruns would choose to eviscerate the Great Mandolini. He'd never been much of a single combat player, so it was likely going to be quick and bloody.

"You came running into my class like a bull was chasing you," Bruns said. "And, typically, there aren't bulls in the hallways here, save Neanderthals like Guthrie over there."

A thick-necked kid in the front row laughed once and shook his head. "That ain't right, Mr. Bruns. You know that ain't right."

Bruns ignored him, his full attention on the Great Mandolini.

"So, Masterson. Are you going to come running into my classroom again like a bull was chasing you?"

"No, sir."

"Excellent. Moving on."

The Great Mandolini rushed toward his desk. When he sat down next to Brezzen, the Great Mandolini was eyes-forward for the first few minutes of class. But once Bruns lost his mind because Alice in the office paged his room in the middle of what he called a "soliloquy on the capitalist agenda," the Great Mandolini turned to Brezzen and shot him a dirty look.

"I was waiting for you at the front door, man."

"I got here early," Brezzen said, speaking out the side of his mouth. He watched Mr. Bruns stand on a desk and disconnect the wires from the speaker, all to the applause of the classroom.

"It's fine. I was just making sure you made it to class. But it looks like I worried for nothing."

Eventually Mr. Bruns went back to his lesson and the class returned to its normal, if not frenetic, pace. When the class ended, Brezzen stood up before the Great Mandolini. Alaina gave him a smile.

"See you around, Brendan."

"Okay," Brezzen said.

"What just happened."

Brezzen turned around and the Great Mandolini was slack-jawed and smiling, a combination Brezzen wouldn't have thought was possible until he saw it.

"What?"

"Why is Alaina Mitchell talking to *you?*"

"We were in Mrs. Tate's class together. Mountain View Elementary School."

"*And?* You know, I was in that class, too," the Great Mandolini said. "I literally sat right behind her!"

"I don't know what to tell you," Brezzen said. "She said it was nice to see me."

"*What*," the Great Mandolini said. "This is madness. Utter madness."

"I have high charisma."

The Great Mandolini laughed loudly.

"Yeah, that's not true. Do you remember that time you went into that inn at the start of the Two Brothers Campaign because you wanted some—what? Lamb stew?—and your complete lack of social skills and abilities made the owner of the inn pull a knife on you."

Brezzen laughed.

"Luckily I'm fast."

"Now, *that* is true." The Great Mandolini looked at the doorway, now empty. "But Alaina Mitchell? Jesus, dude. She's *way* above your level."

The Great Mandolini hadn't told Bork about the new plan for TA period, because when Brezzen walked into the room, Bork had already loaded the computers—and was now complaining loudly.

"C'mon man. I want to play *Interdiction*. It's, like, the perfect length. And we'll never be able to finish a campaign in the same amount of time. It will take forever."

The Great Mandolini was pulling out a bag of dice and some character sheets they must've used at some point in the last couple of years. They wouldn't be current, which normally would bother Brezzen, but it didn't matter at the moment.

Bryan Bliss

He'd spent most of the last night working through the various things Iaophos had said to him. Tried to think about what he was supposed to find or discover and why she was so intent on messing up even the simplest game mechanics. But then, frustrated and almost ready to fall asleep, he remembered something else she'd said.

He looked happy.

Or at least, in his near-REM state, that's how he interpreted it now. And it wasn't even happiness, necessarily, but instead something he could only describe as *expectation*. He was looking forward to something that, while familiar, was also new. And he couldn't remember the last time he had fallen asleep at night anticipating anything.

"Plus, I have a great idea," the Great Mandolini said. "Brendan, pull out the map you made."

Brezzen hesitated, not only because the reaction to the old map had not exactly been positive in almost every case, but also because Bork looked ready to rip apart the next thing he set his eyes on. Reluctantly, Brezzen pulled out the new map and laid it flat on the large project table that stood between all of them.

"Whoa," the Great Mandolini said. "You made a new one?"

"You said make a new map. So I made a new map."

"The other one looked like he'd drawn it with his left

hand," the Great Mandolini said to Bork. "Oh, wait—maybe he did it with his eyes closed."

Bork laughed, which made Brezzen feel a little more comfortable. The Great Mandolini spun the map so Bork could see it a little better.

"It's the school. It's Ford," Bork said.

"Think about this: what if we ran a campaign—an otherwise normal Wizards and Warriors campaign—but it took place here in the school? Like, we can make the various teachers monsters. Or other students. Whatever we want!"

The Great Mandolini threw his hands around excitedly as he painted a picture of the campaign, waiting for Brezzen and Bork to match his enthusiasm. Bork rubbed his chin and looked at the map and then to Brezzen, and then back to the map.

"Okay, I'm not going to lie. That's a good idea."

The Great Mandolini grabbed Bork by the shoulders, shaking him happily. Bork, laughing, pushed him away and went to turn off the computers. When the last one powered down, he spun around, finger and thumb pinching his ear, and said, "Player."

"Shit." The Great Mandolini grabbed his own ear. And quickly said, "*Player.*"

Brezzen was a second too late—well, five. And that's when

he realized that he was going to be stuck being GM, which wasn't bad, per se. But you always wanted to play. Especially in a campaign like this one. The sort of thing that would yield countless stories later.

"I feel like we need three players on this one," the Great Mandolini said carefully. He was watching Brezzen, who would never admit that he was disappointed by being GM. It was considered crass, even among high school boys.

But he was excited to play with them again, even if he ended up guiding the campaign.

"Oh, great. Does that mean we have to ask Hunter to be the GM? That guy never gives loot and I swear he gets off on killing my characters."

Brezzen had only done one campaign with Hunter, a senior who liked to wear fingerless gloves and a sleeveless denim jacket, no matter the weather, and always smelled like a campfire.

"He's free this period," the Great Mandolini said. "I always see him in the library, looking up different lores and mythologies. Okay, you're right. We can't let him GM."

Bork sat down and put his feet up on the table, his hands behind his head. "Understand that I'm not trying to sabotage us when I say this . . . but we could just play *Interdiction* today and then do the campaign at my house this weekend."

"There's something subversive about doing it at school," the Great Mandolini said. "But I don't know. Maybe that is just easier. What do you think, Brendan?"

Brezzen didn't want to play *Interdiction*, but he also didn't know how to solve their GM problem. Of course, he could just take one for the party and be the GM—he was good at coming up with campaign stories, always had been. But the Great Mandolini was right when he said this felt like a campaign they should to do together. For old time's sake. For restarting their friendship. Hell, just for the fun of it.

"I have an idea," Brezzen said, starting for the door. He could feel the Great Mandolini tense up, but before he could object, Brezzen said, "Trust me."

Brezzen walked into Mr. Bruns's room just as he was about to open his sandwich, which looked exactly the same as the one he'd eaten yesterday. Mr. Bruns stared at Brezzen like he'd just stormed into his house. Naked. With his ax.

"Yes?"

Brezzen froze.

Mr. Bruns seemed legitimately pissed at his presence, even though he'd told him to stop by if he needed anything. And he definitely needed something now. But the way he glared at Brezzen led him to believe he might not be interested in

Bryan Bliss

being the second-choice GM for a bunch of kids who he might actually loathe.

"Speak or be gone," Mr. Bruns said.

"I—no, *we*—were wondering if you'd help us out and be the GM for a little campaign we're trying to run here at the school during your free period."

Mr. Bruns didn't wait even a second.

"No."

He wielded the word like a one-handed ax, a stealth dagger, a weapon pulled out before you knew what was happening. Just a flash and then, damage.

Brezzen stepped back.

"Oh. Okay. Well, never mind."

"Thank you for the invitation. And I'll see you in class tomorrow."

Brezzen stood there until Mr. Bruns hit him with those laser beam eyes, burning right through him. Brezzen backed out of the room, as if Mr. Bruns was a fifth-class creature, cornered and snarling, and ran back to the computer lab.

The Great Mandolini and Bork were on their phones, scrolling mindlessly. The Great Mandolini saw him first.

"Dang, man. Where did you go?"

"To the comic shop. To buy a GM," Bork cracked.

"I went to talk to Mr. Bruns."

"What. God. Why?" The Great Mandolini seemed personally and morally offended by even the mention of the teacher's name.

"He plays. Or played. He and his friends used to play during their gym class, under the bleachers."

The Great Mandolini was shocked.

"You've been back in school for, like, four days. How do you know all of this?"

Brezzen shrugged.

"The guy is a psychopath," Bork said, looking to the Great Mandolini for confirmation, which he immediately got. "He's undeniably worse than Hunter. He would probably come in here, start talking about the industrial revolution, and then when that made us fall asleep, he'd say that we'd all been killed by the bourgeoisie or something."

"And there's no way he gives loot," the Great Mandolini said.

"Oh-oh!" Bork slapped the table, laughing. "No, you'd get loot and then you'd have to redistribute it to the masses."

They were all laughing now.

Brezzen felt like he should defend Mr. Bruns, or at least make a stronger case for his candidacy. The man was obviously just like them—or had been at one point. He'd basically said that they used Wizards & Warriors to escape in high school. It seemed perfect for Bruns, who seemingly would love a campaign that unabashedly lampooned the teachers and students in the school.

It was the guy's brand. Or so Brezzen had assumed.

"Listen," Bork said. "We'll play at my house this weekend. I'll see if my brother will GM. If he's not working, he'll give us at least one Saturday night. Trust me when I say, he's not using them."

It was almost time to go to their next class, which only made the feeling that they'd wasted a precious opportunity sharper. Brezzen imagined the built-in urgency of every encounter, every roll, if they had to play with limited time. He didn't know if speed Wizards & Warriors was a thing, but the idea of it seemed not only natural, but maybe preferable.

"So, this weekend," the Great Mandolini said. "That works for me. Are we doing an old-school, Friday-Saturday campaign?"

"I'm down," Bork said. "Brendan?"

When they were kids, really only a few years younger than they were now, but it seemed like a lifetime ago, they would run home from school. Stop at their houses long enough to grab whatever snacks they could pillage and, if their mothers were around to force them, a spare set of clothes and a toothbrush, neither of which would be needed the second they were back together.

They played all night. All day. They barely stopped for bathroom breaks, let alone meals. And if you had to go or you were hungry, well, you better move fast because the time was limited and maybe that was the genesis of everything between them.

They never felt the same urgency during the long, hot summers when days were endless. Only on the weekends. Only when they knew it was going to end.

The weekend would be fine, but it still felt different.

"I'm down," Brezzen finally said.

Iaophos wanted to know whether the glasses had helped, but Brezzen hadn't even thought to use them. Instead, all he talked about was this new campaign. His plans for the weekend. And, for a brief second, the way Mr. Bruns had savagely declined his invitation.

"And how did that make you feel?" Iaophos asked.

"It pissed me off!" Brezzen said, feeling almost frenetic with energy. "I'm sorry for the language, Iaophos. But sometimes you just have to say how you feel."

She laughed. "I would agree with that, with the added caveat that, maybe, Mr. Bruns had his reasons for not wanting to GM a student Wizards and Warriors campaign on his only off period of the day."

Brezzen still thought it was a missed opportunity for the man.

"I guess. Anyway, this campaign is going to be classic," he said. "We're going to use my map but, like, we'll play our characters—so like, orcs and tieflings and, hell, maybe even a dwarf or two, all running around Ford High School. It's just . . ."

He sighed. It was epic. That was the best and only word to describe it. The word had been so de-fanged that now, when a truly epic thing occurred, Brezzen couldn't properly describe how he was feeling.

But *this* was going to be epic. And they were going to play it accordingly.

"So, you made a new map?" Iaophos said. "Tell me about that."

He pulled the map out, flattened it in front of them. "The other one was just for me. We needed something better for the new campaign."

Iaophos reached down and picked up the map, turning it so she could see the details he'd continued adding throughout the day.

"So tell me what excites you about the new campaign."

Brezzen wasn't sure where to start. "Well, it's a unique idea. Like, I've never once heard about something like this. And

I really missed my friends, so getting to play with them is going to be great. I mean, no offense. I like our campaigns. But this is different."

"None taken," Iaophos said, smiling.

"And . . . I won't be able to use any of the items I've gotten with you," Brezzen said. "You understand. It's fun and everything, but they're all so overpowered. There's no way the Great Mandolini or Bork would allow me to bring them. It would ruin everything."

Iaophos gave him a strange look.

"Oh," he said, clearing his throat and shifting his weight in the chair. "Theo. And Kenny."

"Well, I'm sure Theo and Kenny will understand if you ever need to use any of the items," Iaophos said.

"Yeah, maybe. But sometimes it's just fun starting over—having to build the character and figure things out."

"I think that makes perfect sense," Iaophos said, crossing her legs and waiting for Brezzen to say more.

But he was ready to go home, to speed through the rest of the day—the rest of the week—ready to reclaim a little part of his childhood and go running home on that Friday night. To spend every waking moment rolling and running and fighting whatever appeared in front of them.

Bryan Bliss

CHAPTER SEVEN

THAT DAY HAD STARTED OFF THE WAY MOST DAYS started.

He woke up, put on clothes—smelling the "I roll to seduce the dragon" T-shirt he'd worn over the weekend. If he steered clear of his mother, it would be fine.

And he did.

He snuck out without saying good-bye to either her or his dad, one of them in the shower and the other getting dressed in their room. The walk to school wasn't far and the winter had been light so far—no snow, no wind, and the sort of cold that was subjective at best.

So he started walking up the paved road that spun around one of the foothills that, miles away, turned into actual mountains. And then onto an unpaved driveway to pick up Theo, who lived in an old farmhouse on fifty acres that had once been for cattle, but now were nothing more than a chore and a constant source of bitching for his friend.

They walked together, the way they had as kids, headed to school.

Still kids.

When Ford came into sight, something inside of him dipped.

He used to believe that he had some kind of special power, a kind of mental ability that allowed him to see into the future, hazy as it might be, in a way that bypassed his eyes and went straight to his gut. It made him think about the old science fiction novels he'd found on his father's bookshelf, stories about poor farmhands who lived in a world without magic—or so they thought—only to discover that they were the last, or maybe the first, person to possess those skills in generations.

That morning something dipped, but they kept walking because magic had never proven itself to be real outside of their weekly Wizards & Warriors campaigns.

At school Kenny hopped up from the bench he'd been waiting on, shoving his phone into his pocket and telling them something—Brezzen couldn't remember what he said now—that got all of them laughing until they split up with barely a good-bye, going their separate ways, down different hallways that had never felt very far from one another.

He was walking slowly, his head in his phone. The first person running didn't make him look up. And neither did the second. The third one ran into him and he saw her face. That look would be written across his memory for the rest of his life. Before she could say anything, he heard the first shots. One after another, maybe fifteen. Twenty. He stood there with his phone in his hand, right in the middle of the hallway, everybody running around him.

Then he ran, too. West, toward an exit most kids used to sneak out of school early. He ran as fast as he could, his feet barely touching the ground, when all of a sudden the crowd of students changed direction, the way a herd moves to avoid a predator. Two dropped. And then another.

At the end of the hallway, the Medusa. Paralyzing him.

From his left, something massive moved toward him.

The coach ran across the hallway, away from the wrestling room door he'd just closed, and grabbed Brezzen by the collar. He growled out one simple instruction.

Hide.

More shots. The sound of people running and falling and getting back up.

The coach pushed Brezzen under a staircase, next to the

two girls—all of them huddled together, closer than he'd ever been to another person, like it was the only thing that could save them.

The last thing he remembered was that same gravelly voice, yelling as he charged forward.

Brezzen woke up screaming, clawing at the covers until he was in the corner of his bed, pinned against the headboard only because he couldn't move any farther away from the darkness, the shadows that claimed his bedroom.

His parents turned the lights on and rushed toward him, but the shadow was still there in the corners. Under the bed. On top of him and he started wailing, shrieking.

"Brendan—*Brendan.*"

His mother said his name as his father held him, close to his chest so he could hear and feel his heart—beating just as hard.

Brezzen sat in Dr. Ivy's office, his hands wrapped around one another. She wasn't in her typical professional clothing, but jeans and a T-shirt. It was early, not even time for breakfast, let alone a therapy session.

"Can you tell me about the dream?" she asked.

Brezzen could tell her every single moment of the dream.

Bryan Bliss

It's one he'd had since the very first day—but also one that hadn't happened in months.

"The Medusa," he said. "The same as always."

The first month, maybe two, of their sessions had been all about the dream. About the darkness that overtook his mind every time he slept. About waking up, covered in sweat and exhausted, like he'd just run a marathon.

Dr. Ivy nodded. "And how long did it take for you to realize it wasn't real?"

"A few minutes," he said. "But I still feel it—like, right now. I can feel it."

"The Medusa?" she asked.

Brezzen shook his head.

"No. I can feel my heart beating and the blood going through my veins. I'm aware of every single molecule. At least that's how it feels. Like I'm about to combust. Or maybe turn into a superhero."

She smiled. "Let's hope for the latter."

"Can I—can I ask you a question?"

"Of course."

Brezzen sat there for a minute, trying to pick the words from his brain in exactly the right order. Words that would help clarify a question that he'd never really asked.

"Is this going to keep happening?"

Iaophos leaned back in her chair and ran her fingers through her hair, which was not up in its usual ponytail. When she was finished, it looked like she'd just gotten off a ride at the state fair. Out of a car.

"The honest answer is: I don't know. Maybe? Maybe not?" Brezzen's eyes dropped and she said his name. "We can't control everything in our life. All we can do is work on our healing. We can take fifty steps forward, even if there are forty-nine others going the other way. Does that make sense?"

"I didn't do anything," he said.

Iaophos was surprised and perhaps a bit confused. Before she could respond, Brezzen said, "I didn't do anything in the dream. To help. I never do."

"Brendan—you did. You protected yourself. That's all you needed to do. And you're fighting right now, battling to get better. I can't think of a braver thing."

Brezzen nodded.

"You are a warrior," she said.

He tried to brush her off, but she wouldn't let him.

"No, listen to me. You are a *warrior*. Do you understand what I'm saying?"

Everybody played alt characters, but he had always been class monogamous. There was something about the straight-up brawler, the fighter, the warrior that appealed to him. Something that called to him, even when he wasn't playing, giving him a weird irrational strength that had gotten him in trouble more than a few times.

Calling out a bully.

Standing up for his friends.

Walking through school, everyday life, being exactly who he wanted to be, no matter what other people said.

Until the one moment when he didn't.

"Just without the armor," he said, attempting a joke.

Iaophos moved her head back and forth and shrugged.

"Everybody puts on armor of some kind. A little armor helps get us through the day. It's just when we forget to take it off that it becomes the problem. When we forget that we don't always need it."

Brezzen's armor was heavy and he wanted to take it off. But what then? How did you live without a constant fear that you were about to get into some shit?

"Just know that you are incredibly strong, Brendan. And you are incredibly kind. And those two things can defeat almost anything they go against."

Brezzen expected to go to school, but his parents and Dr. Ivy had another plan, so he found himself sitting at Carol's, picking at a sausage biscuit and trying to read his parents' faces.

"I'm fine," he said.

They looked at each other and then at him. The breakfast crowd was long gone, leaving them alone in the restaurant. The walls, once white, were yellowed by grease and, before it became illegal, decades of cigarette smoke. Brezzen could still smell it sometimes when he sat in one of the booths.

"Eat, bud." His dad pushed the plate a little closer to him. "Get something in your stomach. It will make you feel better."

He picked up the biscuit, part of it crumbling back down onto the plate, and took a big bite. It was wonderful and it did make him feel better, if only for a second. By the time he took a second bite, the magic was gone.

"So, maybe we rushed you into this," his mother said, looking at his dad, who agreed. "Dr. Ivy said you might not be ready after all, which is fine! We don't have to have a timetable!"

Brezzen lifted the biscuit back up to his mouth and took another bite. This one fell into his stomach like a stone.

"Am I going to school today?"

They shared another look.

"Honey, you're exhausted," his mother said.

Bryan Bliss

"Let's just take this one day at a time," his dad said. "And when we figure out the right decision, we'll all make it together. The most important thing is that you are feeling supported and ready."

"What does that mean?" Brezzen asked.

"It— " His dad struggled to find the right words, which was never the case. "Just eat and we'll get everything figured out."

Brezzen looked down at his biscuit, only a few bites left. But he wasn't hungry now. When he stood up, they both jumped out of the booth, too, flanking him like he might go running out of the restaurant screaming.

But he didn't. He simply said, "I'm ready to go home."

As soon as he was in the house, he went to his room and got in his bed, not because he was tired, but because he didn't know where else to go. He didn't want to talk to his parents, didn't want to go online, or fall into any of the other routines he'd established over the last year.

He stayed in bed until his mom knocked on his door at lunch and brought him homemade mac and cheese, which he ate without tasting a single bite. When he finished, he put the bowl on his bedside table and eventually his mother came back in and got it, looking down at him with eyes that were so sad, he didn't know where to start. Outside his window the light began to drop and he still didn't move, only falling asleep on accident.

The next knock on his door was so soft that he thought it might be a dream. His mom's head peeked through the door. She smiled when she met his eyes and whispered, "Are you up for some company?"

Brezzen expected his aunt to come walking through door, or maybe the youth pastor from the church they all pretended to attend. So when the Great Mandolini entered a moment later, Brezzen sat up quickly and, for some reason, smoothed his hair down.

"Don't worry," he said. "Your hair never looks good."

Brezzen laughed as his mom hovered behind the Great Mandolini, before finally leaving and then returning a few seconds later with a package of Oreos and a couple of bottles of Gatorade.

She backed out of the room, smiling at both of them.

"So you weren't at school," the Great Mandolini said, picking up the Oreos and popping one into his mouth. "You missed absolutely nothing, I'm happy to report. Well, except Eleanor Boone is officially everybody's favorite person again."

At the mention of her name, Brezzen tensed up momentarily. He grabbed a cookie, pulling it apart and then putting it back together before eating it in one bite.

"Oh, well, there was one other thing," the Great Mandolini said, the tone of his voice changing. "Alaina. She was *very* worried that you might not be coming back. She gave me this . . ."

He reached out a folded slip of paper with a phone number written in loopy pen.

"That's the most she's ever talked to me," the Great Mandolini said. "So, thank you? I guess?"

Brezzen tucked the piece of paper underneath his Wizards & Warriors player's manual, which took up the majority of his nightstand. When he accidentally bumped the book, his d20 fell to the floor.

"Eighteen. Not bad," the Great Mandolini said, reaching down to scoop up the die. He tossed it between his hands as he talked. "So is that what's going to happen? You're not coming back again?"

Brezzen didn't know. But maybe he did. It felt as if his parents—Iaophos, perhaps—had already made the decision and it settled inside his head felt like a dense cloud. Like he had no control over something important.

A die roll wasn't going to decide this one.

The Great Mandolini sighed. He picked up another Oreo, ate it, and then grabbed two more and stuck them in his pocket. His parents had moved here from Oregon when he was a baby, but that time hadn't kicked them from their West Coast, vegetarian, "Our kids don't eat sugar" beliefs. The Great Mandolini, of course, was an addict.

"You can take them all," Brezzen said. "I'm not hungry."

He didn't hesitate. Dumped the entire package of cookies into the top of his backpack, making both of them laugh.

"I can't bring the package home. It's not recyclable."

They stopped talking, listening as Brezzen's dad yelled from the garage—something about needing a broom. In the silence that followed, the Great Mandolini stood up and shouldered his backpack. A single rogue Oreo fell out of the top and rolled under Brezzen's bed.

"Don't worry about it," Brezzen said. "I'll grab it later."

The Great Mandolini turned to leave Brezzen's, but then he stopped.

"Shit, I almost forgot."

He tossed the d20 to Brezzen and it landed softly on his comforter, right below his hand.

"Thanks," Brezzen said, reaching down and picking it up.

"Hey, don't forget about me," the Great Mandolini said, cringing at himself. "I mean, you know what I'm saying. I missed having you around."

"I won't," Brezzen said.

But he'd made the same promise when he was first taken

Bryan Bliss

out of school last year. And then again, months later when he was feeling more stable—more like himself. But he never picked up his phone. Never sent a text, maybe scared that the Great Mandolini and Bork had somehow moved on without him.

"I still want to run that campaign," Brezzen said.

"Hell yeah," the Great Mandolini said. "*Hell. Yes.* Let's do it. This weekend. As long as you're feeling better. What do you think?"

Brezzen looked down at his blanket, wanting to agree. But he wasn't sure when he might be better—what that even meant.

"We need your ax, Brezzen," the Great Mandolini said. "Remember that."

CHAPTER EIGHT

THE NEXT MORNING BREZZEN WAS UP WITH THE BIRDS.
This was the first time, maybe in his life, that he'd woken
up without a constant prodding or some kind of electronic,
beeping, won't-be-snoozed, alarm.

At first he considered just leaving the house. He'd leave
a note, of course, but he didn't want to give his parents any
chance to dissuade him.

Instead, he made himself some peanut butter toast and
sat at the table, waiting for them to wake up. They were
notorious morning people, always up at dawn, singing and
talking loudly—which always felt strangely aggressive to the
normally sleepy Brezzen.

When they finally walked into the kitchen, looking a little
more bleary-eyed than normal, they were clearly surprised to

see him at the table, eating breakfast, fully dressed.

"Hey, bud. Glad to see you up and at 'em," his dad said.

"Everything okay? I figured you'd want to stay in bed a little longer," his mother said.

"I want to go to school," Brezzen said.

He'd spent half the night rehearsing in order to make sure it came out exactly how he wanted it to sound. Confident, but not desperate. Hopeful, but not scared.

He nailed it.

His parents looked at each other and then at Brezzen, who had already stood up and was putting his dish in the sink.

"You don't have to push yourself," his mom said.

"Yeah, bud, Dr. Ivy said it was fine to take few days to, you know, feel better."

He could hear the fear in their words. That the nightmare the other night was something bigger and—if pushed— Brezzen might crack completely, straight down the middle, and they'd lose him forever. He couldn't imagine what it took for them to let him walk out of the house now, after everything.

And if this had been last week, he would've jumped on the opportunity to stay with them. He would've spent the rest of his life moving from his bedroom to the kitchen to the TV room, nothing more.

"I want to go to school," Brezzen said.

"Honey, you will," his mom said, rubbing his arm as she spoke. "When you're ready."

"Yeah, bud. Taking a few days off isn't going to hurt anybody."

But that wasn't true. And Brezzen knew it.

He tried to keep his voice even but failed. It broke after the first word.

"I—I just." He wiped his eyes, refusing to let this devolve into something bigger, a tsunami of emotions that would whisk him away. Prove their point. "If I don't go now, I'm afraid I won't go back. I'm afraid I'll spend two or three days here and it will start to feel comfortable. And then I'll forget."

"What are you going to forget, honey?" His mom took his hand and squeezed it. "Is it schoolwork? You'll catch up."

He shook his head.

"I'll forget that it's safe," he said, not sure if that was the best way to explain it. Whether it was or not, it hit both of his parents like a truck. His mom pulled him into a hug and his dad stood behind them, tears in his eyes.

"Oh, honey. You're going to be fine. You won't forget."

"I will," Brezzen said. "I will because it's easier and . . ."

He wasn't sure if his parents could handle the rest. The

realization that he'd been stumbling toward for the past year. But he needed to say it—maybe for the first time.

"I don't think I'm better yet," he said. "And that will never change if I stay here."

Brezzen walked through the front doors of the school, hurrying to make it to Mr. Bruns's class. He dodged a couple of lost-looking freshman and slipped into the classroom seconds after the bell rang.

Before he could get back to his seat, Bruns stopped him and the entire room grinded to a halt.

"Mr. Hicks. You are late to my class."

Brezzen nodded. "I know. I was—"

Mr. Bruns raised his hand. "Were you being chased by a hawkbear?"

Brezzen did a double take. Mr. Bruns crossed his arms across his chest and cocked his head to the side, waiting for a response. The rest of the class was more confused than usual. Even if they played Wizards & Warriors, they might not know about the hawkbear. It was the size of a bear, with the beak and talons of a hawk. It didn't normally fly—too large—but if properly inspired, usually by the idiotic actions of a party member, it could get off the ground. And then you were really in some shit.

But as the *Creature Manual* expanded, it disappeared—its simple brutality no match for the newer, more complex creatures. So, if you hadn't played first edition, you wouldn't know a hawkbear from a harpy.

"Wouldn't fit in the hallways," Brezzen said, hoping the tone was right—cheeky, not challenging. This time Mr. Bruns blinked. He uncrossed his arms and gave Brezzen the slightest of smiles, then motioned to Brezzen's desk.

"Don't miss my class again. And don't be late."

Brezzen nodded and walked back to his desk, where he was greeted first by Alaina and then by the Great Mandolini, who looked positively confused.

"Dude. What are you doing here?" he whispered.

Brezzen shook his head and motioned to Mr. Bruns, who had already started teaching—a rant that was picking up steam, whether they were ready or not, and quickly turned into an hour of their lives.

Once the period ended, the Great Mandolini leaned over and said, "Okay. What happened?"

Brezzen had no idea where to start. And as Alaina stood up, touching his shoulder and giving him a smile, he decided that a few words would suffice.

"I just needed to take care of some things," he said.

The Great Mandolini gave him a weird look, and then

Bryan Bliss

laughed loudly. As he was laughing, Mr. Bruns came up behind them and tapped the desk.

"You realize there's another class of eager learners hoping to come in here and break the chains of their preconceived ideas and assumptions, right?"

The Great Mandolini gave Brezzen a look that said, *psychopath*.

They stood up to leave, and just before they were out the door, Mr. Bruns said his name.

"Brendan, that was a good pull on the hawkbear," he said.

He turned around, the Great Mandolini on his hip, just like he'd always been in so many campaigns before. And for the first time, Brezzen knew exactly what he should say.

"You just have to know what you're up against."

We sing too.

Songs of hope.

Songs that never stop,

Ringing in the ears of every person

who says they can't hear,

and things can't change.

You've heard their song.

Now hear ours.

ACKNOWLEDGMENTS

FIRST AND FOREMOST, I HAVE TO THANK MY AGENT, Michael Bourret, and my editor, Martha Mihalick. I can't imagine doing this without either of you.

Also, my family—Michelle, Nora, and Ben. I'm sure they get tired of my constant and seemingly never-ending monologue about the books I'm writing, professional wrestling storylines, and various other Very Important Topics. I promise the next book will be a "happy" one. Maybe.

I'm also lucky to have a lot of great friends, writers and not. They are a constant source of inspiration, levity, and wisdom. In no particular order, Sara Zarr, Dan Kraus, Tara Altebrando, Corey Ann Haydu, Steve Brezenoff, Kate Bassett, Carrie Mesrobian, Christa Desir, Amanda MacGregor, Marc Olson, Kirstin Cronn-Mills, Emma Berquist, Greg and Jess

Andree, Richard Lewis, Dustin Wilhelmy, Jill Braithwaite, Chris Hoke, Aaron Guest, Paul Luikart, Seth Riley, Matt Slye, Cameron Dezen Hammon, Lauren Winner, Joy Caires, Lona Caires, Elissa Zoerb, Scott Marsalis, Jim Morehouse, Michael Moore—the entire St. Clement's community—and probably a hundred other people I'm forgetting, thank you. You make my life better.

Andrew DeYoung deserves a line to himself for coming up with the title for this novel.

Thank you to the therapists and childhood trauma experts who graciously pointed out the places where I got things wrong and helped me, hopefully, make this book an honest picture of healing after trauma. Lindsay Miesbauer Wilhelmy, Dr. Robin Gurwitch, PhD, and Dr. Melissa Brymer, PsyD, PhD. Thank you for your willingness and your work. Any mistakes that remain are my own.

And finally, I want to thank everybody who, like me, has had enough. The survivors. The activists. The everyday people who simply won't let this keep happening.

Keep going. Keep going. We can fix this.

Bryan Bliss